WITH THIS RING

AMY CLIPSTON

THORNDIKE PRESS
A part of Gale, a Cengage Company

Copyright © 2025 by Amy Clipston.
Thorndike Press, a part of Gale, a Cengage Company.

ALL RIGHTS RESERVED
This novel is a work of fiction. Names, characters, places, and incidents are either products of the author's imagination or used fictitiously. All characters are fictional, and any similarity to people living or dead is purely coincidental.
Any internet addresses (websites, blogs, etc.) in this book are offered as a resource. They are not intended in any way to be or imply an endorsement by the publisher, nor does the publisher vouch for the content of these sites for the life of this book.
Thorndike Press® Large Print Christian Romance.
The text of this Large Print edition is unabridged.
Other aspects of the book may vary from the original edition.
Set in 16 pt. Plantin.

**LIBRARY OF CONGRESS CIP DATA ON FILE.
CATALOGUING IN PUBLICATION FOR THIS BOOK
IS AVAILABLE FROM THE LIBRARY OF CONGRESS.**

ISBN-13: 978-1-4205-2027-9 (hardcover alk. paper)

Published in 2025 by arrangement with Thomas Nelson, Inc., a division of HarperCollins Christian Publishing, Inc.

Print Number: 1   Print Year: 2025
Printed in Mexico

For my super-awesome, amazing, fabulous, talented critique partner, Kathleen Fuller. I'm beyond grateful for your precious friendship. You are the absolute best!

Chapter 1

Dakota swiped her hand over her forehead and moved the steamer over a wedding gown. Nearby, a dehumidifier and air-moving machine hummed. Her arm ached, but she ignored the pain and glanced around the large workroom at the back of her boutique, the Fairytale Bridal Shop. Several racks of gowns waiting their turn to be restored stared back at her.

It had been a month since late January, when the pipes had burst in her store. The leak had not only damaged the floor, ceiling, and walls but also waterlogged the first shipment of this year's spring line — a huge investment that had cost her thousands. And thanks to the twenty-three-page lease agreement she barely understood and the ridiculously high deductible on her insurance policy, her only choice was to steam and try to restore the gowns herself. She didn't even want to think about the money she'd lost on the ones that couldn't be saved, but she wasn't giving up. She would find a way to recoup as much as she could. She was a Jamison, after all, which meant she wasn't a quitter. She'd keep fighting, no matter the obstacles.

But first she had to work on getting these gowns back out on the floor. Trying on dresses was a vital part of the bridal shopping experience, and customers couldn't imagine a wrinkled gown being their dream dress. She was losing business, and if she continued to do so, she'd see her own dream — that of owning this boutique — go up in flames after only two years. Or maybe more accurately, in this case, the dream would go down the drain . . .

Dismissing her negative thoughts, she continued steaming the chiffon A-line gown before her. Its bikini neckline and asymmetric draped bodice had made it one of her favorites from the spring line. She was certain this was one gown that would sell as soon as she hung it back out front with the rest of her collection.

The bell on the front door dinged, and Dakota jumped with a start.

Customers!

She turned off the steamer and stowed it before brushing her hands down her gray top and black pencil skirt. Hoping she looked presentable, she hurried out to the front, where an instrumental version of Jason Mraz's "I'm Yours" serenaded her from the speakers placed throughout her boutique. She shook her head and smiled. She had tried to create the perfect romantic playlist, hoping it would give the customers warm feelings about the dresses in her shop. She'd always believed the little details of her store mattered. But now as she moved past the half-empty shelves of shoes and clutches, the sparse racks of wedding gowns and bridesmaids' dresses, the displays of tuxedos, and the elegant chairs and chaises arranged in front of the dressing rooms, she worried her limited stock would do just the opposite and discourage customers from purchasing.

"Welcome to Fairytale. I'm Dakota. How may I help you?" Her black stilettos clacked along the white tile floor as she came around the counter. Waiting for her were two young women who appeared to be in their midtwenties, clad in matching cranberry-colored puffer coats. Based on their similar facial structures, she assumed they were related — possibly even sisters. Their matching coats made them look cute and youthful.

One of the women held up a catalog opened to a page featuring a gown Dakota immediately recognized. The figure-hugging dress had a V-shaped neckline, long sleeves, a fine lace bodice adorned with sparkling beads, and a train that extended from the mermaid skirt.

This gown was supposedly going to be all the rage this season, and Dakota had planned to order at least two of them before the pipes burst.

"Do you have this dress?" the young woman asked.

Dakota's attention was drawn to the young woman's left ring finger, where a large diamond in a platinum setting sparkled. She did her best to keep a smile on her lips. "I don't have that exact gown, but I have something similar." She nodded toward the racks behind her and then took in the woman's figure. "I would imagine you're a six."

The woman blinked with shock. "How'd you know that?"

"Lucky guess." She'd always had a gift when it came to sewing, which included sizing up her clients on sight. "Would you like to see what I have?"

The bride-to-be and her companion shared a look before they followed her to her racks of gowns, where she located a satin dress with an organza ruffle mermaid skirt and a sweetheart neckline. Although both dresses featured a form-fitting bodice, this one did not have beading or a train.

"This gown is lovely and will be perfect on you," Dakota told her. "It's 30 percent off too. Would you like to try it on?"

The customer frowned. "That's not exactly what I'm looking for."

"Isn't that style out of season?" The other woman leaned toward her companion and whispered, "That must be why it's on sale."

Dakota did her best to hide her disappointment. It *was* out of season, but classic never went out of style. The mermaid shape was always a favorite, with or without sequins and beads. "I have a few others you might like." She pulled out three more dresses, but the women shook their heads.

"Well, thank you for your time," the bride-to-be said.

"I don't know why Karen recommended this shop. What a disappointment," the second woman muttered on her way to the door.

"I'll have newer dresses soon," Dakota called as the women stepped onto Main Street, sending a gust of late February air into the store. "I hope," she added with a wince.

If only she had the means to purchase more of this year's gowns. She needed to call the insurance company again to demand they reimburse her for her lost stock, if only so she could afford more inventory.

When the door burst open and the bell rang, another blast of cold air filtered in.

"Auntie!"

Dakota managed a smile as her niece barreled toward the front counter, her long dark ponytail swishing behind her. She dropped her backpack on the floor behind the counter and began shucking her black coat, revealing a light-pink sweater that complemented her gray skirt and black boots.

"Hey, Skye." Dakota joined her at the counter. "How was your Monday?"

Her niece hopped up onto the stool behind the counter. "I'm so done with high school."

"Tomorrow is the first of March, and before you know it, June will be here and your junior year will be over."

"I know, but everyone is so juvenile." Skye leaned forward, resting her elbows on her knees. "I told you last week that Ashley was obsessed with Tommy, right?"

Dakota nodded. Although she wasn't a fan of teen gossip, she was grateful her niece trusted her and felt comfortable confiding in her.

"And today all she talked about was Bart." She waved her hands around, flashing her coral-colored nail polish. "It was Bart this and Bart that all day long. She talked about him in the hallway between classes. She babbled about him during lunch. How cute he is. How he has the best smile. How he's so funny and athletic."

Skye yanked her sparkly fuchsia insulated water bottle from the side pocket of her rose-colored backpack and took a drink. Dakota smiled at how committed to pink her niece was. "I love Ashley like a sister, but she's boy crazy. I sure hope I never act like that. I mean, we're sixteen, but we can still be mature, you know?"

Dakota bit back a grin. Her niece was all grown up, or at least partway there. Gone was her little buddy who tried to do everything just like "Auntie Kota." Instead, Skye was complaining about boys. At least one thing remained the same: Dakota was still a cool aunt in her niece's eyes, and having Skye working with her at the bridal shop after school for the past year had helped them grow even closer.

Kayleigh, Dakota's best friend, had always called Skye Dakota's mini-me, and with the same dark hair, dark eyes, and height of five feet seven, Dakota agreed they resembled each other. In fact, they were often mistaken for sisters, which Dakota took as a compliment since they were fourteen years apart.

"Sweetie, you're mature for your age, but sometimes girls just get caught up in the drama, you know? They get excited and let their crushes take over their lives. Someday you might meet a guy who sweeps you off your feet."

"Sure." Skye gave her a look of disbelief. "But I doubt that will happen when I'm in high school. What are the chances of anyone actually marrying their high school sweetheart?"

An image of Hudson Garrity filled Dakota's mind. She could still see those bright-blue eyes that melted her insides, and she could even hear the deep baritone laugh that always made her toes curl. He'd been her crush in middle school and her boyfriend in high school and college — then her one big heartbreak and regret as an adult when he'd chosen a career in New York City over their plans, their life together.

She touched her naked finger where a small diamond engagement ring had once sat. Hudson had given it to her when they were twenty-one, and she could still remember how it felt to wear it. But it was a promise that had never come true. She shook her head, also trying to shake off the grief that suddenly appeared.

Why was the wound in her heart still so raw after seven years?

Skye's voice brought her back to the present. "If you fall in love in high school, won't you outgrow each other?"

Dakota knew there was a ring of truth to Skye's words. At least for her and Hud.

"I mean, my parents met in college," Skye continued, "and I bet you really find yourself during those years. That's why, statistically, high school relationships are doomed to fail. It makes sense to me." She shrugged and took another sip of water.

Dakota bobbed her head in agreement. "Right." Then she cleared her throat. "So, I had a customer in shortly before you got here, but it didn't go the way I'd hoped."

As Dakota shared the story, Skye's pretty face transformed into a frown. "I'm sorry she didn't like the mermaid dress."

"That's why I need to keep steaming the damaged dresses I can salvage. We need more variety available for customers."

"Can't you pay Miller's next door to do it

instead?"

"I wish, but it's too expensive." Dakota's savings were nearly gone, and her credit card was maxed out thanks to the burst pipe and her lousy landlord. Though she knew Mr. Miller would dry-clean the dresses for her at reduced cost, she couldn't even afford his help at a discount.

When her phone dinged, she pulled it from her skirt pocket and found a message from Parker Bryant.

Hey, just wanted to tell you I had a great time Saturday. Hope you're having a good Monday.

"Mr. Bryant texted you?"

Dakota looked up and found her niece leaning over the counter, straining to read over her shoulder. "Hey, Miss Nosy Pants!" she teased. "I don't try to read your text messages." She dropped her phone back into her pocket and started toward the back of the store. "You cover the counter while I go work in the back, okay? Call me if you need me."

"Whoa, Auntie." Skye trailed after her. "You didn't come to Nana's yesterday for supper, so I never got the details from your date."

Dakota shook her head as she walked through the doorway to where her small office, a sewing and workroom, a restroom, and a small break room were located. "There's nothing to tell."

"That can't be true," her niece whined. "I deserve to hear the details. I set you up with Mr. Bryant because you need to get out and have some fun. All you've done since the pipes burst is work long hours in here, cleaning up and steaming gowns. You need to have a life, Auntie."

Dakota picked up the steamer and turned it on. "Dating isn't a priority right now, Skye. You know I'm trying to get things back on track so I don't lose my boutique and my house."

"But you haven't been in a relationship for, like, three years."

Dakota spun to face her. "That's not true."

"When was the last time you had a boyfriend?" She rested her hands on her slim waist.

Dakota's mind drew a blank.

A grin spread on Skye's face, and she pointed a finger at her aunt. "See? I told you. The last guy you dated was the one who rear-ended your car after he dropped you off at the apartment complex where you used to live."

"How on earth did you remember that

disaster?"

Skye lifted her chin. "Because I'm the observant sister. Aubrey is the whimsical sister. You're the fun aunt. Dad just kills the vibe. We all have our roles in the family — and don't change the subject!" Her eyes sparkled with excitement. "I bet you hit it off with Mr. Bryant. He's, like, the best teacher we have at Flowering Grove High. The best art teacher, at least."

"He was . . . nice." Dakota had liked him. He was polite and funny, and he had an easy sense of humor. In fact, she had no complaints about the date at all. It truly had been nice. A nice date with a nice guy at a nice coffee shop followed by a nice walk. Their conversation had flowed fairly easily, and Parker was certainly easy on the eyes with his dark eyes and strong shoulders.

Even so, the spark was missing. He was her type to a T— good with kids, attentive, laid-back, polite. So why did the date leave her feeling so lukewarm?

"And . . . ?" Skye folded her hands and bounced on the balls of her feet. "Are you going to see him again?"

Dakota hesitated. Although she'd liked Parker, she couldn't see herself in a relationship with him. Besides, when would she fit a relationship into her busy schedule? Not only was she trying to get her business back on its feet, but she also taught skating lessons on Friday and Saturday nights at the Flowering Grove Rollerama. Oh, and her house was a disaster too. She didn't even have time to clean — let alone date.

"Come on, Auntie. I know he's, like, nearly forty, but you have to admit he's good-looking, even for an old guy."

Dakota guffawed. "First of all, he's only thirty-three, and second, forty is not ancient, young lady. Your dad is forty-two, and your mom is forty-one."

"Yeah, and they're old. But Mr. Bryant is so nice." Her eyes seemed to search Dakota's. "At least tell me why you don't like him."

Dakota began steaming a gown while she considered the question. "I do like him."

"Then what's the problem?"

Dakota shrugged. "I just don't have time for a relationship."

"Ugh!" Skye rolled her eyes. "You always say that, but if you want something, you can make time for it."

"It's not that simple," Dakota said, moving the steamer up and down the gown's lace bodice.

"But you sell wedding gowns, for goodness' sake. Don't you want to get married and have a wedding of your own? Have a family?"

"Of course I do."

"Well, that won't happen if you don't make time for a relationship."

Dakota wished it were that simple. She loved helping brides dress for the wedding of their dreams, which was why she opened this boutique. Witnessing the pure joy glowing on her customers' faces when they found the perfect gown felt almost magical. In fact, she eventually wanted to have a place where she could not only sell gowns but also host weddings. An all-inclusive wedding venue with a boutique and a large restored building — such as a barn or an old mill where couples could have their ceremony and reception — would be perfect. Perhaps one day she'd find a farm to purchase, but first she'd need the funds to open the place . . .

Until then, she'd continue to sell gowns and help brides plan their dream weddings and their happily ever afters. After all, she believed in fairytales for the brides-to-be who shopped with her, though she didn't believe she'd ever experience her own. She'd just have to live vicariously through her customers instead — which meant getting the restored gowns out to the floor as soon as possible.

She turned her attention back to her niece. "Would you please go out front in case we have customers? I have that bell on the door, but it's more appealing to be welcomed by someone in the showroom."

"You're just deflecting because you know I'm right." She pointed to Dakota's pocket. "Are you going to text Mr. Bryant back and ask him out?"

"Maybe later, when my hands aren't occupied." She pointed to the dress.

Skye moved to the doorway, then turned to face her aunt again. "You really should text him back. I think you two would make a super-cute couple."

"I'll think about it," Dakota promised.

"Good." Skye's smile was back. "By the way, have you thought about playing more hip music here?" She pointed to the speaker above her. An instrumental version of "All of Me" by John Legend was barely audible above the hum of the dehumidifier and air-moving machine, which were supposed to be helping rid the store of its water damage smell.

Dakota sighed. "Studies have shown that bridal shop patrons are more apt to purchase a gown and other accessories if classic romantic music is playing in the boutique."

Her niece seemed unconvinced. "Well, this is Flowering Grove, after all. I think the customers would appreciate hearing a Kirwan song every once in a while since the lead singer married a local."

"Skye . . ." Dakota's voice held an undercurrent of warning.

"Fine, fine. We'll keep playing the boring old-people music, but I'm singing a Kirwan song in my head." With a flourish she disappeared from the doorway, her footfalls sounding on her way back to the front.

Dakota set down the steamer and yanked her phone from her pocket. Then she placed it on the table beside her. Maybe she'd think about texting Parker back later. *Maybe.*

Hudson stared at his computer screen in his dark office. Horns blasted and traffic hummed from the Manhattan streets below. The sounds had become comforting to him since he'd moved to the city years ago.

A tap sounded on the doorframe, and he looked up just as Darren Jensen, his best friend and business partner, leaned in. "Hey, Hud. Don't you know what time it is?"

Hudson glanced down at the bottom

right-hand corner of his screen. "It's 8:38."

"That was rhetorical," Darren deadpanned. "Why are you still here?"

"For the same reason you are — working."

"Yeah, but we worked until nine every night last week. Get outta here and get a life."

Hudson gave him a wry smile. "You're the one with the life, so *you* get outta here. The only thing waiting for me at home is the television, and I'm not even streaming anything right now."

"Man, that's your own fault. You could have all the dates you want, but you picked being married to the company instead."

"And it worked out well for both of us, huh?" Hudson leaned back in his chair, and it groaned in response. Their company, D&H Software Solutions, had finally been sold — and once the deal was complete, Hudson and Darren would have to decide what to do next.

Darren's phone pinged, and his hazel eyes moved to the screen.

"Lauryn?" Hud asked.

Darren swept his fingers over his stubble, the light-brown hair barely visible in the dim office lighting. Meanwhile, Hudson's own five o'clock shadow probably could've been seen from the street below. "Yeah. I promised her I'd meet her at seven. This is the fourth time she's texted me."

"So quit talking about it and leave."

Darren turned toward the doorway, then turned back and pointed his phone at Hudson. "You should seriously consider Bahrain."

Hudson grimaced. "I don't know . . ."

"It's a great offer, Hud. We could whip that company into shape, help sell it, and move on again."

"What about Lauryn?"

Darren smiled. "I'm going to ask her to go with me. You need to say yes."

Hudson shrugged. "Maybe I will."

When Darren's phone started to ring, he held it up. "Gotta run. See you tomorrow."

Before Hudson could respond, his best friend was gone, talking on the phone as he hurried down the hallway. Hud yawned and rubbed his eyes, then got up and stretched his legs.

He walked to the window and peered down at the headlights illuminating the streets of Manhattan. Taxis and cars moved past, horns blaring every once in a while. He smiled. After so many years of hard work, he finally felt he had accomplished something.

It had been seven years since he'd left his hometown of Flowering Grove, North Carolina, and moved to New York City to chase his dream of running a software company. He'd started out at the bottom of the first company that hired him, then worked his way up to the top. He'd met his business partner, Darren, along the way, and together they had taken a chance and started their own firm. After only four years, they now had a sale and more money than Hudson ever could've dreamed of.

He walked back over to his desk and sat down, taking in the neat piles of papers. He was grateful for his financial gains, since they had allowed him to take care of the two people who meant the most to him — his baby sister, Layla, and his aunt Trudy. His aunt had raised him and Layla after their parents died in a car accident, when Hudson was eight and Layla only a year old. Thanks to his success, he'd been able to pay off Trudy's house, allowing her to retire. He'd also paid for Layla's college education.

But now he was at a crossroads and had to figure out what to do. Although he'd enjoyed living comfortably, he had no ties to New York. No family and definitely no girlfriend. But he was too busy providing for his aunt and sister to worry about that. His parents would've wanted him to take care of them, and they were the only family he needed.

As he hit the button to power down his computer, his cell phone started to ring. He picked up and saw his little sister's name on the screen.

"Hey, Layla," he said.

"Hud!" The excitement in her voice was palpable. "I have news."

He hit the speaker button on the phone and grabbed his coat. "Do tell, baby sis."

"I'm engaged!"

Hudson froze, his coat half on. Surely he hadn't heard her correctly. "You're *what*?"

"Engaged. I'm getting married." She giggled with joy.

He let his coat drop to the floor, then sat down on his chair. He clutched the phone and switched off the speaker. "To who?"

"To my boyfriend, of course. You met him when you came home for Christmas."

Hudson searched his memory, trying to recall meeting Layla's boyfriend. Then a vision of a skinny, nondescript guy filled his mind. "Shawn?"

She expelled a frustrated puff of air. "It's *Shane.* You need to pay better attention, Hud."

He brushed his hand down his face. Now he remembered talking to the guy during Christmas dinner. He clearly recalled thinking Layla could do much better. "He mows lawns, right?"

"No, he's a landscaper," she corrected him. "You have to see what he did for Aunt Trudy's backyard. The flowerbeds look awesome, and he added a cute little birdbath in the corner. He put in a bench and a path too. He's very talented."

Hudson couldn't stop his snort. "Do landscapers make enough money to support a family?"

"Of course they do."

He ignored the irritation in her tone. "Don't you think you're rushing into this?"

"Not at all. Today is our three-month anniversary, and we've known we wanted to get married since our first date. Remember how we reconnected at the coffeehouse? We were both there on our lunch breaks. I saw him and recognized him from high school."

"Wait a minute," Hud said as his conversation with Shane returned to him. "Didn't he mention at dinner that he was always in trouble in high school?"

"Yeah, and we laughed about it. He's changed just like I have." She paused for a moment. "He earned his GED and got his life together. He's a really hard worker, Hud."

"That's great and all, but three months isn't long enough. Marriage is a serious commitment."

"I *know,* Hud," she muttered. "We're both ready to commit."

He rolled his eyes. "But you're only —"

"Don't you dare tell me I'm too young to get married," she snapped. "I'm almost twenty-three, and you got engaged at twenty-one."

"And look how well that turned out. Please don't make the same mistakes I did." He pressed his lips together as a vision of Dakota Jamison gripped his mind. He closed his eyes and tried to stop the familiar heartbreak from creeping into his chest.

Dakota had been the love of his life. At least, that was what he'd believed — until she dumped him without any explanation.

"Did you hear what I said, Hud? We're getting married in June."

Her statement brought him out of his thoughts. "June?"

"Yes, June," she said firmly.

Hudson glowered. "Layla, I don't approve of this."

She sniffed on the other end of the line. "I don't need your approval, Hud. You don't have to be such a jerk all the time."

"I'm just looking out for you —"

Click.

Hudson stared at the screen. As moments ticked by, worry sifted through him. He shook his head. He knew what he had to do.

The sale of the company would take a few months before it was final, which meant he could come and go from the office as he pleased. He would pack up his essentials and head to Flowering Grove.

He shrugged on his coat, grabbed his laptop, and called a cab.

It was his job to take care of his baby sister — and he wasn't about to let her make the biggest mistake of her life.

Chapter 2

The bell above the door rang the following Tuesday afternoon just as Dakota was walking out of her workroom and toward the front of the store.

"Kayleigh!" Dakota called out in greeting. "What brings you out this way?"

Her best friend since kindergarten placed a stack of flyers on the counter. "I'm passing these out along Main Street, and I thought I'd stop in. We're trying to drum up publicity for the '80s-themed night at the rink on Saturday."

"Ugh, you know I love a leg warmer moment. Hand me one to put up in the window!" Dakota reached behind her desk for the tape. "My best friend buying the rink is maybe the fifth best thing ever to happen to me."

"Only fifth? I'd have thought we'd rank higher since you seem to be on the rink every night." Kayleigh laughed. "But for me too. The car dealership's business is great and all, but since it has been in Brice's family for so long, he wanted something fun that was just ours. I'm glad I let him convince me we should buy the rink when it went up for sale."

"And you two have been doing a great job ever since!" Dakota beamed. "My best friend breathing new life into the Flowering Grove Rollerama — saving our community from a life without disco balls, teaching a whole new generation to love skating. A true hero."

Kayleigh laughed again. "Thanks, friend. Brice thinks we'll bring in more business if we try more theme nights."

Dakota pulled a piece of tape off its dispenser. "We all know the success is due to your two amazing roller-skating instructors." Dakota loved teaching others how to skate. It took her back to when her mother had taught her in the cul-de-sac in front of their house when she was only six years old.

"We are the best, aren't we?" Kayleigh agreed.

Dakota hung one flyer in the window and then taped another on the door before returning to the counter. "How's little Gigi doing?"

"She's a mess." Kayleigh yanked her

phone from the back pocket of her jeans. "You gotta see what she wore today." She angled the screen toward her friend.

Dakota chuckled as she took in Kayleigh's six-year-old, clad in a violet dress and purple rain boots with periwinkle bows on her curly blond pigtails. "Oh, Kay. She's such a cutie pie."

"She's decided it's time to choose her own outfits for school, so she insisted on wearing the dress Brice's mom got her last year. I'm surprised it still fits. Of course we all have to wear rain boots with our best dresses, right?"

With her bright-blue eyes and angelic face, Gigi was the spitting image of her mother — but she was just like her dad in personality. Little Gigi was determined, and when she set her sights on something, she went for it. It reminded Dakota of how sure Brice had been about Kayleigh when they started dating eight years ago. They'd locked eyes from across the skating rink one evening, and that was it. He said it took just one lap for him to know she was *the one.*

That was the type of love Dakota wanted. Someone whose devotion was unwavering, who picked her every day. And she'd thought, once upon a time, that maybe she'd found it . . .

But that heartache was behind her. She had her friends, her family, and her own slice of happily ever after with her store.

"She looks just like you," Dakota said.

"My mom says she acts like me too. Stubborn as an ox."

"As we all should be." Dakota gave her a high five, and they laughed again.

Kayleigh picked up the remaining flyers. "I'd better get running. I have to pick Gigi up from school in about an hour." She pulled Dakota in for a side hug. "I'll see you Friday night at the rink, right?"

"Don't you always? Tell Gigi and Brice hello for me."

"Will do." Tossing a wave behind her, Kayleigh hurried out onto Main Street.

Dakota returned to her workroom full of dresses in need of care. She'd had a half dozen customers stop by so far this week, and five of them were disappointed with her selection of gowns. The sixth didn't purchase a dress, but she did try one on and promised to come back with her mother. Dakota tried her best to keep her worry and disappointment at bay. Sales were going to get better. They had to. She just needed to keep steaming the gowns and getting them out onto the floor.

Dakota finished the gown she was working on and was adding it to a rack when she heard the front doorbell ring. She looked up and saw Layla Garrity hurrying into the store, her aunt Trudy close behind.

"I'm engaged!" Layla flashed a small solitaire diamond in a gold setting at Dakota. In her right hand she held a small tote bag.

Dakota examined the ring, then hugged Layla as a warm burst of affection overwhelmed her. "Congratulations! It's just lovely. I'm so happy for you, Layla."

The young woman beamed and pushed her long, thick dark hair off her slight shoulders. "Thank you. Shane asked last Monday. It was our three-month anniversary, and he took me to our favorite restaurant, which was where we had our first date. Then we went for a walk, and he got down on one knee."

Dakota smiled. She had observed Layla and Shane together at the roller rink, and he seemed like a sweet young man. He hung on Layla's every word and studied her like she was the most interesting and attractive woman in the world.

A dreamy sigh escaped Layla's lips. "When you know, you know, right?"

Dakota nodded, though she wondered what it would feel like to know for sure she'd found the love of her life. She'd thought she'd known once, but . . .

Memories of Hudson and their happier times flashed through her mind all too often. She tried to ignore them and focus on Layla, but it was the second time in the past week he had snuck back into her thoughts. She might not be sure about her love life, but she was positive she'd left Hudson in the past, where he belonged. What was wrong with her?

"Have you set a date?" she asked, hoping to kick Layla's older brother out of her brain for good.

Layla's sky-blue eyes twinkled, and she shared a smile with her aunt. "The second Saturday in June."

"That only gives us three months to pull everything together," Trudy Garrity chimed in, rubbing her niece's shoulder. "I'm sorry we didn't make an appointment, Dakota, but Layla happened to get the afternoon off."

"This is the perfect time. Do you have a gown in mind?"

Layla bit her lower lip and pulled a framed photo out of her tote bag.

Dakota sucked in a breath as she took in the portrait she immediately recognized — Layla's parents, Daphne and Chandler

Garrity, on their wedding day, posing in front of the altar at their church. The portrait hung in Trudy's den, a room where Dakota had spent countless hours with Hudson — watching movies, snuggling on the sofa, kissing, talking late into the night, playing games with his aunt and sister, and making plans for a future they'd never share.

Stop, stop, stop!

"What do you think, Dakota?"

Her gaze moved to Layla's, and heat crawled up her neck. "I'm sorry. What did you say?"

Layla's expression was hopeful. "My mom's gown. Can you make it for me?"

Dakota shook off her embarrassment and focused on the dress. Confidence hurtled through her. She'd much rather sew than steam gowns.

She quickly assessed the dress's details. The white, early '90s gown had a sweetheart neckline, short sleeves, a full skirt, a chapel-length train, and copious amounts of beading and ruffles. Oh boy.

"I can make it for you, but I'm not sure I can get it done by your wedding. And creating one from scratch is expensive." She tapped her chin with a light-pink manicured nail. "By any chance, do you still have your mom's gown? If you do, then I can alter it for you."

Layla and her aunt exchanged a sad expression. "No."

"Chandler and Daphne moved around a lot before Hudson was born," Trudy said. "I remember Daphne once mentioning the gown had been lost in one of their moves."

Dakota recalled the stories about Hudson's parents. They'd always struggled financially, with his father jumping from job to job.

"I wish I had it. I would have cherished it." Layla's voice was small, and her stricken expression squeezed Dakota's heart.

Dakota snapped her fingers. "I have an idea." She beckoned Layla and her aunt to follow her over to the racks of gowns. She quickly found a similar white one from two seasons ago with short sleeves and a chapel-length train, sans the beading and ruffles. "What do you think about altering this to look more like your mom's?"

Layla's pretty face lit with excitement. "You can do that?"

Dakota nodded.

"Thank you, thank you! I mean, I know it's a rush job. Not that I doubt your sewing skills!" Layla was almost bouncing with excitement. "Oh my gosh, remember those matching shirts you made for you and Hud . . ." She paused a little awkwardly. "Of course, I mean, a wedding dress is, like, a way bigger project, and I'm sure you don't remember some silly shirts from fifteen years ago . . ." She trailed off.

Dakota didn't know what to say. The silence was almost painfully loud, but she tried to keep smiling through it.

"Anyway, you're a lifesaver, Dakota!"

Dakota gripped the hanger but kept her expression blank. "Well, let's see if the dress fits first. I think this is your size. Would you like to try it on?"

"Oh yes, please." Layla and her aunt slipped into the nearby dressing room.

A few moments later when they returned, tears pricked Dakota's eyes at the sight of Layla stepping up onto the small platform in front of the wall of mirrors. This was her favorite part of the job — when the future brides gazed at their reflections, and their faces shone with joy and anticipation. She loved helping them create their fantasy wedding. Many of them declared they felt like princesses, and that was her goal. It was the main reason she'd named her store Fairytale Bridal.

Trudy covered her mouth with her hands, and her bright-hazel eyes gleamed with tears. "Oh, Layla. You're positively glowing."

"I agree," Dakota said.

Layla moved back and forth in front of the mirror, the satin softly swishing. A wide smile took over her face, and she met Dakota's gaze in the mirror. "How'd you know this was my size?"

Dakota shrugged. "I've measured a lot of dresses." Then she pointed to the gown. "If you'd like, I can add the ruffles and beading. I'll do my best to match your mother's dress."

Layla examined herself at different angles. "Do you think Shane will like it?"

Dakota and Trudy shared a knowing look before Trudy said, "He'll love it, honey."

"He sure will," Dakota agreed.

Layla spun to face them. "*This* is the dress." She grinned. "I'm so excited I could pop."

"Perfect." Dakota couldn't wait to dive into the alterations. Happiness swelled inside her as she imagined adding the details to match Layla's mother's gown. She already couldn't wait for the final fitting, when Layla would stand in front of the mirrors again and see her reflection in the finished dress.

"How much will it be?" Trudy asked.

"Why don't we talk at the counter, and I'll look it up for you?"

After Layla changed back into her jeans and hoodie, she and her aunt met Dakota at the counter. Trudy handed Dakota the wardrobe bag, and she hung it on a nearby hook before pulling the ticket out of a pocket on the bag.

Dakota scanned the barcode, and the price filled the computer screen. She opened her mouth to share the figure just as Skye flounced through the front door of the shop.

Dakota greeted her niece, who dropped her purse and backpack behind the counter.

"This is my niece," Dakota said. "And this is Layla and her aunt, Ms. Garrity."

Trudy smiled. "I remember when you were knee-high to a grasshopper, sweetheart. Call me Trudy."

"Nice to see you, Ms. Trudy." Skye nodded toward the gown. "When's the big day?"

"The second Saturday in June," Layla told her. Then she turned to Dakota. "How much did you say it was again?"

Dakota calculated the cost of the alteration, adding in beading and ruffles, then told her the price.

Layla blanched. "Oh. I had no idea." She turned to her aunt. "I don't have that much saved up. I want a small wedding, but I've always dreamt of looking like my mom on my wedding day to remember and honor her."

Her aunt patted her hand. "Sweetie, I'm sure your brother would help cover the cost if you asked him. He'd do anything for you."

Layla's face fell again, and her aunt turned back to Dakota. "Before we commit, I'll have to talk to Hud about it."

"I understand." Dakota hesitated, and the strange urge to help her ex-fiancé's sister took hold of her. "I'm happy to give you the friends and family discount. That will save you 10 percent on the gown and the alterations." Dakota felt Skye staring at her, but she didn't budge.

"You'd do that for me?"

"Of course I would."

"I appreciate it so much. Would you possibly hold the gown for me so I can come back to pay for it later this week?"

"I'm happy to." Dakota gestured toward the photo of Layla's parents. "I'll need to make a copy of that so I can match the dress to it."

"I can make a copy in the back," Skye said.

Layla handed her the photo, and Skye hurried to the back office.

Trudy turned to Dakota. "Have you found yourself a special fella yet?"

Dakota shifted her weight on her feet. Why were people so interested in her love life all of a sudden? "Not yet, I'm afraid."

Trudy shook her head. "I'm surprised to hear that."

For a moment, Dakota considered asking Trudy about Hudson. Had he settled down? Was he married? Did he have a family? Had he bought a large house close to the city and adopted a couple of dogs?

But then again, why should she care? He didn't care enough to ask about her, let alone start his company in Flowering Grove so they could've built a life together.

Dakota was grateful for the distraction when Skye headed back their way.

Her niece gave the photo back to Layla. "Your gown is going to be amazing. My auntie is the best seamstress around."

"I remember that about her." Layla gently returned the portrait to her tote bag. "She made Barbie clothes for me one year for Christmas. I had the best-dressed Barbies out of all my friends."

"Really?" Skye asked, glancing at Dakota. "I didn't know that."

Dakota nodded. That was the year she and Hud had started dating.

Stop with the memories already!

"It's so great to see you again, Dakota." Trudy waved at Skye. "Thank you both for making Layla's wedding dream come true."

Dakota told them goodbye and then started a ticket for the dress, filling in Layla's name and Trudy's address, which she still knew by heart.

"How come you didn't ask for their address or phone numbers?" Skye asked, perching on the stool beside her aunt.

"Because I already know them." Dakota sighed. "I was engaged to Layla's older brother."

"That's Hud's sister?"

She lifted an eyebrow. "You remember him?"

"Of course I do. He gave me books from my favorite author for my birthday one year."

Dakota chuckled. "I actually picked them out but *let* him give them to you."

Skye rolled her eyes. "Cool, so . . . when was the last time you saw him?"

The day I broke up with him. "It's been a long time. Last I heard, he'd moved away."

"And he never comes back home to see his family?"

Dakota hit the button to print the ticket. "If he has, I haven't run into him." *And*

43

thank goodness for that.

They were silent as Dakota attached the ticket to the gown's wardrobe bag.

"You know, Auntie, if you give everyone the family and friends discount, you won't have a bridal shop anymore."

She spun to face her niece. "What does that mean?"

"You're selling older gowns at a discount already, and then you gave her a discount on top of it." Skye's lips formed a thin line.

Dakota sighed. "You're right. But I've known Layla almost as long as you've been alive." She shook her head. "You heard what her aunt said. It's my job to give people the wedding of their dreams."

"But dreams won't pay the lease on this place."

Dakota tilted her head. "Where'd you get your business sense?"

"I'm a Jamison. From my dad, of course." Skye smirked and headed toward the back of the store.

Dakota pressed her lips together, silently acknowledging again that Skye was right. She shouldn't have given Layla a discount, but she had to make Layla's wedding dress more affordable. Layla and Trudy were almost her family. No matter her feelings about Hud, she would make sure Layla had the wedding she always wanted.

Chapter 3

Later that evening, Dakota steered her ten-year-old blue Ford Focus sedan into her driveway. Exhaustion covered her as she killed the engine. She slumped in her seat and rested her forehead against the steering wheel as a yawn overtook her. Pulling herself up, she looked ahead at her little house. When her phone started to ring, her father's name flashed on the screen. She stared at it for a moment, then decided to ignore the call as she climbed out of the car.

Dad had insisted that Dakota was taking on too much by buying a house while her business was still blossoming. Yet when the two-bedroom home came up for sale, Dakota fell in love with it. She scraped together a down payment and snatched up the house before anyone else could grab it. Its one-car garage, galley kitchen, two small bedrooms, family room, laundry room, and tiny deck were all she needed. And it was hers. Well, technically, it belonged to the bank, but it would officially be hers someday.

After grabbing her mail from the mailbox and unlocking her door, Dakota stepped inside and was met by her orange tabby. "Hey, Trouble. How was your day?"

The cat meowed and walked circles around her feet, rubbing her shins while she set her keys, purse, and tote bag on the bench by the door.

"Mine was less than stellar, but thanks to Layla, it wasn't a complete wash." She deposited the mail on the kitchen counter and scanned the cabinets that showed their age. A few of the doors were hanging at odd angles, in desperate need of an update — or at least a coat of paint. She'd get around to that . . . eventually. She turned to the cat yammering at her feet. "Are you hungry?"

The cat sang a chorus of meows while continuing to massage Dakota's shins.

"I thought so." She opened the cabinet door to retrieve the cat food, and the hinges came off, sending the cabinet door and her arm sailing onto the counter with a *thwack*. Dakota blinked and then grimaced. Great. Just what she needed: something else to fix. But she'd have to worry about that later. She couldn't take on one more task until her store issues were handled.

She picked up Trouble's bowl and filled it with canned food. Tonight's flavor was Tuna Delight. Yucky smelling, but Trouble loved it. "Enjoy," she said, setting the dish in front of him.

He purred and dug in.

Dakota made her way down the short hallway to her bedroom. When she stepped inside, she kicked off her heels and then halted. "Oh no!"

Sheets of toilet paper decorated the floor. She brushed her hand down her face, turned toward the open bathroom door, and groaned. How could she have forgotten to close the bathroom door this morning? Trouble loved dragging toilet tissue all over the room.

She picked up the mess, but when she entered the bathroom, her mouth dropped open. The cat not only had wasted an entire roll of paper but also had pulled the toilet paper holder out of the drywall. If only Dakota had fixed the loose holder sooner. It was her fault for letting it get to that point. She leaned against the doorjamb. She had enough problems to work out at the store, and she had no budget or time to fix her house.

After placing a roll of paper on the back

of the toilet tank, she closed the bathroom door. She'd worry about fixing the holder another day. Right now all she wanted was to put up her sore feet after working late into the evening, trying to salvage more gowns.

Dakota changed out of her skirt and sweater and pulled on her favorite yoga pants and gray hoodie before returning to the kitchen. When she found her cat taking a bath in the corner, she wagged a finger at him. "Trouble, you're a bad kitty. I cleaned up the mess, but you need a time-out."

The cat ignored her and continued licking his paws.

With a sigh, she opened the fridge and pulled out the chef's salad left over from yesterday's lunch. She wished she had more time for cooking an actual meal. And cleaning. And doing yard work in the spring and summer.

Dakota plopped down on her sofa, rested her aching feet on her coffee table, flipped on the television, and chewed a forkful of salad. Opening the messages on her phone, she looked at the few she had traded with Parker during the past week. They'd mostly made small talk about how glad they were March was here and the weather was finally starting to warm up a little. But she hadn't committed to seeing him again.

She frowned, set down her phone, and pulled out the sketch she'd created for Layla's dress, continuing her dinner as she studied the drawing. As her thoughts moved to Layla and her wedding plans, she couldn't help but think of Hudson too. She hoped he wouldn't come back to Flowering Grove until the wedding. If he did, she'd have to find a way to avoid him.

Dakota took another bite of salad as another thought hit her: Hudson Garrity had always been so career- and money-driven that perhaps he wouldn't bother to show up for the wedding at all.

And that would be fine with her.

Hudson steered his SUV down Main Street in Flowering Grove, his headlights guiding his way past the landmarks that had painted the backdrop of his life from his childhood until he'd moved away seven years ago.

He motored past the Barbecue Pit restaurant, where he'd eaten more meals than he could count, then the library where Aunt Trudy took him and Layla every Saturday afternoon when she didn't have to work. In the distance he spotted the sign for Vet's Field, where he'd attended the Fourth of

July fireworks every year until he moved north.

He merged onto Lincoln Avenue and drove past Ridge Road, the street that led to the home where he lived for a couple of years before his parents died. He could still remember every detail of that little house his parents had rented — the chipped gray paint on the front porch, the worn beige carpet in the family room, and the creaky stairs that led up to his small bedroom, where he'd lined up his Star Wars figures on the wooden shelves. He could almost hear the sound of his mother singing to his sister as she rocked her to sleep in the next room, and his father's laugh while they played catch in the small backyard.

Hudson pushed that image out of his thoughts and flipped on his right blinker before turning onto Zimmer Avenue. He stopped at a stop sign and drummed the steering wheel to the beat of a country music song playing on the radio. It felt strange to be back in Flowering Grove, especially in March. For the past several years he'd managed to come for just a few days at Christmas, but now he was planning an extended visit.

Hudson gripped the wheel. He hadn't yet decided on the best way to talk his sister out of her crazy idea of getting married. Since he couldn't get through to her over the phone, he hoped discussing it with her in person would help her see she was making a huge mistake. Maybe she would listen to the voice of reason if they were sitting in the same room together. And if she insisted on getting married, then maybe he could convince her to postpone the wedding for a year — or maybe even two.

As he steered into his aunt's driveway, his headlights swept across her white Cape Cod–style home. The paint on the house and the gray shutters were starting to show their age, and he made a mental note to have the house painted this spring.

He slipped his gray Infiniti QX80 into Park. His best friend and business partner, Darren, liked to remind him that the Infiniti was completely unnecessary since they lived in Manhattan. Still, the SUV was one of the few splurges Hudson had allowed himself since he'd become a CEO. He enjoyed his spacious, four-bedroom apartment with its balcony and spectacular views in a great building, along with tailored designer suits, which were necessary in his line of work. Other than that, his money was invested, saved, provided to his aunt and sister, or given to his favorite charities.

He climbed from the SUV and trotted up the front steps. Just as he raised his hand to knock, the door swung open. His aunt stared up at him from across the threshold. "Hudson," she exclaimed. "Wh-what are you doing here?"

"After the way my last conversation ended with my sister, I thought I'd better come see her in person."

"Well, I'm sure glad you're here."

He allowed his aunt to pull him in for a warm hug, and he breathed in her comforting scent — Bengay mixed with baby powder. It seemed like only yesterday that he had to stand on his tiptoes to hug her, but ever since he'd hit his full height of six foot three at the age of nineteen, he'd adapted to bending to meet her five-foot-four height.

She patted his cheek. More wrinkles lined his aunt's bright-hazel eyes, and her medium-brown hair was highlighted with more gray, but she insisted her spirit was much younger than sixty-five. "I suppose you're here to discuss her wedding plans?"

"That's right." He glanced at Layla's gray Toyota Camry, which he'd purchased for her last year when her older Hyundai started having problems. Then he met his aunt's curious expression. "Is she home?"

"Right now she's on the phone. She'll be

so surprised to see you." She beckoned him into the house. "Bring in your luggage. I'll make up the cot in the craft room for you, just like we do at Christmas."

"Thanks, but I booked an Airbnb a few blocks from here."

Aunt Trudy's eyes lit with excitement. "You're back to stay for a while?"

"Possibly." They fell into step on their way inside the house. "Darren and I are in the process of finalizing the sale of the company, and I have a few offers on the table for my next position. I figured I'd spend some time here before I decide what to do next."

Aunt Trudy rubbed his bicep. "Maybe you'll decide to stay in Flowering Grove."

"Don't get your hopes up, but I'll be here for longer than usual."

"I guess I'll take what I can get."

He followed his aunt into the small family room, where Layla was sprawled on the sofa, her cell phone to her ear. When her blue eyes met his, they rounded.

"I have to let you go," she said into the phone. "My brother is here. Love you too, Shane." She disconnected the call and dropped her phone onto the sofa beside her. "Are you here to tell me what a jerk you've been and how sorry you are for hurting my feelings?"

Hudson sank into the armchair across from her and rested his elbows on his knees. Normally Layla was happy to see him during his brief holiday visits, but she was obviously still upset with him. She hadn't responded to his voicemails or text messages since she'd hung up on him last week. While her silence pricked at his heart, he still hadn't changed his mind — she was too immature to get married, and he was here to tell her so whether she wanted to hear it or not.

"Layla . . ." He sighed. "I just want to talk to you."

"Okay. I'm listening."

He licked his lips. "I'm sorry I hurt you."

"You are?" She sat up straight.

"But I don't approve of this wedding." He hated seeing his baby sister's face fall, but she was moving way too fast. *Again.* Layla had a bad habit of finding "true love" every other week. Sure, Shane had stuck around the longest, but Layla was a hopeless romantic — emphasis on *hopeless* — who picked out baby names after a first date. She also had a terrible habit of giving her true loves money — a situation Hudson had bailed her out of more than once.

Aside from that, Shane had a sketchy past. Layla had told Hudson that Shane had been kicked out of school for drugs and alcohol and fighting — all of which didn't make him the best choice for a husband. "I'm here to talk some sense into you."

Her blue eyes narrowed to slits. "I don't need you to talk sense into me."

"Layla," he began, his voice holding a hint of warning, "remember what you put Aunt Trudy and me through when you were in high school? You made some pretty bad decisions back then."

His sister hopped up to her feet. "You're bringing that up now?"

He stood, looking down at her. "You ran around with the wrong crowd and got into a lot of trouble back then. How am I supposed to trust your judgment after all of that?"

Her face turned as red as a tomato. "That was seven years ago, Hud. How dare you hold that against me? I'm not the same person I was."

"You were impulsive back then, and you're being impulsive now. You haven't known Shane that long. Three months is a blip in time, and marriage is a big commitment. I think you should date him for a while longer and see where it goes."

Aunt Trudy touched her chin, her gaze

bouncing from Layla to Hudson and back again.

Layla's hands balled into tight fists. "I don't need your lectures or your advice. I'm a grown woman, and I've made my decision." She pointed to the door. "Why don't you just go back to New York City where you belong?" Then she turned and bounded up the stairs to her bedroom before slamming her door.

Silence filled the den. Hudson kneaded his forehead, a headache brewing behind his eyes. This might have gone even worse than expected.

Aunt Trudy sighed from across the room and took a seat on the sofa. "You know you have to let her grow up, Hud. She's a young woman now, and she knows what she wants."

"She's not ready to get married."

"How do you know that?"

He rubbed his eyes. "I helped raise her, remember?"

His aunt's expression warmed. "And I raised you both."

He sat down again and rested his hands on his lap. He should have known that lecturing her wasn't going to work. After all, it hadn't worked last week on the phone.

He didn't want to lose his sister. He also

wasn't going to win this argument. As Layla's older brother, he believed it was his duty to pay for her wedding — but he would have to make it clear he couldn't support her choices in good conscience. Perhaps he could help her see the light before her wedding day and stop her from ruining her future.

He stood and started for the stairs.

"Where are you going?" his aunt called after him.

"To fix this."

Outside his sister's bedroom, Hudson knocked on the door and waited.

"What do you want?" Layla called from inside her room.

He leaned against the door. "Look, I don't approve of this wedding."

"You've made that crystal clear. Now go away."

Hudson looked up at the ceiling and closed his eyes. As much as he hated to do this, he made the pledge: "But I'll pay for it."

There was a beat of silence before footsteps sounded. Then the door opened. "You will?"

He nodded.

Layla studied him. "Does that mean you've changed your mind and you'll give us your blessing?"

He shook his head. "No. I think you're rushing into this."

"But you'll pay for it anyway?" she asked. When he nodded again in response, she pulled him in for a hug. "Thank you."

"Truce?" he asked.

"Truce." She smiled, and relief filtered through him. "You'll change your mind about my wedding, Hud. I know you will."

I doubt that.

Layla took his arm and yanked him toward the stairs. "We have a coffee cake, and I'll make your favorite coffee too."

They made their way to the kitchen, where she brewed three cups of coffee in the Keurig. Soon the three of them were drinking coffee and eating cake together.

Hudson pulled out his phone and began making a to-do list for his aunt's house, adding *Find a local paint company* to the top.

"You're working now?" Layla asked.

He shook his head. "I'm making a list of what needs to be done around here. I noticed the house could use a fresh coat of paint. If you know of a local company who can take care of it in the spring, I'll pay for it." He picked up his mug of coffee and grinned at his aunt. "Unless, of course, you'll let me buy you a nice condo, which would mean no maintenance." He was determined to spoil his aunt, even though she repeatedly turned down his offers.

Aunt Trudy remained silent and sipped her coffee.

"We could find you one where all of the upkeep is included, so you won't need to worry about finding someone to mow the yard. The really nice ones have fitness centers and a lot of social activities too," he added.

She swallowed a bite of cake and shook her head. "I don't need a fancy condo. This is where I raised you two, and it's enough for me."

"We'll talk about it later then." Maybe he'd just buy her a condo and then insist she move in. That might work. "What about a new car?" he asked. "Your Honda is starting to show its age."

She pressed her lips together. "There's nothing wrong with my car, and I happen to like it."

Layla turned to her brother. "How long are you staying?" she asked.

"At least until the wedding."

"Oh. That's good." She folded her hands. "I found a wedding dress today." Her face seemed to glow as she explained how she wanted a dress that looked like their mother's, but instead had found a similar one to have altered.

"How much money do you need for it?"

Layla shared a look with their aunt and then told him the price.

He pulled his wallet from his back pocket and opened it. "Use my card to pay for it."

"I'd like to pay for part of it."

"Don't be silly." He held his black credit card out to Layla. "Take it."

"No, you always pay for every —"

"Layla, Mom and Dad would want me to take care of you. I'll pay for the dress."

His sister's brow wrinkled. "I can't get to the store until later this week."

"No problem." He pushed the card back into his wallet and shoved it into his pocket. "I need to run some errands tomorrow anyway. Tell me where the shop is, and I'll take care of the dress."

Layla turned to their aunt, and Aunt Trudy gave Layla a quick nod. Then Layla turned back to Hudson with a sly smile. "That's a wonderful idea, Hud."

Had his sister's attitude just done a one-eighty? He cocked an eyebrow as suspicion filled him. "Am I missing something?"

"No, no." Layla's smile was bright. "I found the gown at Fairytale Bridal. It's on Main Street between Miller's Dry Cleaners and Swanson's Hardware, near Treasure Hunting Antique Mall." Her expression warmed. "Thank you for offering to pay. It means a lot to me."

"Of course." He cut himself another piece of cake. "How's work?"

"Great," she said. "We've been getting a lot of new patients, which doesn't surprise me since Dr. Warner is an excellent dentist."

Hudson took another crumbly bite and studied his sister. "Have you ever thought about going to dental school?"

"No." Layla laughed, then sobered as if surprised he wasn't laughing too. "Why?"

"So you can stay in a field you enjoy but make more money. If you want to go to dental school, I can —"

"I don't want to be a dentist. I love my job as a hygienist. I enjoy helping the patients and working with Dr. Warner. And even if I did want to go to dental school, I'd figure out a way to afford it myself," she said, her tone growing terse.

He set his fork down. "Layla, you have so much potential. You could become a dentist and then own your own practice. I could help you set it up."

"Hud," she began, leaning forward on the table, "believe it or not, not everyone wants to be the boss. And besides that, I don't need you to take care of me for the rest of my life. I can take care of myself."

Irritation coursed through Hudson on his drive to the Airbnb. His whole purpose in coming to Flowering Grove had been to stop his sister's wedding, but so far his sister was staying her course. She also dismissed his career advice, and his aunt rebuffed his offer of buying her a new condo or car. Nothing had gone right this evening.

When he reached the rental house, Hudson parked in the driveway. The large colonial on Oak Street was more than he needed, but it was the only Airbnb in Flowering Grove available for an extended stay.

He climbed out of his vehicle and looked toward the small house next door, where a blue Ford sedan sat out front. A warm yellow glow in the front window illuminated an orange cat lounging on the sill. Hudson shook his head. He couldn't imagine what it would feel like to not have a care in the world.

He gathered up his backpack and two suitcases and unlocked the front door with the keypad. With most of his stuff in storage and his apartment being sublet to a friend, he just had the basics with him. As he made his way through the large foyer, the house was still and quiet. *Too* quiet. He was used to the hustle and bustle of the big city, and silence unnerved him.

He climbed the stairs and found the master bedroom down the hall, past three large bedrooms and a bathroom. He began unpacking, grateful to have left most of his custom-made Armani suits behind. Although they were essential to his line of work as a CEO, he was still most comfortable in jeans. He supposed that was due to his upbringing in a small town with mostly blue-collar workers. He was grateful for the luxury of providing for his family, but he would never forget where he came from.

While hanging the two suits he'd brought with him in the closet, he wondered what it would be like to take the offer and move to Bahrain. Did he want to be that far way? If something happened to his aunt, it would take hours to get home.

But he couldn't even think about that right now. First he had to deal with his sister — and considering how the day had gone, convincing her to cancel her wedding was going to be even more complicated than he'd imagined.

Chapter 4

Dakota sat up straight at her desk the following morning despite tossing and turning all night. With the hums of the dehumidifier and air-moving machine serenading her, she tried to ignore the worry pressing down on her shoulders. She held her phone to her ear while the hold music played. She'd practiced her speech during her drive to the store this morning, and she was finally going to confront her insurance company about paying her for her lost dress stock.

"This is Francine," a woman on the other end of the line said.

"Good morning. This is Dakota Jamison, and I wanted to discuss the flood in my store." Her hands shook, but she worked to keep some pep in her voice.

"Give me a moment to look you up in the system," the woman said.

"Yes, of course." Dakota held her breath while the sound of keyboard clicks filled the line. She took a few moments to regroup. She was going to convince this woman that the insurance company should reimburse her for her lost gowns, and the outcome would breathe new life into her store. Then everything would be just fine. It had to be.

After a few beats Francine said, "I found your information. How can I help you?"

"Before the flood, I had ordered a line of wedding gowns for my bridal shop. The dresses were then water-damaged, so I feel I should be reimbursed for them." Dakota worked to keep her tone even and sunny. "I've lost thousands of dollars in stock."

"I'm sorry, ma'am, but according to your insurance policy, this loss isn't covered. I see from your file that you've already discussed this issue with a representative." Impatience radiated in Francine's voice.

"That doesn't make any sense to me. Without gowns to sell, I have no store." When her voice started to shake, she took a deep breath. She had to be strong. She couldn't allow this woman to destroy her hope. "What is the purpose of my insurance policy if my stock isn't covered?"

"Ma'am, if you review the policy, you'll see that you are responsible for items that are considered stock. If you'd like, I can highlight those paragraphs in the policy for you. Just give me a few minutes, and I'll pull that up on my screen."

Dakota closed her eyes while the woman continued to talk. She wasn't getting anywhere. She was wasting her breath and her time.

"Do you have any further questions?" Francine asked.

"No, thank you."

"Thank you for calling, and have a nice day," Francine said before the line went dead.

Dakota massaged her temples and closed her eyes. Then the bell at the front of the shop rang, and she sat up straighter. Thank goodness she had a customer. She collected herself, then hurried to the front of the store, stopping by the mirror in the workroom to assess her gray pantsuit and red top. *Good enough,* she thought to herself. She'd tried to disguise the shadows under her eyes with makeup, but they still peeked through.

Dakota pushed through the door into the storefront. And stopped in her tracks.

A tall man with dark-brown hair cut short seemed to be examining the jewelry case, standing with his back to her as he did so.

Wow.

Broad shoulders, muscular back and arms.

Her eyes moved from his long-sleeved gray Henley shirt, which was tight around those glorious biceps, to his jeans. She smiled as she noticed how the jeans fit his trim waist in all the right places.

"Welcome to Fairytale," she began, her chunky red pumps clacking along the tile floor. "How can I —" Both her words and her steps faltered when he spun around.

She was face-to-face with Hudson Garrity. The man who had destroyed both her heart and her faith in love seven years ago.

His bright-blue eyes widened for a second, and then a guarded expression overtook his face.

Her belly clenched as she studied him. A few days' worth of stubble lined his chiseled jaw, and his features were more mature than she recalled.

She mentally took hold of her herself, lifted her chin, and shot him the coldest expression she could muster. "How may I help you?" she asked as she slipped behind the counter.

"I'm here on behalf of Layla," he said, joining her by the cash register. "She sent me to pay for her dress."

Dakota nodded and focused on her computer, but her thoughts kept swirling like a cyclone. She'd never expected to see him in her store, but here he was, standing in front of her in the flesh.

"Let me find the invoice," she mumbled, taking her time and deliberately making him wait longer than necessary.

"This place is yours?" he asked.

She trained her eyes on her computer screen. "Last time I checked."

"Wow," he quipped. "I wouldn't have expected you to own a place in Flowering Grove."

"Stranger things have happened." She narrowed her eyes and pasted a wry smile on her lips. She supposed he couldn't have imagined her ever being successful in their tiny town, which he'd once called a dead-end place for people trying to make ends meet.

A few beats of silence passed between them, and an instrumental version of "I Will Always Love You" filled the awkward silence between them.

After deciding she'd made him wait long enough, she pulled up Layla's invoice. "Here we go." She told him the total.

Without batting an eye, he yanked a leather wallet from the back pocket of his jeans and handed her a black credit card.

She was careful not to allow their hands to touch when she took it from him. She stared down at his name — Hudson Nathaniel Garrity — words that felt familiar and foreign at the same time.

She could tell the card was exclusive — the kind only successful people would carry. A strange feeling rippled through her. Hudson had made it just like he always planned to. Surely he thought he was better than everyone else who chose to stay in their sleepy hometown.

Dakota felt his eyes scrutinizing her as she ran the card. She held her breath, grateful the confirmation popped up quickly.

"Sign this copy," she told him, handing him a pen and a printed receipt.

He took the pen in his left hand, and while he scribbled his name, she noticed his ring finger was naked. The only piece of jewelry he wore was a silver watch on his right wrist. Such a watch might've been worth more than her car.

Was he still single?

She chided herself for bothering to wonder. All she wanted was for him to leave — *quickly.*

Hudson left the signed receipt on the counter and then perused the itemized invoice. His brow furrowed, and he lifted his eyes to meet hers. "Friends and family discount?"

She nodded.

He snorted. "Why?"

"Because I like Layla, and I want her to have the wedding of her dreams," she said curtly.

His lips formed a thin line, and a look of disbelief overtook his face as he folded the extra receipt and pushed it into his pocket. "Don't I need the dress?"

She shook her head. "She asked me to alter it so it resembles your mother's."

"Oh. Right." He cast his gaze in the direction of the racks of gowns behind her. "She mentioned that."

"Plus, she'll need to come in for fittings."

"I see." His blue eyes scanned the boutique before his focus returned to her face. "Thanks for your help."

"It's been a pleasure, Hudson," she responded, her voice sugary sweet.

He shook his head, then he sauntered out of the store toward Main Street.

When the door to the shop closed, she leaned forward on the counter and let out a pent-up breath. She had *never* imagined she would see Hudson Garrity in her store. He was most likely just in town for a short visit, and he'd left the store in the same way he'd walked out of her life seven years ago.

That was what she'd hope for, at least.

Her cell phone rang, and she jumped with a start. When she saw the insurance company's phone number across the screen, her shoulders tightened even more. She had to push the encounter with Hudson out of her head and concentrate on her business. Maybe this time she'd make some progress with her claim.

The cool early-March breeze whipped over Hudson, and the morning sun warmed his neck as he stalked down the sidewalk. He wasn't sure where he was headed, but he knew he had to get away from Dakota.

For the past seven years, he'd managed to visit his aunt and sister for a few days at Christmas without ever bumping into his ex. Since he had to keep his visits short, he'd slipped in and out of town without one run-in. At one point, he'd assumed Dakota had moved away. No, he'd *hoped* she'd moved away — far enough away that he'd never have to see her again.

Yet today, only his second day in town, he'd managed to come face-to-face with her before noon. He'd told his aunt and sister years ago that he didn't want to discuss Dakota, and they had kept their promise not to update him on what she'd been up to. Dakota had always talked about working as a seamstress, but he never expected she'd open a store in Flowering Grove — especially a bridal boutique.

He couldn't help but notice that her left hand was bare of a ring. He'd always figured she'd be married by now, maybe with a few children. Or maybe she'd gotten engaged again — or even a few times — since him. Had she given those rings back too, leaving a trail of destroyed men in her wake?

Why should he trouble himself with speculation? She'd broken up with him without any explanation, and then he'd left town without looking back.

Hudson stopped at the crosswalk and then loped toward the other side of the street. He pressed his lips together while contemplating his baby sister's face last night when she'd asked him to pay for the dress at the boutique. That strange look that had passed between his aunt and Layla now made sense. Layla had set him up to run into Dakota, which was ridiculous.

Dakota Jamison was the last woman on the planet he'd ever want to be involved with. In fact, if she were the last woman on the planet, he'd choose to remain a bachelor. He'd learned his lesson.

Also, how laughable that she'd given Layla the friends and family discount. As if she could ever be a true friend to him or his family members after how she'd dumped him.

Hudson glowered and made his way down the sidewalk until the delicious smells from Bloom's Coffee filled his senses. A mochaccino would hit the spot right now.

He reached the door but paused when he found the same flyer hanging in the window that he'd noticed in the bridal boutique. The fluorescent pink paper advertised an '80s night at the Flowering Grove Rollerama on Saturday. The rink was a popular hangout when he was a teenager, but he was surprised to see it still operating.

"Hud?"

Hudson turned and found one of his best friends from school standing behind him. "Gavin!"

"Hey, man." Gavin thrust out his hand. "How's New York City?"

Hudson returned the handshake. "Great, but I'm here visiting for a while. Do you have time to grab a cup of coffee?"

"Absolutely."

They went through the line, then found a deserted booth at the back of the shop. Hudson took a draw from his cup. Ah, as good as he remembered. While he enjoyed a good cup of coffee back in the city, nothing beat a cup from Bloom's.

"So," Gavin began, "how are things with your software company?"

Hudson wrapped his hands around the warm cup. "Great, actually. We're in the midst of selling it."

"Dude, that's amazing. Does that mean you're retiring?"

"Not exactly." Hudson couldn't imagine ever retiring, especially at the age of thirty. Working seemed to be a part of his DNA, despite his impressive bank accounts. "I have some offers on the table for other positions. There's one in Bahrain that my business partner thinks I should seriously consider."

"That's pretty far away. What are you doing home now?"

Hudson scrubbed a hand over his face. "My baby sister has decided she's getting married in June."

Gavin leaned forward. "Little Layla is getting married?"

"Yeah. But she's only known the guy three months." He explained how he met Shane at Christmas. "I'm not thrilled. She's not ready for this."

Gavin shrugged. "I'd known Jeannie for less than a year when we got married. Sometimes when you know, you know."

Hudson couldn't imagine what that felt like. The few relationships he'd had over the past several years hadn't lasted more than a few months. To him, the idea of a soul mate was a foreign concept. "How's your little one doing?" he asked, referring to Gavin's daughter.

"Great." Gavin touched the screen of his phone and held it up, revealing a photo of a little blond. "I can't believe Anissa is five already."

"She's adorable."

"Thanks." He set his phone down. "Are you seeing anyone?"

"Nope. No time for a relationship." He pushed away thoughts of his failed attempts at dating and instead considered the good times he'd had with Gavin in high school. Then he grinned and lifted his cup. "I miss the old days when we worked together at Smith's Construction."

Gavin laughed. "We did have fun building that new neighborhood over in Wadesboro. I think of it every time I drive by it."

"It was hard work. But it was rewarding to see the finished product." He could still recall his aching muscles, as well as how proud he'd felt when a house he'd helped build was sold.

"Yeah, but I'm sure software is much

more rewarding. After all, you and Darren designed something that was ahead of its time."

"Maybe so, but you know I only studied computers to support my family. I still miss working construction."

Gavin rubbed his chin. "Sometimes I wonder what it would feel like to sit in an office all day long."

Hudson nodded toward him. "How's business for you?"

"I finally opened my own company a little over a year ago."

"That's great, man. What are you working on?"

"You know that old music store building across the street?"

"The one that's been empty since we graduated?"

"Yeah. My company was hired to remodel it for a new restaurant. We start work in a couple of weeks."

"Congratulations. How do you like running your own company?"

Gavin settled back in his seat. "It's . . . a lot."

"But it's gratifying."

"Sometimes." Gavin took a drink of his coffee.

Hudson's eye once again landed on the

pink flyer hanging in the coffee shop window. "By the way, is the rink still the place to be on weekends?"

"Believe it or not, yes! My daughter loves to take lessons there." Gavin looked like he was going to say something, but then he stopped. "Anyway, Friday nights are family nights. We go there every weekend. Kayleigh and Brice Hayes bought the place a while back, and they've been breathing new life into it."

"Kayleigh and Brice, huh?" Hudson moved his fingers over his cup. Kayleigh had been Dakota's best friend since they were kids, and she'd married Brice not long before Hudson left for New York.

"You should see it during the holidays. They even have roller-skating Santas. Brice likes to plan theme nights. They had a Valentine's Day skate a couple weeks ago, and the entire place was decked out with heart balloons and cupids on the walls. Anissa loved every minute of it." Gavin glanced down at his watch. "Oh, wow. I'd better get going, man. I have a meeting in twenty minutes with the architect."

They both stood to leave. "You should come to the rink," Gavin said. "It's a lot of fun."

"Maybe I will," Hudson said, not meaning it. If Kayleigh owned the place, then most likely Dakota would be there too.

They walked to the exit together, and when Hudson stepped out onto the street, he cut his gaze to the Fairytale Bridal Shop. He'd do his best to avoid Dakota for the remainder of his time in Flowering Grove, but in such a small town, that just might be impossible.

Chapter 5

"Hello, this is Dakota Jamison at Fairytale Bridal on Main Street in Flowering Grove," Dakota said into the phone later that afternoon. "I'd like to arrange for the fans and dehumidifier to be picked up."

"How about tomorrow afternoon?" the woman on the other end of the line said.

"Perfect," Dakota said. She ended the call just as the bell above the front door of the store rang, and her niece rushed toward her with a bright smile on her pretty face.

"Auntie, you are not going to believe it." Skye dropped her backpack on the showroom floor and twirled in the middle of the store, almost knocking over a rack of shapewear.

Dakota steadied her. "Are you okay?"

She let out a dreamy sigh. "I'm in *love.*"

Dakota put her hand on Skye's forehead. "No fever." When Skye's brow wrinkled, Dakota felt her lips twitch. "But you *must* be sick because you said you were immune to boy-crazy fever."

"Very funny," she deadpanned, lifting her bag back onto her shoulder. She let out a frustrated huff and started for the back office. "Forget it. I thought I could talk to you, but never mind."

Guilt nipped at Dakota, and she hurried to catch up with her niece. "I'm sorry, sweetie. I was only kidding. You know you can tell me anything."

"Okay." Skye spun to face Dakota, her bright smile returning. "The *cutest* guy I've ever seen transferred to our school a few weeks ago, and he ate lunch with *me* today." She let her heavy backpack fall again with a thud at her feet. "His name is Gunner Crenshaw. He's super tall, and I like tall guys just like you do. He has blond hair and green eyes. And he has the coolest Southern accent. It's stronger than ours since he's from Alabama. I'm hoping he'll ask me to prom."

While her niece rambled on about the cute young man, Dakota tried not to think about the two proms she and Hudson attended.

"You okay, Auntie?"

"Yeah. Of course." The truth was, she'd been reeling all day since Hudson had appeared in her store. She'd tried to keep herself busy with steaming more dresses and gathering materials for Layla's alterations, but Hudson still hijacked her thoughts. The memories of their life together seemed to be grabbing her by the throat.

"Gunner's cute, huh?" She tried to smile, but it felt more like a grimace.

Skye breathed out another moony sigh. "Extremely."

"He must be something special to have captured your attention."

"I think he is. He's so different from all the boring guys here in Flowering Grove." Her niece pulled her large cup from the backpack's side pocket and took a long drink of water. "What have you been up to today?"

"Let's see . . . I steamed another dress and started putting together what I'll need for Layla Garrity's gown, but I need her to come in for a formal fitting before I can get started. I've gotten a few phone calls, and I've set up an appointment with a new client for Friday morning, so that's exciting."

Skye took another long drink, and her dark eyes seemed to assess Dakota. She could almost hear her niece's thoughts since Skye was never one to hold them back.

"Just say it, Skye."

"What do you mean?"

"I know that look. Just say what's on your mind."

Her niece hopped up onto the stool and then crossed one long leg over the other. "Auntie, I have an idea." She gestured widely. "I've been thinking about what we can do to boost sales."

"I'm listening." Dakota leaned on the counter in front of her.

"We need to start taking online orders," Skye said. "I'm good at managing your website and —"

"No."

Skye blinked. "You're not even going to let me finish explaining my idea?"

"I appreciate your concern, but I don't want to get into online sales."

"Why not?" Her niece held her palms up. "We have to stay relevant. I've been researching it, and online sales are crucial to a business's survival. You're an amazing seamstress. Women could send you their measurements, and you could make gowns to order."

Dakota stood up straight. "I just can't manage it right now — not until I get past this mess the flood caused. I'm still rearranging the displays and trying to salvage the purses and shoes that were damaged."

"But brides often know what they want

before they come into the store. There's a real demand for gowns that are made to order." She hopped off the stool and scooted around the counter. "Auntie, we can do this." She held her hand up as if to stop Dakota's protests. "I know this would mean more work for you, but you can price the gowns so the work is worth your time. I'll handle all of the orders for you — respond to the customers and make sure they send their measurements and payments. This could work. And it would put this boutique on the map."

Dakota frowned. While she needed the customers, incorporating Skye's idea was overwhelming. She couldn't handle another thing on her plate. "I'm grateful that you want to help, but I can't think about it right now. We can talk about it again later. I promise."

"Okay," Skye said, her mood a little subdued. She started toward the offices. "Do you want me to help steam dresses?"

"That would be perfect. I need to get started on Layla's gown since the alterations will take some time." And she couldn't wait to get started.

Hudson found his aunt and sister sitting on the back deck later that evening. The cool evening air penetrated his shirt as he climbed the steps to where they sat drinking tea. His sister was dressed in pink scrubs, and her long dark hair was pulled back in a thick braid.

"I was hoping you'd come by this evening." His aunt smiled up at him. "What'd you do today?"

He took a seat at the round table. "I ran some errands around town, then I bumped into Gavin Wallace at the coffee shop. We stayed and talked for a while."

"Wasn't he your lab partner in biology?"

Hudson nodded. "And then we worked at Smith's Construction together after graduation."

"I remember him," Layla announced.

Hudson fished the receipt for the dress from his pocket, then handed it to Layla.

A slow smile overtook her lips as she examined the receipt. "Thank you so much. How was your visit to the boutique?"

Hudson studied her reaction, and irritation pricked him. "Why didn't you tell me Dakota worked there?"

Layla shrugged, but her smile betrayed her display of disinterest.

"If you're trying to play cupid, you can just forget it."

"Well, you and Dakota are both single,

and a lot of time has gone by . . . ," Layla said.

So she *was* single. That information shocked him.

Not that he cared.

"Hud," Layla began, "you and Dakota are meant to be together. Neither of you has settled down with someone else, so you should give it another chance."

"Don't even start, Layla," Hudson warned. "I have no interest in getting into a relationship, and if I did, Dakota would be my last choice."

Aunt Trudy sat straight in her chair and made a sweeping gesture toward her yard. "Hud, did you see what Shane has done here with my landscaping?"

He surveyed the backyard, taking in the strategically placed shrubs and landscape timbers, an impressive slate path, and the organized flowerbed. A birdbath and birdfeeders were nice touches as well. "Looks good."

His sister beamed. "He does fantastic work. I'm so proud of him."

Hudson nodded. Shane obviously had talent, but talent didn't necessarily translate to financial success. And it also didn't mean he'd gotten his life together after running with a rough crowd and getting himself expelled from school.

"Are we still meeting his family at the country club tomorrow night?" his aunt asked.

"The country club?" Hudson lifted an eyebrow. "For supper?"

"No," Layla hissed. "We're considering having our reception there, but it might be out of our price range. Want to come with us?"

"I guess," he said, feigning a long-suffering sigh. "I don't have anything else to do."

Layla smacked his arm, and he chortled.

"Of course I'll go." He would offer to pay for the reception too — though he was still determined to make sure there would be no wedding or reception at all.

Hudson glanced around the large open reception hall at the country club. While he'd been invited to his ten-year class reunion here a couple of years ago, he hadn't bothered attending. He'd been too busy with work, and it felt as if his high school years had been another lifetime.

"What do you think, Hud?"

He turned to Layla, her expression expectant. "I'm sorry, can you repeat that?"

"Do you think this is a nice place for the reception?" She worried her lower lip. "I know it's pricey, but it's nicer than the other halls we've seen."

Hudson glanced across the room to where Shane stood with his parents, Patrick and Libby, and his younger sister, Melody, who looked to be around eighteen. They seemed to be analyzing how the lighting coming in from the balcony overlooking the golf course would illuminate the reception. Nearby the banquet manager, Ms. Anderson, and Aunt Trudy discussed options for the menu.

Hudson's eyes met Layla's, and the urge to make her happy overwhelmed him. "Is this where you *want* your reception to be?"

She shrugged, but the glimmer in her eyes told him all he needed to know. She angled to her right just as Shane joined them. "What do you think?"

Shane stuck his hands in the pockets of his jeans. "I know you love it, babe, but it's out of our price range." He hesitated, then lowered his voice. "In fact, all of the places we looked at were pretty expensive. Maybe we should just get married in your aunt's backyard."

"If this is what you really want, I'll make it happen," Hudson said.

Layla faced Shane, and an unspoken conversation passed between the couple before she turned back to Hudson. "What if we paid half?"

"Layla —"

"For the thousandth time, you don't have to pay for everything. You've already covered my gown."

Hudson crossed his arms over his chest, not budging.

Shane frowned at Layla while a tight smile overtook her lips.

"Okay, fine. Thank you, Hudson." Layla hugged him. "How about we talk about this later?" Then she started toward the banquet manager. "Ms. Anderson, what sort of down payment would you need to hold the date for us?"

Hudson pivoted toward Shane and held out his hand. "I don't think I've had a chance to congratulate you on the engagement."

"Thanks." Shane shook his hand, but his expression remained unsure or possibly annoyed. Maybe a little of both?

"The landscaping you did at my aunt's house is impressive."

Shane nodded.

"Are you out on your own now or still working for a company?"

He brushed his hand over his neck. "I work for Robertsons' Landscaping."

"Oh." Hudson studied him, and Shane scratched his palm. As they stared at each other, the awkward moments ticked by.

"Hud?" Layla beckoned him to join her by the banquet manager. "Could we discuss the deposit before we go to dinner?"

"Excuse me," Hudson said, and a muscle ticked along Shane's jaw. He walked over to his younger sister and retrieved his wallet from his jacket pocket while the banquet manager informed them of deposits and final payments.

After he finalized the deposit, Aunt Trudy sidled up to Hudson. "Are you going to join us for dinner with Shane's family?"

"Of course."

She smiled. "This will be fun."

A short time later, they were all seated for dinner. Hudson had suggested they go to the Grove Grille, one of the fancier places in the area. He had noticed Shane's scowl when he suggested the place, but Hudson planned to pick up the tab.

"Hudson, I hear you live in Manhattan," said Libby, Shane's mother, from across the table. "That must be exciting."

"Yes, ma'am, it's a great place to live." Hudson lifted his water glass and took a sip.

The server had already taken their orders

and their menus, and now a buzz of conversations hovered around them, along with the delectable aroma of steak.

Libby chose a roll from the basket in the center of the round table. "What exactly do you do?"

"I began working as a computer programmer, then later on I started my own company." He briefly explained the software he and Darren had written and how they had recently sold the business.

Patrick, Shane's father, nodded. "Impressive."

"How about you two?" Hudson asked.

"I work in sales," Patrick said. "And Libby teaches kindergarten at Flowering Grove Elementary."

Hudson glanced over at Layla and Shane, who were engrossed in a quiet conversation. He'd spent the ride to the restaurant contemplating the comment Shane had made at the country club about how he thought they should get married in Aunt Trudy's backyard. It annoyed him that Shane wouldn't want his sister to have the wedding and reception of her dreams, and Hudson's jaw tightened at the thought of her settling. He had worked hard to provide a better life for his aunt and sister, and he believed Layla deserved better than Shane.

He didn't want her to struggle, even for a moment, and if she married a landscaper who couldn't afford a decent wedding reception, then she'd surely spend the rest of her life living paycheck to paycheck, just like their parents had.

"It's a wonder that we have both lived in Flowering Grove for so long but haven't gotten to know each other," Libby said. "Where did you work, Trudy?"

"I was a receptionist at the Carolina Pediatric Group. But that was years ago."

"Oh," Libby said. "We know where that is. Right, Melody?"

Her daughter smiled. "I see Dr. Santucci. She's the best."

"I don't know her. She must be a newer physician." Aunt Trudy unrolled her silverware and laid the cloth napkin across her lap.

"Melody feels very comfortable with her, which is so important," Libby said.

Aunt Trudy nodded.

The server appeared with their meals, and after each plate was distributed, the sound of utensils scraping dishes filled the air.

"So, Shane," Hudson began, "have you considered starting your own business?"

Shane swallowed. "I like the company I work for. The other guys on the crew are like family." He hesitated, then added, "And we work well together."

Hudson found his response strange. How could Shane ever reach his full potential if he continued to work for someone else? He picked up his steak knife and cut into his filet mignon. "Layla, have you and Shane talked about the future?"

His sister looked up from her shrimp and grits. "What do you mean?"

"Have you discussed a budget for rent or a mortgage? Or where you're going to live?"

Shane stiffened, and a hush fell over the table. He swept his hand over his mouth. "We haven't found a place yet, but we'll be fine."

"What kind of houses are you looking at? What price point?"

Shane and Layla shared a look, and her brow puckered. "We're planning to live with Aunt Trudy at first. Then we'll figure the rest out when the time comes," Layla said, her words measured.

"When the time comes?"

"Yes, when the time comes," she repeated. "Right now we're focused on having a wedding and saving money for our own place." Her expression warmed as she turned toward their aunt. "She said we can stay with her for as long as we'd like, right?"

Aunt Trudy smiled. "Of course, sweetheart."

Hudson set down his fork and knife. "Layla, you can't hide in our aunt's house forever. You need to face reality, and you'd better do it *now*. Life is expensive."

"I know that, Hud," she said, then set her jaw.

"Do you really?" he challenged. "Buying a house is a big deal."

Her nostrils flared.

"First, you need to get approved for a mortgage — that's if you can afford one," he continued. "Or you'll need to sign a lease if you have to rent. You'll have to come up with either a down payment for a house or a security deposit, along with first and last month's rent for an apartment." He shook his head. "I'm not convinced you and Shane are ready for that."

All eyes around the table focused on Hudson. As if on cue, Shane's parents both set down their utensils. Layla's and Shane's eyes rounded, while shock flickered across Aunt Trudy's and Melody's faces.

Hudson turned his attention back to his sister and her fiancé. "I can help you both with that, but will you be able to make the payments?"

Ire sparked in Layla's eyes. "We have it

handled, Hud, but thanks for the tip."

"Do you *really* have it handled?" Hudson turned to Shane's parents, who watched him with expressions of displeasure. "Layla, it's time to grow up. A marriage is more than a wedding and a pretty dress."

Patrick leaned forward, resting his arm on the white tablecloth. His lips formed a thin line. "I think they're old enough to make their own decisions."

Hudson felt his aunt place her hand on his elbow, but he ignored her. "Do you agree, Mrs. Simpson?"

"Yes, I do." Libby's expression was unflappable. "Shane and Layla are responsible young adults, and we're excited for their future."

"Now, Melody," Aunt Trudy began, her sunny tone sounding a bit forced, "I hear you're looking to go to UNC Charlotte in the fall. What do you plan to study?"

Hudson cut into his steak while his aunt forced a subject change with Melody. He glanced around the table, taking in the awkward silence and sober expressions as Layla, Shane, and Shane's parents kept their focus on their meals. He decided it best to keep the rest of his thoughts to himself — not understanding why he was the only one seeing the reality of Layla and Shane's situation.

Later that evening, Hudson steered his SUV into his aunt's driveway. The ride home from the restaurant had been almost silent, aside from the country music playing from the speakers. Though Layla had kept her eyes on her phone, he'd felt tension radiating from the back seat.

Aunt Trudy gathered her purse from the floorboard. "Thank you for dinner. I hope I'll see you soon." She gave Hudson a quick pat on the arm.

"You know you will."

Aunt Trudy climbed out of the SUV and started toward the porch. Then Layla pushed herself out of the back seat and followed her.

When she didn't even say goodbye, Hudson leapt out of the car. "Hey, Layla," he called after her. "What's wrong now?"

His sister spun to face him, her face a mask of fury. "I think you've reached a new low, Hud. It was bad enough that you questioned Shane about his work, but calling us both out at dinner was even worse."

"Calling you out?" His voice rose. "I was only asking if you've thought about the future —"

She held up her hand. "Save it! I've had

enough, Hud. I don't need you lecturing me about what it takes to be an adult. From now on, you can keep your opinions to yourself because I don't want to hear them."

"Layla, I'm only trying to help."

"Well, keep your help to yourself too." She pushed the front door open and pinned him with a glare. "And our truce is over."

"Is it?" he asked. "But you'll take my money to pay for your wedding?"

Her mouth opened and then closed, her gaze sharpening with every second.

"If you're such a grown-up, Layla, maybe you should pay for your own wedding."

"Layla?" Aunt Trudy called from the front porch. "It's late, and you have to get up early for work tomorrow."

"I'm coming," his sister responded before glowering at Hudson. "Then keep your money," she hissed before shutting the door behind her.

Frustration boiled under his skin. He climbed into the front seat, slammed the door, and backed out onto the road, then started toward the Airbnb a few blocks away.

He ran his tongue over his teeth. He had no idea how to get through to his stubborn sister, especially if Shane's family and his aunt were all supporting the wedding. He was at a loss as to how to stop it. What kind of a future would she have with Shane? He couldn't stand the idea of his sister marrying a guy with no career goals.

When his phone rang, he connected the call over Bluetooth. "Hey, Darren," he answered, trying to sound upbeat despite the irritation plaguing him.

"I was wondering how things were going down there in Flowering Glen."

Hudson shook his head. "Flowering *Grove*. And unfortunately, things are a little tense here."

"Tense?" his business partner asked.

"Yeah. I've paid for my sister's wedding dress, and today we booked the country club for the reception."

"Sounds fancy."

"It is, but I don't see how she and her fiancé are going to make it in the real world."

"Well, man, the best way to learn is to get out there. Have you been thinking about the offer in Bahrain?"

"Yes and no," Hudson said, flipping on his blinker.

"Well, a couple more offers came in. Positions in Los Angeles *and* in Europe." Darren continued to discuss the other opportunities while Hudson drove to Oak

Street and parked in the rental house driveway. "We could always accept offers at the same place and keep working together since we make a great team. What do you think?"

"It's been a long day, man. Can you send me the info?"

"Will do."

"Thanks." Hudson switched off the ignition.

Darren was silent for a moment. "For what it's worth, just because they're young doesn't mean they won't make it."

Hudson rubbed the back of his head. *If only life were that easy.* "Yeah, I know. G'night, Darren."

"Night."

Hudson strode toward the front door, punched in the code, and headed into the warm house. Maybe if he spent the rest of the evening looking over the offers from Darren, his mind would get a break from his worries about his sister and her dubious future.

Chapter 6

Dakota rushed out her front door Friday morning, balancing her purse, tote bag, and lunch bag. Her heart hammered in her chest, and her black suede round-toe heels clicked along the stone path to her car. She was late, thanks to forgetting to set her alarm last night. She had only twenty minutes before her appointment would arrive, so she had to hightail it to the store. Impressing this bride-to-be was critical. She *needed* this sale.

She glanced over at a fancy SUV parked in the driveway of the large colonial Airbnb next door, but she kept moving forward. She unlocked the back door of her car and shoved her bags in the back seat. She started to open the driver's seat door and —

Oh no.

She halted at the sight of a flat tire.

This was the last thing she needed today. She was already running late, and now she had to change a tire in her best suit and heels. She looked up at the sky, stomped her foot, and kicked the flat tire in futility. As if that was going to help.

"Great," she muttered, opening the front door and popping the trunk. She hurried to the back of the car and let out a groan. Her trunk was full of bags of clothes and odds and ends she had meant to drop off at the donation center last week.

She had no choice but to unload the trunk, bag by bag. Out of the corner of her eye, she spotted the garage door opening at the house next door. She tossed each bag down on the driveway, yanked up the trunk liner, and grabbed the tire iron and scissor jack.

As soon as she'd gotten her learner's permit, her father had made sure she knew how to check her oil, measure her tire pressure, and change a tire. She could handle this, no problem — even in a nice pantsuit and heels.

"Do you need help?"

She froze, the muscles in her neck and back tensing. She recognized that voice. Dakota peeked around the trunk and, sure enough, found Hudson Garrity standing on the strip of grass separating her yard from the Airbnb.

Not again.

She straightened, maintaining a death grip on her tools. "What are you doing in my driveway?"

He scowled. "You live here?"

"Obviously." She glanced around, and her stomach sank as she took in the open garage next door. "Don't tell me —"

"We're neighbors? Okay, I won't, even though it appears to be true."

What were the chances her ex-fiancé would be staying at the house next door? And that he was the owner of that impressive SUV? Coupled with his upscale black credit card, it looked like Hudson had achieved his dream of making a lot of money.

Well, good for him.

Her nostrils flared.

Hudson pointed to the car. "You have a flat tire."

"Thanks, Hud, but I already figured that out on my own." She lifted the tire iron.

He took a step toward her. "Need some help?"

"Nope. This isn't my first flat."

He gestured toward her. "You're not exactly dressed for the task." He brushed his hands down his black hoodie and faded jeans — which fit him oh so well. "Let me do it for you."

"No, thanks. I'm sure you have more important things to do today." She shooed him away with her hand. But despite her brush-off, he was beside her in a few long strides. She shot him another dark look. "I don't need your help, Hudson."

He shook his head. "Some things never change."

"What's *that* supposed to mean?" she demanded.

"Stubborn as always." He held out his hand. "Give me the tire iron, Dakota."

She huffed a breath and for a moment considered telling him off. But she was running out of time. If she was late for her appointment, she could lose this customer — and as much as she didn't want Hudson's help, he could change the tire faster than she could. After all, last time she'd changed her own tire, she'd spent a lot of time fighting with the lug nuts. Plus, if she smudged grease on her suit, she'd have to change her clothes — which would no doubt make her late.

Her shoulders slumped as she handed over the tire iron. "Fine."

Squatting down, he slipped the tire iron onto the first lug nut and spun it as if the lug nut had never been tightened. As he loosened the remaining lug nuts, she folded her arms over her middle and observed the muscles in his shoulders flexing under his hoodie.

Hudson stood up to his full height and pushed a hand through his short dark hair. Then he scooted around the car, returned with the scissor jack, and quickly lifted the car. After removing the flat tire, he slipped on the spare and replaced the lug nuts.

"How long have you lived here?" he asked, tightening everything into place.

"A little over a year."

He lowered the car and shielded his eyes from the sun. "What's your cat's name?"

Had he been spying on her? "How'd you know I have a cat?"

He pointed to the window. "I think that's his favorite place to sit. He was there when I got home last night and the night before."

"Trouble."

He rolled the flat tire toward her trunk. "What?"

"His name. It's Trouble."

Hudson actually smiled, and her stupid, traitorous heart skipped a beat.

He leaned the tire against the bumper and then loaded the scissor jack and the tire iron. "I'm sure the folks at Barton Automotive can fix the flat. I could even drop it off for you."

"Why do you care?"

He sighed. "Do you need me to take the tire for you or not, Dakota?"

"Nope. I got it."

"Fine." He loaded the tire into her trunk, then reached around the flat and pulled out an old towel that must have fallen out of one of the donation bags. "Can I wipe my hands on this?"

"Sure." She began placing the bags of donations into the back seat. She would have to drop them off today on her way home.

When he closed the trunk, she faced him, and they stared at each other for a moment. But enough was enough — she had to get going. She pulled her keys from her pocket, and they jingled. "Thanks, Hudson."

"You're welcome, Dakota." Nodding, he started toward his SUV. She couldn't help but notice that his faded jeans, simple hoodie, and sneakers were a stark contrast to his expensive-looking vehicle.

Her hands shaking, she hopped into the driver's seat and motored out of her driveway. She ended up at her shop with only two minutes to spare.

Later that evening, Dakota flipped off the

lights in her store, turned the Open sign to Closed, and locked the front door. Relief wound through her as she made her way to the back door. Today had been the most successful day she'd had in more than a month. She'd managed to sell the new client a gown, and she'd even found bridesmaids' dresses she liked. The woman also said she'd send her groom back with his attendants for their tuxedos.

Layla had finally come by in the afternoon for her first fitting, and though Dakota hadn't been able to get Hudson out of her mind most of the day, she had managed to steer their conversation away from Layla's older brother. More than anything Dakota just wanted to go home, flop on her couch, and veg out, but she had less than two hours to get ready for her skating students.

After powering down her computer and turning off her office light, Dakota slipped out the back door and drove down the block to Barton Automotive. She paid for her tire repair before Carter Donovan installed it for her. She was grateful he had been able to fix it, and the cost was much less than a new tire would have been.

When she walked back out to her car, a delectable whiff of coffee filled her senses, and she gazed down the street toward

Bloom's. Her thoughts turned to Hudson once again, and she imagined he liked his coffee black like his heart. She snickered.

Then another thought hit her. Hudson had gone out of his way this morning to change her tire for her. Without his assistance, she would've struggled to do it herself and most likely would've had to either change her clothes or call her father for help.

But now that Hud had helped her, she felt indebted to him, which made her uncomfortable. She didn't want to owe him anything, and she certainly didn't want him to think she still had feelings for him. Giving him the wrong impression would make the situation even more awkward now that he was staying next door.

One way to solve that was to get him a gift card for the coffee shop as a thank-you. That way, she'd no longer owe him, but she'd be showing him gratitude for his help — something her mother had always taught her to do. Sending thank-you notes was important, and a simple gift card would do the trick.

Dakota drove to the coffee shop and parked in front. Then she hurried up the sidewalk and inside the coffee shop before taking her spot in line to purchase a gift card.

Later Dakota nosed her car into the driveway. After leaving the coffee shop, she had dropped off the donations, but now she had to eat something, change, and hurry off to the rink. It would be a long night, since after she and Kayleigh gave their lessons, Dakota planned to stay past closing time to help Kayleigh, Brice, and the rest of the team decorate for tomorrow's '80s night.

Turning toward the colonial next door, she saw the empty driveway. While she was grateful Hudson wasn't home, her curiosity got the best of her. Was he having supper with his aunt and sister?

She removed the gift card from the side pocket of her purse, located a pen, and then wrote on the envelope: "Thanks for your help with the tire. Enjoy a cup of coffee on me. Sincerely, Dakota."

After grabbing a tape dispenser from the desk in her office, she zipped over to the colonial and taped the gift card to the storm door. Then she scampered back to her house, thankful to have avoided another run-in with him. When he found the gift card, they would be square.

She returned to her house and fed her

yammering cat before changing into jeans and a t-shirt. She made a turkey sandwich and leaned against the counter to eat while watching the news and scrolling through social media on her phone.

When her phone chimed with a text, she pulled up a message from Parker.

Sorry I haven't texted. It's been crazy at work. Would love to see you again.

Dakota swallowed the last bite of her sandwich. She kneaded her forehead and considered her niece's words about how she'd spend the rest of her life alone if she didn't make time for a relationship. Despite Skye's words, Dakota wasn't convinced she could create a connection with Parker if it wasn't already there.

At the same time, Parker was easy to talk to and genuine, which were qualities she admired.

Dakota poised her thumbs over the phone and began to type:

Maybe we can plan something for next week? Things should slow down for me.

Conversation bubbles appeared almost immediately.

Sounds great. I'll reach out next week.

After setting her plate in the dishwasher, she sighed. Maybe Skye was right and she needed to get back into the dating game.

But if that was true, then why did she feel so reluctant?

Chapter 7

Hudson slipped his wallet into the back pocket of his jeans before exiting the bank's walk-up ATM. The bright Saturday afternoon sun was high in the sky, and birds sang in the trees lining Main Street. The light breeze brought with it the scent of coffee. He stepped to the edge of the sidewalk, allowing a group of giggling teenage girls to pass before he came to Bloom's Coffee.

His gaze flitted over to Fairytale Bridal, where he found that the Open sign had been switched to Closed. He shook his head, contemplating the generous gift card Dakota had left taped to the storm door of the colonial last night. The gesture had confused him. What was she up to?

Why would she give him a gift card if they weren't even friends? She wasn't anything to him anymore but an acquaintance, and even that would be a generous title. Her expression when she'd seen him yesterday made it clear he was more of an annoyance. Still, he couldn't stop himself from offering to help her with the tire. After all, he hoped another man would do the same for his aunt or sister.

The appetizing smell of coffee reached him, and he considered using the gift card to grab a cup. Instead, his eyes moved to a lemon-yellow logo adorning the front window of Heather's Books 'N' Treats. He picked up his pace, recalling his aunt's excited phone call the day the shop had opened. The residents of the little town were buzzing about finally having a bookstore, and since it was paired with a bakery, the prospect was even more thrilling.

Hudson moved his hand over the stubble on his neck and tried to remember the last time he'd read a book for pleasure. It had to have been at least six months, and that was too long. Since he was between jobs, he had no excuses now.

He recalled recently seeing an ad for a new book by one of his favorite suspense writers. Surely he could find the book in this store. Maybe a good book would help take his mind off his argument with his sister. She hadn't called him since their tiff in his aunt's driveway, and as much as he tried to put his irritation out of his mind, it still lingered there.

He yanked open the door, and a bell trilled as the delicious aromas of chocolate, cake, and icing wafted over him. Chipper conversations buzzed around the space. A young woman wearing glasses and a lemon-yellow t-shirt featuring the store's logo stood by a cash register, beaming as she rang up a stack of books for an old man with a receding gray hairline.

Pop music filtered through the shop's surround sound, and an autographed framed photo of the world-famous pop band Kirwan sat proudly on the bakery counter at the back of the store, serving as a reminder that Heather, the owner, had married the band's lead singer. At least a dozen customers waited in line to purchase one of the sweet treats from the glass case featuring cakes, scones, cupcakes, pies, muffins, and cream puffs.

"Excuse me," Hudson muttered, weaving through the sea of patrons until he found the suspense section. Signs were strategically placed above the stacks, recommending books paired with the bakery's bookish desserts — such as Plot Twist Cinnamon Rolls with Emil Zimmerman's *The Man in the Window* and Elise Harvey's *Where Did She Go?* with Suspenseful Shortbread.

Hudson grinned. *Brilliant marketing.*

He folded his arms over his chest and scanned the shelves in search of his favorite author — Sebastian Harris.

The titles of three of his novels filled his vision, and he chose the two that didn't sound familiar — *Hide* and *The Obsession.* He flipped one over and started reading the blurb.

"I know, I know," a woman said nearby. "I promise I won't be late. I'm aware it's a big night. I'm just stopping in here, and then I'll go home and change."

The voice sounded familiar, but Hudson continued reading the blurb.

"Okay. I'm in the suspense section. What was the author's name again? Sebastian Harris?" she continued. "You've mentioned his books at least a million times." She chuckled. "Yes, I'll add it to the list of things I *should* do. If I find the book, I'll pick it up for you, and I'll read it when I have time, which will be never."

That sounds like . . . Oh no.

Hudson looked up just as Dakota moved in his direction. Her eyes were focused on the books in front of her as she held a cell phone to her ear. The muscles in his neck and shoulders tensed. She seemed so consumed with her book search and her phone call that she hadn't even noticed him standing less than three feet from her.

In an effort to ignore his ex, he returned his attention to the blurb on the back of the book. His eyes read the same sentence over and over, but his brain refused to comprehend it.

"Sebastian Harris . . . ," Dakota murmured softly. "Here he is." She tilted her head. "I see two books, and they're both copies of *The Dark House.* I don't see *The Obsess* —" She took two steps to the right, and her high heel smashed down on the toe of Hudson's sneaker.

Pain radiated up to his ankle, and he bit the inside of his cheek to stop a yelp from escaping his lips.

Dakota spun and gasped. "I'm so sor—" She froze, and pink tinged her cheeks. Then she squared her shoulders, and her eyes narrowed. "Excuse me."

"No, excuse *me,*" he quipped.

She stared at him at him while addressing the person on the other end of the line. "Give me one sec, Kay." Then she turned to Hudson. "Guess I didn't see you there."

"Obviously." He shot her a sardonic grin. "Unless, of course, you were aiming that stiletto for my toes."

"No, I wasn't, so that was pure luck." She

turned back to the shelf and her phone conversation. "I don't see *The Obsession.*"

Hudson sighed, and before his brain engaged, he held the book out to her. "Dakota."

She faced him again, her expression hesitant.

"Take mine."

She peered down at the book and then back at him. "No, thanks."

"Just take it."

She shook her head. "It's fine."

"Take the book, Dakota. I insist."

She pushed it back toward him. "No, I insist you keep it."

"I can ask the store to order me another copy. It's yours."

She lifted an eyebrow. "No, I'm good."

"Stop being ridiculous and *take* the book."

Dakota grabbed it, and he slipped the copy of *Hide* back onto the shelf before retreating to the next aisle. He located another author he enjoyed, chose a few books, and headed to the cashier.

As he turned the corner, he almost ran right into Dakota, who was holding the copies of *Hide* and *The Obsession* in one hand and her phone in the other. She met his gaze, and her body went rigid.

He made a sweeping gesture toward the

cashier. "After you."

She shook her head. "After *you.*"

"I insist."

She lifted her chin. "*I* insist."

"Nope." He took two steps to his left and made another sweeping motion toward the cashier. "After you."

The skin between her eyes pinched, and he could almost feel her irritation coming off her in waves. He was getting under her skin.

Good!

He worked to stop his lips from tipping up in a grin.

"Fine," Dakota muttered. She pursed her lips and took her place in line behind a woman holding a plastic shopping basket full of paperbacks, each featuring a ridiculously muscular man in desperate need of a shirt.

"Sorry about that," Dakota murmured into the phone. "I'll explain it to you tonight. So what did Gigi say to Brice's mom?" She listened for a moment and then laughed.

Hudson tried to pass the time by reading the blurbs on the backs of the three suspense novels he had picked. When it was her turn, Dakota walked up to the cash register, quickly paid for the books, and thanked the cashier before fleeing the store without looking back at him.

Buh-bye.

He had almost thanked her for the suspicious coffee shop gift card, but he'd been having too much fun irritating her.

Hudson set the books on the counter and paid for them before stepping back outside and into the warm afternoon sun.

Hopefully that would be his last awkward run-in with Dakota for the week. Or maybe even the next three weeks.

At least, he could hope.

"Let's try skating from one end of the rink to the other." Dakota clapped her hands from the middle of the rink at the Flowering Grove Rollerama. "Who's ready?" she asked the kids' class.

"Me! Me! Me!" Gigi waved both arms in the air, and Dakota grinned. Kayleigh's six-year-old daughter was a near-expert skater who loved to participate in their classes, usually acting as a mentor to the other children. Tonight she was dressed in an '80s-inspired rainbow-themed t-shirt and pink jeans, with matching fluorescent pink ribbons on her curly blond pigtails.

Dakota had stayed past midnight on Friday to help decorate the rink, which was now adorned with streamers, inflatable boom boxes and cassette tapes, musical notes, neon balloons, giant Rubik's Cubes, and banners illustrated like walls of graffiti.

Anissa Wallace, Gavin and Jeannie's daughter, was also wearing fluorescent clothes. She raised her hand and said, "I'm ready too."

The other half dozen children agreed.

Kayleigh glided on her skates while directing her class of teenagers on the other side of the rink.

"Now, let's start skating toward the other class," Dakota said. "Take your time. We'll build up speed when we feel more confident."

A peppy Duran Duran song played overhead, serenading them.

Gigi took Anissa's hand, and together they led the group forward.

"Great job, Jack!" Dakota told the shy little boy at the back of the group when he wobbled past her. "You're getting this."

Dakota's class reached the other side of the rink, then turned and skated back to the center. They continued going back and forth, all to the soundtrack of nostalgic '80s songs.

When they finished thirty minutes later, Dakota clapped. "Y'all did a fantastic job," she said. "That's it for tonight. Keep practicing."

"Dakota?"

She turned at the sound of her name, and Jack's mother, Rose, sidled up to her. "Hey! Jack is doing great."

Rose looked embarrassed as she wrung her hands. "It's because you're a great teacher. But it was a slow week at the diner, and I was wondering if I could pay you next week."

Dakota's heart clutched for Rose. She was aware of her situation — working hard to raise her son on her own. She understood what it was like to struggle, especially lately. "That's no problem at all."

"Thank you. I really appreciate it, Dakota."

Jack appeared next to his mother and pulled on her sleeve. "Can we get a drink, Mom?"

"Of course." Rose smiled down at her son and then at Dakota. "We'll see you next week."

Dakota was grateful Kayleigh and Brice gave free concessions coupons to all the skating students so Rose could get Jack something to drink.

Kayleigh skated over and smiled at Rose and Jack before taking Dakota's arm. "Are you ready for the adult class?"

"Can I help teach?" Gigi asked.

Kayleigh leaned down and touched Gigi's nose. "Why don't you help Daddy in the DJ booth instead?"

"Okay!" Gigi set off to find her father.

Dakota and Kayleigh moved back to the center of the rink, where a group of a dozen new skaters ranging in age from nineteen to sixty stood waiting for them.

For the next forty-five minutes, Dakota and Kayleigh taught the basics. By the time the class ended, the rink was buzzing with patrons, most of them dressed in '80s clothes. A line had formed by the snack bar, and others stood by the half wall, waiting for the general skating time to begin. Kayleigh headed toward the DJ booth while Dakota glided off the rink floor.

"Good evening, folks." Brice's voice rang out over the speakers as the lights dimmed and disco balls reflected around the rink. "Who's ready for an '80s all-skate?" A Bon Jovi song began, and cheers broke out around the rink.

Dakota grinned as people poured out onto the floor and began skating counterclockwise.

Kayleigh appeared next to her balancing a tray with two pieces of pizza and two sodas.

"Want a slice?"

"Sure. Is Gigi staying in the booth with Brice?"

Kayleigh nodded toward the DJ booth. "Yup, so we can talk."

Dakota followed Kayleigh to a booth, where she sat across from her best friend and took a bite of pizza. "You know, hands down, this is the best pizza in Flowering Grove," she said, raising her voice to be heard over Bon Jovi. "I don't care what anyone says."

"Thanks for the loyalty, bestie. And I'm always grateful to hear that the food is good." Kayleigh lifted her cup and took a drink of soda.

"Our classes went well tonight. We had a good turnout too." She leaned forward and shared what Rose had said about paying for the classes. "If you need me to cover her, I will."

Kayleigh waved her off. "I don't expect you to pay for Jack's lessons. We can give her time." She gave Dakota a look. "Besides, you have your own financial concerns now."

"That's true, but I don't want Jack to miss out."

Kayleigh reached across the table and touched Dakota's arm. "You have such a generous heart." Then she pointed toward the rink. "We didn't really have a chance to get caught up last night since we were busy with lessons and then decorating. Have you heard from Parker?"

Dakota nodded. "He texted me last night."

"Really?" Kayleigh rested her elbow on the table and her chin on her palm. "What'd he say?"

Dakota summarized their brief conversation.

Her best friend seemed to study her. "Do you *want* to see him again?"

Dakota shrugged. "We talked about making plans next week."

"You should see him," Kayleigh said. "It would be good for you."

Dakota nodded. Kayleigh was probably right. Parker was sweet, thoughtful, handsome, and genuinely interested in her. Maybe he was the guy who would warm her heart if she only gave him a chance.

"Has Layla come in for a fitting yet?"

Dakota swallowed a bite of pizza and wiped her hands on a napkin. "She came in yesterday." She proceeded to gush about her plan for altering the gown to look like Layla's mother's. Though she still had gowns to save after the flood, her true joy was in alterations. "There's a lot of work to do on her gown, and I can't wait to get started." She hesitated and looked down at her plate.

"Hey." Kayleigh leaned forward. "What's up?"

She frowned. "Hud paid for the gown."

"You saw him at the shop?"

"Yup." She moved her straw around in her drink. "And he changed a flat tire for me yesterday." She held up her pointer finger. "Oh, and that's not all. Then I saw him at the bookstore today. He actually handed me one of the books you recommended, then hassled me about getting in line ahead of him to pay."

"What?" Kayleigh's blue eyes glittered. "Tell me everything."

Dakota explained how Hudson was staying in the Airbnb next door and how he had discovered her and the flat tire, then went on to describe everything else that had happened between them during the week.

"Interesting." Kayleigh lifted her cup. "It stinks that he's staying next door to you. You'll run into him constantly. So awkward."

Dakota rolled her eyes. "You got that right. But the good news is that if he's in a rental house, he'll only be here temporarily." She sighed. "I just wish he'd leave already."

"Well, I hate to tell you . . ." Kayleigh leaned forward, her voice low. "But he's here."

Dakota's stomach dropped. "Where?"

"At the snack bar."

Dakota spun around. Sure enough, Kayleigh was right.

"Don't stare," Kayleigh said.

Dakota peered toward the snack bar, where Hudson, Gavin, Jeannie, and Anissa stood. "Oh no," she muttered.

"Just ignore him," Kayleigh said.

"Right, right." But that was easier said than done. She swallowed against her suddenly dry throat.

Kayleigh glanced around the rink without a care in the world. "The theme night turned out great, and I'm thrilled that our patrons are wearing their '80s garb." She grinned in the direction of a group of women. "Check out that redhead over there. Her MTV shirt and multicolored pants are fabulous."

Dakota nodded, trying to focus on what Kayleigh was saying — but she couldn't resist sneaking a glance at the snack bar, where Hudson still stood with Gavin and his family. She was stunned to find Hudson's bright-blue eyes focused on her.

■ ■ ■ ■

Hudson looked over at Dakota despite Gavin's discussion of his week at work. She and Kayleigh wore stonewashed jeans, pink leg warmers, and similar orange fluorescent shirts decorated with pink peace signs. Their wrists were covered with colorful jelly bracelets, their hairstyles were teased up high, and they both wore copious amounts of blue eyeshadow. They definitely looked the part of 1980s roller girls.

"Hud, are you going to skate tonight?" Gavin asked.

Hudson turned toward his friend. "I doubt it."

"But you were a great skater back in the day. I remember you winning all of the relay contests. You were the fastest guy out there."

Hudson shrugged. "That was a long time ago."

"It's like riding a bike," Jeannie insisted. "It'll come back to you as soon as you get out on the floor."

Gavin looped his arm around his wife's slight shoulders. "That's right."

When Prince's "When Doves Cry" started playing over the speakers, Jeannie gasped. "I love this song." She looked around at her family. "Who wants to skate?"

Anissa took her mother's hand and pulled. "We do! Right, Mommy?"

"Of course." Jeannie gave her husband a look. "You're coming too, Gavin."

"And you too, Hud," Gavin said.

Hudson shook his head. "But I don't have skates."

"They'll give them to you." Anissa pointed to the rental counter.

Hudson smiled at the cute little girl. It had been a while since he'd been around kids.

"Yes," Gavin agreed. "Now stop being such a stick in the mud and come out with us. Let's have some fun."

"Yeah," Anissa insisted.

Hudson couldn't disappoint Anissa. "Okay," he finally agreed. "I'll see you out there." He weaved through a sea of people toward the rental booth and paid for a pair in his size. Then he sat down on a bench and pulled them on.

Once his skates were secured, Hudson stood and scanned the area. The rink was now packed with people skating to the beat of a lively Madonna song. Gavin, Jeannie, and Anissa sailed around the floor, obviously enjoying themselves.

Hudson took his time as he glided toward

the rink, dodging people loitering near the snack bar and chatting beside booths. He reached the entrance to the rink, stopped, and leaned on the wall.

Dakota whizzed past him. She had always made skating look effortless, and she still had the gift. She gracefully turned to skate backward, her long legs keeping time with the music. She spun again, and her dark hair fanned around her face. Even her over-the-top '80s outfit complemented her tall and athletic frame.

Kayleigh joined her, and they fell into a routine of skating back and forth, sharing high fives before spinning and skating backward.

Hudson waited until Dakota and Kayleigh were on the other side of the rink before he stepped out into the flow of the crowd. He hit his stride and continued around the rink, keeping pace with the music.

When he wound up behind an older couple, he slowed, hoping for an opening to pass. Movement out of the corner of his eye caused him to turn just as Dakota glided up beside him. She glanced over at him and then took off, expertly weaving past the slower folks. Her moves were just as crisp as when they were teenagers.

Unable to stop himself, he followed.

She sailed past a group of teenagers as a group of older men appeared around her, boxing her in. She moved to the right, and Hudson caught up to her, their gazes locking for a moment.

Then an older man in front of them started to teeter, his arms flailing. When Dakota stumbled, both she and Hudson pivoted — but instead of getting out of the way, they crashed into each other.

Chapter 8

As soon as Dakota collided with Hudson, his feet went out from under him. He twisted his body in an effort to cushion her fall, which slammed him down on his back. Dakota landed in a heap on his chest, knocking the breath from his lungs.

"Oof," he grunted.

He raised his head and saw her eyes were still closed. She hadn't even moved.

"Are you all right?" he asked despite the pain radiating up his back and shoulders.

Her eyes flew open, and she scrambled off him to sit on the floor. Wincing, she rubbed her right knee. "I'm fine."

"You don't look like it." He touched her shoulder, and she shifted away from him.

A group of skaters gathered around, and the overhead music stopped.

But Hudson ignored the crowd and kept his focus on his ex. "Do you think you can stand?"

Dakota ignored him and continued to rub her knee.

He struggled to stand on his own, then held his hand out to her. "Take my hand."

She peeked up at him, hesitating.

Oh, she's infuriating!

"Dakota, stop being so stubborn and take my hand," he said, his words measured.

Reaching up, she linked her fingers with his, and he lifted her to her feet.

Kayleigh skidded to a stop beside them. "Are you okay?"

"I'll help her to a booth," Hudson said. "Could you find her an ice pack?"

Kayleigh gave him a strange look before hurrying off toward the snack bar.

"Can you skate?" He looped his arm around her waist to hold her steady.

She sucked in a breath, and her dark eyes glittered. "I'm not sure."

"Do you want me to carry you?" he offered.

She shook her head and gripped his shoulder. "No, I'll skate."

"Fine. But take it slow."

The crowed parted for them, and they slowly made their way to the booths, where he helped her sit. She slid to the far end and stretched out her right leg, blanching at the movement.

"Do you want me to take you to the ER?" he asked, sitting down across from her.

"No." She sniffed. "I'm sure it's just a bad bruise."

Silence expanded between them, and she kept her focus on her leg.

"Thanks for the gift card."

She finally met his gaze. "Thanks for helping me. And for the book."

"Were you able to get the tire fixed?"

Dakota nodded. "Carter Donovan took care of it."

"I remember him from school."

Hudson opened his mouth to speak again but was interrupted when Kayleigh arrived with an ice pack. "Here you go."

Dakota placed the ice on her sore knee and winced once again. "I think both my pride and my knee are bruised."

An unspoken conversation passed between the women, and Hudson sensed Kayleigh's disapproval. That was his cue to leave.

He slid out of the booth and stood.

"Hud," Dakota called.

He froze before spinning to face her.

"Did I hurt you when I fell on you?"

For a moment, he studied her gaze. That couldn't possibly be genuine concern sparkling in her dark-chocolate-colored eyes, could it?

He moved his hand over the back of his neck, ignoring the pain still radiating up from his lower back. "Nope."

"You sure? I landed on you pretty hard."

"I'll be fine."

"Well . . ." Her voice trailed off. "Thanks again."

He nodded before skating away from them.

"Did you have fun, Hud?" Jeannie asked, walking through the Flowering Grove Rollerama parking lot between Gavin and Hudson.

Gavin carried Anissa, who was fast asleep with her head resting on her father's shoulder.

Hudson shrugged. "Yeah. Did you?"

"Oh yeah." She grinned. "We always have fun here."

"Glad to hear it." He glanced back toward the door, looking for any sign of Dakota.

The last time he'd seen her, she was sitting on a stool by the snack bar talking to a few of the teenagers who worked at the rink. She had taken off her skates and replaced them with black high-top Converse sneakers, and she still held an ice pack on her knee. He'd considered checking in with her again, but he thought it best to steer clear of her.

Even better, maybe he could forget she even existed.

Yeah, right.

"Did you see the party rooms behind the snack bar?" Jeannie continued. "We should have Anissa's birthday party here."

"That's a great idea," Gavin agreed.

When they reached Gavin's four-door Dodge pickup, Hudson shook Gavin's free hand. "Thanks for inviting me."

"Of course. We'll have to do it again," Gavin told him.

Hudson nodded. "You all drive safe." He waved and continued to his SUV.

His phone dinged with a text just as he climbed inside. He pulled it from his pocket and found a message from Layla: *Tux fitting at Fairytale Bridal Wednesday, 3 p.m.*

He stared at his sister's message. He hadn't heard from her since their argument on Thursday. He texted back: *You okay?*

Hudson expected the message bubbles to appear right away, but after several moments, they still hadn't. He ran a hand through his disheveled hair. Being on the outs with her was a new feeling, and he didn't like it at all.

Then the speech bubbles suddenly appeared.

I'll be okay when you have some respect for my fiancé.

Hudson rubbed his eyes. His sister was always so dramatic. He responded: *Does that mean you and Shane are paying for the wedding now? Should I plan to only cover the cost of my own tux?*

When his phone lit up with her number, he answered it.

"Is that your idea of an apology?" she asked.

"Not exactly."

She was silent, but he could almost hear her seething over the phone. "How about this? We agree to disagree. I think you're a jerk, and you disagree."

"Layla —"

"Look, are you getting a tux or what? Are you going to give me away, or should I ask Aunt Trudy to walk me down the aisle?"

"You still haven't told me who's paying for this shindig."

"If you're going to treat my fiancé and me like children, then I guess we'll be paying. That's all you care about anyway." Her voice sounded thick. "You really embarrassed me at dinner with his family. I can't believe you did that to me."

Hudson leaned back, allowing his head to hit the seat behind him. "I was only speaking the truth."

"Well, you could've been a whole lot nicer and less snobby."

"So you think I'm a snob?"

"Yes, a very big one." She sniffed.

He looked out the window toward the line of cars heading out of the parking lot. "I don't want to fight with you."

"There's a simple fix for that. Stop being a jerk."

They were both quiet for a moment.

"Are you going to give me away or not?" she finally asked.

He blew out a puff of air and debated how best to convince her to see things from his point of view. Fighting obviously wasn't working. "Of course I'll give you away."

"And you'll go to the tux fitting?"

"Yes, I'll go to the tux fitting." He drummed his fingers on the steering wheel. "And what about the wedding? Should I send you a receipt for the down payment on the country club, so you and Shane can discuss making payments to me?"

She was quiet.

"Does your silence mean you need me to pay for the wedding?"

"I still don't like how you embarrassed

me in front of Shane and his family."

"And I still don't think you need to rush into this. You should take your time and get to know him better."

"Like I said — what if we agree to disagree?" she asked.

"Fine."

"Fine."

"Good."

"Good. And bye," she said before the line went dead.

Shaking his head, he started his SUV. What on earth would help his sister see the light?

Dakota hurried over to the front counter of her store as the phone rang Wednesday afternoon. "Fairytale Bridal, this is Dakota. How may I help you?"

"Hello," a woman said. "My daughter is getting married in July, and she's looking for yellow bridesmaids' gowns. Do you have any yellow dresses?"

"Yes, ma'am. We have almost every color you can imagine."

"Now, when you say you have *every* color I can imagine, does that mean you have butter yellow?"

"I sure do. Different styles too. Would you like to make an appointment to come and see them?" She balanced the receiver on her shoulder and peered out the window just as a gray Infiniti SUV pulled into a spot in front of her store. *Uh-oh. That can't possibly be . . .*

Hudson climbed out of the vehicle and stood on the sidewalk.

Her eyes rolled heavenward. *Not again.*

Maybe he was going to Swanson's Hardware. Surely he needed something from there and hadn't come downtown just to see her.

"Now, you're positive you have butter yellow?" the woman continued. "I don't mean citrine or oatmeal. I need *butter* yellow, specifically."

Dakota forced her lips into a smile despite the woman's condescending tone. "I'm sure I have butter yellow in several styles."

Out on the sidewalk, Hudson turned toward the hardware store and spoke to another man. She shifted to see the other man's face but couldn't from her angle at the counter.

The woman harrumphed. "Now, you understand that I need butter yellow, right? We've been to several stores, and they tried to sell us canary and lemon chiffon."

"I understand completely." Dakota brushed her hand over her forehead. "I'm sure I have what you need, ma'am. When would be a convenient time for you to come in and see our selections?"

She knew Shane Simpson had an appointment for a tux fitting at three o'clock today. Had he invited Hudson to join him? She pulled her schedule up on her computer and found that both Shane and Hudson were listed at three. Had Skye added Hudson to the appointment and forgotten to tell her?

The bell above the door dinged, welcoming Shane into the store with Hudson right behind him.

Oh no.

She lifted her chin and gave Hudson her best aloof expression while also trying not to stare at him. He was clean-shaven and wore a dark-gray Henley shirt with a snug pair of jeans.

Shane stood to the side, his countenance grave. He folded his arms over his chest, and tension radiated in the room. It seemed the two men weren't happy to see each other, which she found curious.

Dakota held up her finger, indicating she would be off the phone soon, and Shane nodded before crossing to the display of tuxedos. Hudson remained near the jewelry counter, where he perused a row of cufflinks. Yes, they were definitely avoiding each other.

"Now, you're *certain* you have butter yellow?" the woman asked yet again, bringing Dakota's focus back to her tedious phone call. "I don't mean sunflower or bumblebee yellow."

Dakota took a deep breath and mustered up all the patience she had. She had nearly every possible shade of yellow, and as much as she didn't appreciate the woman's attitude, she needed the sale. "Ma'am, I'm positive that I have the color you're looking for. Now, when would you and your daughter like to come in?"

"Friday at ten works for us. We'd like to get these dresses in the works. July will be here before you know it, and my daughter has fourteen bridesmaids. You know how it is when you're in a sorority."

Fourteen bridesmaids! Excitement rushed through Dakota. This could be the financial break she'd been waiting for. "Yes, ma'am. I sure do." Her hands shook as she booked the appointment, taking the woman's information before hanging up the phone and turning her attention to Shane and Hudson.

"Sorry about that." She touched her hair, hoping her French braid was still intact and presentable.

"No problem," Shane said, but his sour expression indicated otherwise. Maybe he wasn't thrilled to be here. Or perhaps his issue was with his future brother-in-law.

She grabbed her clipboard, a measuring tape, and a pencil from under the counter before looping the tape around her neck and joining Shane by the display of suits. "Do you know what style of tux you'd like?"

Shane gave her a helpless look before pointing to the framed poster of a man in a traditional tuxedo. "Layla said she's fine with regular ol' black-and-white."

"Perfect." She checked a few boxes on her tuxedo order form, then divided a look between the two men. "Who wants to go first?"

A cell phone started to ring, and Shane fumbled for his phone in the back pocket of his jeans. "Sorry. Gotta take this. My boss." He rested the phone against his ear and wandered toward the racks of gowns for bridesmaids. "Hey, Ramón."

"Guess that means I'm first." Hudson rubbed his hands together, glancing over at Shane and then back to Dakota. "Sorry for the tension. We should've made separate appointments." He paused. "Layla is just being Layla."

"Oh." She hesitated, hoping he'd elaborate. When he didn't, she wrote his name at the top of the form, forcing her hand to stop quivering. "What's your phone number?" she asked, keeping her eyes trained on the piece of paper.

"It's the same."

"Sorry," she snipped, "but I don't remember it."

"Right. Why would you?" He rattled it off.

She wrote it down, pretending she hadn't known it by heart for so many years. "Do you know your neck size?"

He shared the number, which she wrote down.

"Your chest?" She peeked up at him.

He crossed his arms over his middle and told her the number.

"You must have a tailor in New York."

"I do. I have to look the CEO part."

She tried not to react to the news that not only did he have a tailor, but also he was an actual CEO. He certainly *was* successful, which meant he'd gotten everything he'd wanted — all without her. It was obvious that heading to the big city and leaving her behind with a broken heart had been a great decision for him.

He should be so very proud of himself.

"Well, I won't waste your time if you can tell me all of your measurements." She poised her pencil. "I'm ready when you are."

He shook his head. "Cuts can be different for different suits. You should measure me."

That meant she had to touch him.

Oh boy.

"How's your knee, by the way?"

She blinked at him, surprised to see his expression was a little softer. "Sore but much better. I'll be fine before I have to teach Friday." She consulted her clipboard. "Let's start with your overarm measurement. That's around your chest with your arms at your sides. But I would imagine you already knew that."

"Yup." He stood as directed, and she wrapped the measuring tape around him. Being this close to him was almost too much for her.

"Do you teach skating at the rink every weekend?"

"On Fridays and Saturdays." She felt like an idiot for being so flustered when Hudson seemed completely unaffected by her presence. He obviously had zero attraction to her, which only added to her frustration with herself.

Shane continued to talk on the phone on the other side of the boutique, fully engrossed in a conversation involving bushes, perennials, and landscape timbers.

"Let's get your sleeve length," Dakota said.

She slipped behind him before stretching the tape measure from the base of his neck, over the top of his shoulder, down the back of his elbow, and over his arm to just past his wristbone.

"You like teaching?" he asked. "Skating, I mean."

"I do." She wrote down the measurement. "I need to get your outseam. Would you please stand up there?" She pointed to the platform in front of the wall of mirrors.

Hudson hopped up on it and stood sideways. He started to say something just as the bell above the door rang and Skye rushed in.

Her niece waved and hurried toward Dakota with her backpack bouncing on her shoulders. "Hi, Auntie."

"How was school?" Dakota asked her.

"Good." Skye pointed to the back of the store. "I need to use your computer for a minute." She hurried toward the door that led to the office. "Be right back."

"Take your time," Dakota called after her.

Hudson looked surprised. "Is that Skye?"

"Sure is."

"Wow," he said. "She's grown up quite a bit."

"That's what happens after seven years." She placed the measuring tape on his hip bone, then ran it down to the top of his shoes.

"She looks just like you."

"I hear that a lot." She bent at the waist to complete the measurement.

"Your store is nice. Classy."

She stood and picked up the clipboard and pen from the podium. "Thank you."

"I'm kind of surprised you're so into weddings since you didn't give ours a chance," he snipped.

His comment stung her with such force, she felt as if the wind had been knocked out of her. Grateful she wasn't facing him, she gripped the pen, her body quavering. He made her decision to break their engagement sound so much simpler than it was. It had been the toughest choice she'd ever made in her life. She could still feel the crack in her heart to this day.

Dakota declined to respond and instead tried to shake off her anger. She wrote down the measurement and took a ragged breath to steady herself.

The bell above the door rang, and she fixed her face with a smile. When she turned toward the door, she froze at the sight of Parker walking in.

His light-brown hair was shaggy, as if he'd missed a few haircuts, and his dark eyes twinkled in the fluorescent lights. He was stocky, and when she wore heels, they stood at the same height. He gave her a wave and a hesitant smile. "Hi, Dakota."

"Parker, what are you doing here?" she asked as he came to stand in front of her.

He scratched his throat. "Would you think less of me if I admitted I've been waiting with bated breath for you to text?" Color tinged his cheeks. "I thought maybe if I came to see you in person, we could actually plan another date."

"You came here to ask me out?" she asked, certain she could feel Hudson's eyes burning into her back.

"Yeah." Parker gave a nervous laugh. "So . . . when can we go out again?"

Dakota hesitated. "I-I'm with a customer right now." She stole a glance at Hudson, whose eyes were narrowed. Then she met Parker's eager gaze. "I'll text you after I close tonight, and we'll make definite plans. Does that work?"

Parker's face lit up with a smile. "Great. I'll look forward to it."

As he headed out the door, she spun to

face Hudson again. He was watching her with an expression that seemed to be somewhat stunned. Good. He deserved to be off-balance after his heartless comment. She couldn't stop her smile. "I'm sorry about that interruption. Do you still wear a size eleven shoe?"

He stared at her as he stepped down from the platform. "Yeah."

She chose a shiny black pair from the display and brought them over to him. "Try these."

He sank onto a nearby chair and pulled off his sneakers. "I meant to grab a pair of dress socks before I left the house this morning, but I forgot."

"One sec." Dakota slipped into the hallway behind the showroom and grabbed a pair of the thin socks she offered to customers off the shelf.

Skye rushed over to her. "Do you need my help?"

"No, thanks. I've measured Hudson, and when Shane is done with his phone call, I'll take care of him too."

"I've watched you do it a hundred times, Auntie. Let me try it for once." Skye folded her hands. "You can trust me."

Dakota shook her head. "I promise I'll show you soon, okay? I've got it this time."

Skye's posture wilted, and her lips formed a straight line.

Dakota nodded toward the workroom. "Would you please bring out the gowns I finished steaming earlier? They're in the wardrobe bags on the rack to the right."

"Sure."

"Thank you." She returned to the front, where Hudson sat on the chair, scrolling through his phone. Shane stood by the platform, off his call and ready for his turn. Again, neither man interacted with the other, as if they were strangers instead of future brothers-in-law.

She handed Hudson the socks. "Let me know how the shoes feel." Then she turned to Shane. "Are you ready?"

She quickly recorded Shane's measurements, then gave him his own pair of shoes to try on. Then they all three walked to the counter together.

While she rang them up, Skye came out to the floor and started adding the restored gowns to the racks. Her expression appeared irritated while she worked.

Dakota calculated the tickets and told them the total.

"I'll pay for both." Hudson had his black credit card on the counter in a flash.

Shane speared him with a look. "I don't

need you to pay for my tuxedo," he groused.

"I said I'd pay for the wedding. That means all of it." Hudson handed Dakota the card. "Charge me for both."

"No." Shane handed Dakota his own card.

Dakota paused, an awkward silence surrounding the men. Taking the easiest path, she ran both cards and printed their receipts, which they each signed.

"My groomsmen and my dad plan to come within the next week," Shane said, pushing the signed receipt toward her.

"Fantastic."

The men slipped their receipts and cards back into their wallets.

"Thank you for your business," she told them.

Hudson nodded and followed Shane toward the door.

She kept her eyes on the front window as Hudson said something to Shane. Both men glowered while they seemed to share a heated discussion. Curiosity niggled at her, and she contemplated the tension and their disagreement about the payments. Shane wasn't a fan of Layla's older brother, and boy, would she love to know the story behind their fallout.

"You okay, Auntie?"

Dakota turned to where her niece sat on a

stool. "Yeah. Why?"

"You seem, like, really preoccupied."

"The taller man who just left? Well . . ." Dakota swallowed. "He's Layla's older brother." She paused. "And also my ex, Hudson Garrity."

"I thought he looked familiar. He came to all of my dance recitals with you when I was little."

Dakota turned her attention to straightening the counter and filing the receipts, hoping Skye would drop the subject.

"What exactly happened between you two?"

Dakota shrugged as if it was no big deal at all. "We grew apart." She picked up the socks Hudson used, then turned around and saw Skye on her phone. "Who are you texting?"

"Gunner." Skye kept her eyes focused on her phone, her thumbs moving swiftly over the digital keyboard.

"But you're at work."

"I know, but there's not a ton going on here." She looked up, her brow pinched. "When are you going to let me do more than clean, move the inventory, and update the website?"

"I promise I will someday soon."

"But when, Auntie? I'm smart enough to

take measurements and help customers pick out gowns and tuxes. You need to trust me."

Dakota reached for her arm. "I do trust you. I just need the time to teach you, and right now I don't have it. I promise I will after we get through the fiasco with the damaged gowns."

Skye moved her arm out of reach. "You just want to control things. Is that it? Dad always says you're stubborn like Grandpa," she retorted.

"I suppose stubbornness runs in the Jamison family," Dakota said with a sigh.

"Have you thought any more about adding the online sales?"

Dakota shook her head. "No, not yet. Maybe soon."

"Fine." Skye headed back toward the office, but Dakota could tell her niece was disappointed. Guilt overshadowed her. How long until her business would be out from under its dark cloud?

CHAPTER 9

Dakota couldn't believe she was sitting in the theater on a Thursday night when she had dresses to steam and Layla's gown to alter. But here she was, witnessing a good-looking actor on the screen loudly revving a sports car and chasing a bad guy down a congested highway at top speed as exciting music swelled.

Beside her, Parker scooped a handful of buttery popcorn from the bucket and dropped it into his mouth, his eyes trained on the movie.

Dakota sighed. She'd made a promise to Parker yesterday, and when she'd texted him last night, she'd let him talk her into meeting up after work tonight. She was grateful the date had been platonic so far. He hadn't tried to hold her hand or slip his arm around her shoulders. Instead he'd purchased a ten-gallon bucket of popcorn and two sodas before they entered the sparsely occupied theater and found two seats in the middle of a row.

Conversation before the movie began had been pleasant enough. They'd discussed their days, and he hadn't stopped smiling since he'd met her in the lobby. Their interaction had been . . . nice.

But her mind still lingered on the work waiting for her back at the store. Her leg began to bounce. She didn't have time to waste on movies she wouldn't have bothered to watch even if she'd been desperate to relax at home and could find nothing else to choose from the streaming service.

But Parker was a nice guy, and that's what she needed in her life — a nice guy, a dependable guy, a sweet guy.

Give him a chance.

She did her best to focus on the movie, and soon enough, it was over. She followed Parker out of the theater and to the sidewalk. The sky was dark, and the air was cool. Cars motored by on the street, and most of the businesses had flipped their Open signs to Closed.

"So what did you think of the movie?" Parker asked.

She shrugged. "It was good."

"You hated it."

"Well, I didn't hate it . . ."

He gently bumped his shoulder against hers, and when she turned toward him, they both started to laugh.

"Okay, okay," she said. "I didn't exactly love it, but I didn't hate it. I guess not all action and adventure movies are my thing."

"So what is your thing then?"

"Roller-skating."

His mouth gaped. "Roller-skating?"

She chuckled again. "Yeah, roller-skating. I teach on Friday and Saturday nights." She explained how Kayleigh and her husband had purchased the rink last year, and for some ridiculous reason, she felt the sudden urge to invite him. "Would you like to join me at the rink tomorrow night?"

"Uh, maybe?" He brushed his hand over the back of his shaggy brown hair.

"Hmm," she teased. "You sound as excited about skating as I did about the movie."

"Well, if skating is how I get to spend time with you, then sign me up. Just don't laugh at me when I fall."

"I promise I won't laugh or let you fall."

"I'm going to hold you to that promise too," he said.

She nodded, hardly believing she'd just agreed to another date.

Hudson jogged across the road toward the

site where the old music store building had once stood. He'd been surprised when Gavin had called him earlier and invited him to stop by and talk business. He couldn't imagine what the business was, but his curiosity propelled him down the street, where the streetlights cast a yellow glow, illuminating the dark storefronts and the sidewalk.

As he sauntered down the sidewalk, he spotted a couple standing between the movie theater and the music store. He went to step around them, and his eyes locked with Dakota's. Then he focused on the man standing beside her.

It was the same guy who had barged into her store while she'd been measuring him for his tux. What was his name? He searched his mind.

Parker.

What a stupid name. Yet there she was with him, and he was beaming at her. It looked like he'd gotten the date she'd promised him yesterday, and it seemed pretty clear that Dakota wasn't as single as Layla had insisted.

Well, good for them.

Dakota quickly looked away, and Hudson hurried past them. Then he rushed down the street to the vacant lot, where he found

Gavin waiting for him, standing under a streetlight.

"Hud." Gavin shook his hand. "Thanks for meeting me."

"Sure thing." He glanced past Gavin just in time to see Dakota and Parker disappearing down a side street. Once they were out of his sight, Hudson gave his friend his undivided attention. "What's up?"

Gavin gestured toward the construction site. "Well, as you can see, the building was demolished earlier this week. Kind of bad timing though." He sighed. "A few members of my crew moved on to other jobs, and now I'm shorthanded. Don't guess you'd be interested in earning some calluses and messing up those manicured hands while in town, huh?"

Hudson laughed. "Don't be a jerk." He pretended to examine his short fingernails. "Not all New Yorkers get weekly manicures," he joked. "I'm only going to be here until after Layla's wedding, but . . . if you're really in a bind, I could give it a try. I think I remember some tricks from when we worked for Mr. Smith. Maybe it'll help me work out some of this frustration over my thing with Layla."

Gavin paused. "Wait, for real? Do you remember how to hold a hammer?"

"Believe it or not, yes." He struggled not to roll his eyes, but he was quite sure his tone was still a little exasperated.

"Great, great, that's fine." Gavin pointed at him and grinned. "You're pretty smart. I can teach you anything you've forgotten."

Hudson chuckled. "All right. It's a deal."

"Fantastic." Gavin pointed back to the empty lot. "Now, let me tell you about the plans we have for this place. I already told you it's going to be a restaurant, right?"

As Gavin talked, Hudson rubbed his hands together. As he considered the work he'd just agreed to, he couldn't believe how excited he was to get started.

Kayleigh gave Dakota a high five the following night. "Great lessons! And we had even more kids join our children's class. I'd say that's a win."

Dakota glanced around the rink. The place was buzzing with patrons preparing for the all-skate session, which would begin in five minutes. "I agree."

Kayleigh scanned the lobby, and her smile faded. "There's a line at the rental desk. I should go help Brice since Hayley called in sick tonight."

"I can pitch in too."

"Nope. You wait for your date." Kayleigh

bumped Dakota's shoulder. "I think it's great that you told Parker to meet you here tonight. I can't wait to hear all about it." She grinned before gliding toward the rental desk.

Dakota pulled out her phone from the back pocket of her jeans just as the DJ's voice boomed over the speakers.

"Gooooood evening, everyone. Who's ready for the general skate?"

Cheers went up around the room. A loud bassline began to play, and skaters filed out onto the rink.

"Dakota."

She turned to see Parker weaving through the crowd on the way to her booth. She stood as he approached. "I'm so glad you made it."

"My younger brother loaned me his skates since we're the same size. It's been years since I've actually worn a pair, so we'll see how this goes." He set the pair of worn dark-blue skates on the booth bench before gathering her into his arms for an awkward hug. She patted his back and waited for some kind of spark. Instead, she felt nothing but gratitude for him.

"Are you ready to skate?" she asked him.

"Sure."

As he pulled on the skates, Dakota hoped

she would develop stronger feelings for Parker — and soon.

Hudson found his way to the skate rental booth and took his place in line. He glanced around the rink and spotted Dakota skating hand in hand with that Parker guy. It was bad enough that he'd run into them on the street last night, but now they were together at the rink. Looked like they were really happy together. And that was just fine with him. Still, his lips tipped down.

But he wasn't going to allow their presence to stop him from skating. He would enjoy his night at the rink and just ignore Dakota as she skated with another man.

"What size skates do you need?"

Hudson pivoted toward Brice in the booth. "Hey, Brice. An eleven."

"No problem." Brice retrieved the skates while Hudson pulled out his credit card. Then Brice gave Hudson the skates and ran the card.

"I love what you've done to bring the rink back to life."

Brice handed him a receipt. "Thanks. It's been a little hectic, but Kayleigh and I are having the time of our lives. Thankfully, our daughter is crazy about skating too."

"Coming back here has reminded me how

much I used to love to skate." Hudson slipped the receipt and card into his wallet.

"Glad to hear it. Enjoy your night."

Hudson carried the skates to a nearby booth and pulled them on before heading out to the rink. He joined the knots of people, quickly catching up to Gavin and Anissa. Gavin had mentioned in a text earlier that Jeannie was out with her book club tonight, so the guys were on their own. Hud laughed along with Gavin as Anissa tried her best to show them her tricks.

When Hudson found himself behind Dakota and her guy, he sped up to pass them. Dakota held the man's arm, and Hud overheard her trying to give him instructions. He felt his entire body tense. It was clear the man hadn't skated much and had no idea what he was doing. That, or he was pretending to need help to have a reason to hold on to her. Either way, what a loser.

When the song ended, the house lights came on.

"Hey there, everyone," the DJ announced. "Let's give a warm Flowering Grove Rollerama welcome to the rink owners, Kayleigh, Brice, and Gigi Hayes."

The crowd clapped and cheered when Brice, Kayleigh, and Gigi skated out to the center of the rink. Brice held up a microphone, and Kayleigh stood beside him waving a checkered flag.

"What's up, y'all?" Brice asked, and the crowd clapped some more. "We're so glad you've joined us tonight. Many of us spent the better part of our youth here at the rink." He motioned toward Kayleigh, who beamed at him. "And we loved the roller-skating competitions we had here, especially the relay races. Since this is family night at the Rollerama, we thought we'd have some fun." He scanned the room. "Now, who wants to race?"

More claps and cheers.

Hud folded his arms across his chest. He had won plenty of those races, and so had Dakota. He couldn't stop himself from turning to where Dakota stood with that guy — the joker who was holding on to her arm and grinning at her.

Hudson gritted his teeth. What did he care if she chose to date a dolt who couldn't even stand up on his skates?

Kayleigh took the microphone. "The first relay is for girls ten and under." She pointed to the floor in front of her. "If you're ready to show us what you've got, line up here."

More claps sounded as nearly a dozen girls, including Gavin's daughter, Anissa, came to stand in front of Kayleigh and Brice.

"Let's hear it for our contenders," Kayleigh called, and the crowd whistled and cheered. "Okay, ladies. Now I want you to race as fast as you can around the rink and back here." She pointed to a line on the floor. "This is the finish line." She held up the flag. "Whoever gets here first is the winner and will race the winner from our next group." She whispered to her daughter before handing her the microphone.

Gigi held the microphone up to her lips. "Ready . . . set . . . go!"

And Kayleigh shook the checkered flag.

A clatter of roller skate wheels blended with cheers as the girls began their journey around the rink. Anissa quickly fell to the back of the pack. With her adorable little brow furrowed and her tongue sticking out, she raced with all her might.

Hudson's eyes once again betrayed him, and he found himself watching Dakota instead of the race. She clapped and hopped around on her skates, cheering on the girls. She was mesmerizing with her sparkling eyes and her thick, dark ponytail bouncing off her shoulders.

Suddenly, she turned toward Hudson — and when her gaze tangled with his, his breath caught. She nodded a greeting, and he returned it.

Parker tapped her shoulder. She fixed her dark eyes on him before laughing at something he said, and Hudson's moment with her was gone.

The racers came around the rink, and a girl with bright-green skates crossed the finish line first. Kayleigh shook the checkered flag, signaling the end of the race.

"We have a winner," Brice announced over the roar of the crowd. He beckoned the girl to skate over to him. "What's your name?"

The girl took deep breaths. "Suzy Darst."

"Let's hear it for Suzy Darst and the rest of the young ladies who participated in our first relay!" Brice said.

As the crowd clapped, Anissa skated over to Hudson.

"Did you see me skate, Mr. Hud?" Anissa asked him.

Hudson bent at the waist to talk to her over the claps and whistles. "You did great."

She beamed. "Thanks."

A few more races took place before it was the adults' turn.

"Now," Kayleigh began, "let's have our women ages sixteen and older join us in the middle of the rink."

Several teens and women skated to the other side of the rink and stood on a line.

Kayleigh scanned the crowd and then pointed. "Dakota Jamison, where are you?"

A few people cheered and pointed to where Dakota stood with the guy who couldn't skate.

"Get over here, Dakota," Kayleigh ordered.

Dakota shook her head and held up her arms. "Not tonight."

Kayleigh rested her free hand on her hip. "Why are you saying no?"

"Unfair advantage," Dakota called back.

"Does anyone else think Dakota has an unfair advantage?" Kayleigh asked the crowd, and laughter broke out around the room.

Brice took the microphone. "I think you need to race, Dakota."

Parker said something to Dakota, and she smiled before leaving him behind and skating over to join the race.

"All right," Kayleigh said. "Here comes the legendary Dakota Jamison. I believe you were the champion when we were kids."

A blush crept up Dakota's cheeks, and she waved off her best friend. "That was a long time ago."

Gavin leaned over to Hudson. "And you

were the champion of the guys."

Hudson snorted.

"Well, let's see who'll be tonight's champion," Kayleigh said. "Line up now, ladies."

The contenders did as they were told, and Brice took control of the microphone.

"To make this race more challenging, the first to complete *two* laps will be the winner," he said.

Brice gave his daughter the microphone, and again she yelled, "Ready . . . set . . . go!"

Kayleigh shook the checkered flag, and the women took off around the rink. Dakota was graceful and agile, not showing any sign of the knee injury she had suffered when she and Hudson collided last week. She swiftly moved to the front of the line and battled another young woman for the lead.

The crowd cheered when they finished the first lap side by side. Dakota crouched and pumped her arms, her long legs picking up speed. She shot ahead of the pack, then came around the first curve while the spectators continued to hoot, holler, and whistle.

Hudson couldn't help his grin when his ex lengthened her lead, putting a couple seconds between herself and the rest of the women. She had always amazed him with her athletic prowess. It seemed to come naturally to her, as if she'd been born to skate.

Dakota glided through the next two turns before launching across the finish line, where Kayleigh shook the checkered flag. Dakota slowed and spun before crossing her arms over her short-sleeved green shirt, then worked to slow her breathing.

"The winner is . . . my auntie Dakota!" Gigi cried into the microphone, and everyone clapped.

Dakota hugged Gigi and kissed her cheek.

Brice took the microphone. "Let's hear it for everyone who raced." He said something to Dakota, and she laughed before he addressed the crowd again. "Our winner Dakota has earned herself a gift certificate to the snack bar."

Dakota leaned over and added, "Where else can you find the best pizza ever? Am I right?"

"Thanks for the plug," Brice told her. "At this time I need all of the men who are sixteen and older to come out here. Whoever wins this next round will have to race Dakota."

Anissa pulled on Gavin's arm. "You need to race, Daddy."

"No, sweetie." Gavin shook his head. "I'm

not fast enough. Plus, I can't risk getting hurt and missing work."

Anissa stuck out her bottom lip. "Pretty please. I was brave enough to race. Aren't you?"

Hudson snickered. "I think that was a challenge, Gavin."

"You think that's funny, huh?" Gavin lifted an eyebrow at Hudson. "Are *you* brave enough, Hud?"

"Anyone else?" Brice called into the microphone.

"Yes!" Gavin tapped Hudson on the shoulder. "Right here."

Hudson hesitated but then smiled down at Anissa. He'd always loved skating, and he had to admit, the competition was fun. "Fine, I'll do it."

As he skated off to the starting line, he smiled at the sound of little Anissa cheering him on.

Chapter 10

Hudson joined the other six men who were ready to race at the starting line. He turned to his right, where Dakota watched him with an expression of disbelief.

"No one else?" Brice asked the crowd. A chorus of cheers went up when two more men in the audience decided to join them for the race.

Kayleigh took the microphone. "Let's see which of you is the fastest. Now, this race is two laps, just like the one the ladies just finished. The first to complete two laps will be our winner." She beckoned for Dakota to come over to her, and they both bent down beside Gigi.

Together the three of them chanted, "Ready . . ."

Hudson crouched down.

"Set . . ."

He bent his arms.

"Go!"

Kayleigh waved the checkered flag, and Hudson took off. Adrenaline shot through every cell of his body as he weaved past the slower skaters. He felt like he was floating, flying above the rink floor while he negotiated two curves and then headed down the straightaway. The noise from the crowd became background to his heart pounding against his rib cage.

Out of the corner of his eye, he spotted someone gaining on him. He peeked over at the young man who looked to be at least five years his junior. Hudson quickened his pace, speeding through the curves to the straightaway, where he and his opponent crossed the finish line together for the first lap.

Hudson pumped his arms and legs, and his spirit soared along with his speed through their second lap. The young man gained an advantage on him, but Hudson wasn't about to give up. He caught up with the young man, and they shot around the curves together.

When they reached the last straightaway, Hudson felt a burst of adrenaline that powered him forward. The roar of the crowd echoed in his mind when the finish line came into view. He pushed himself, moving faster and faster, until he flew across the line.

The clapping and whistling continued while Hudson slowed and spun. He swiped the back of his hand over the sweat beading on his forehead.

"Who won?" he asked Brice, still gasping for air.

Brice grinned. "You did."

Hudson skated over to the other young contender and shook his hand. "Great race."

"Yeah." The kid laughed. "I can't believe you beat me."

"Hudson Garrity is our winner," Brice called. "Great job to all of you who competed. Now, we have our final showdown between Dakota and Hudson."

Kayleigh tapped her husband's shoulder and whispered something in his ear, causing him to grin wider.

"We're going to handle this last relay a little differently," he said into the mic. "Instead of Dakota and Hudson skating two straightforward laps, they'll skate forward for the first lap and backward for the final lap."

Hudson held up his hands. "No, no, no." He made a sweeping gesture toward Dakota, whose pretty face seemed full of surprise.

"You're the winner, Dakota. Enjoy your trophy." He started toward the other side of the rink.

"Are you too chicken to race me, Hudson Garrity?" Dakota's voice rang out over the speakers.

A chorus of "Ooh!" sounded, along with some laughs and playful jeers.

He sighed before turning to face her. She had taken the mic out of Brice's hand and was staring at him, her dark eyes glittering. Leave it to Dakota to call him out in front of a crowd.

"No," he responded, raising his voice over the rowdy folks around him. "I just know you'll win."

"I remember when you were competitive and loved to race. Did New York City change you?" Her expression seemed to challenge him.

Hudson shook his head. "No, I'm still that way."

She handed the mic back to Brice and glided over to Hudson. "Then what's the problem?"

"I'm rusty."

She scoffed. "You didn't look rusty to me." She rested her hands on her hips. "What's the real issue, Hud?"

"There's no issue."

"Then why won't you race me?"

He rubbed the scruff on his neck. Why was she making such a big deal about this? "Dakota . . ."

"What is it, Hud?" Her brow pinched. "Am I not good enough to race?"

"Fine," he said. "I don't want to beat you in front of everyone."

"Oh, so you think you'll be beat me then?"

"Yeah, I do."

They studied each other.

"Then prove it," she snapped.

The chorus of hecklers sounded again, while a woman added, "She told you!"

Dakota started to skate backward, away from him. "How about it, Hudson Garrity? Are you going to race me, or are you too chicken?"

"Come on, Hud," Brice yelled. "You gotta represent us guys."

"Yeah, Hud," someone else yelled. "Show her how it's done."

Kayleigh clapped and started a chant. "Race! Race! Race!"

"Okay, okay." Hudson held his hands up in surrender, and everyone cheered.

Dakota grinned, and his heart felt light. For a moment it was as if he'd gone back in time. She was the funny, flirty, outgoing woman he'd fallen in love with when he was a teenager. And this rink had been his home away from home. Being back here sent an exhilaration through him that surprised him.

Brice spoke into the microphone. "Hudson and Dakota, you two line up. Remember, two laps: one forward, one backward."

He took his place beside her on the line, and she crouched down, looking ready to sprint into action.

"Ready?" Kayleigh asked, holding up the checkered flag.

Hudson and Dakota glanced at each other and nodded.

"May the best skater win," Kayleigh said.

Dakota turned her focus straight ahead.

Hudson crouched, and his heart began to pound again.

"Ready . . . ," Kayleigh and Gigi yelled. "Set . . . go!" Kayleigh dropped the flag, signaling the start of the race.

Hudson took off just as Dakota leapt into action. They skated together toward the first curve and both took it via crossovers before picking up speed on the back stretch.

When they came through the next set of curves, Dakota moved ahead of him, but Hudson worked to catch up on the straightaway. They hit the line together, then both spun into their backward skate positions.

Hudson craned his neck to look over his shoulder, skating the scissors move as fast as he could but transitioning to crossovers on the turns. Dakota scooted ahead of him, and he tried his best to gain on her on the straightaway once again.

When she slowed on the curves, he caught up to her, and they headed neck and neck down the second straightway as the crowd went wild. As they came to the finish line, they each sped up.

When they crossed the finish line together, Hudson faltered and overcorrected. He righted himself, gliding to the left, and just before running into her, he held out his arms.

"Whoa!" Dakota cried, reaching for and taking hold of his hands. Her skin was warm, and his pulse rocketed from a mixture of exertion and something more potent. "Steady there, Hud," she said. She continued to grasp his hands, which flabbergasted him. "That was fun. Just like old times, right?"

She grinned, and Hudson felt something warm unfurl inside him.

"Right," he said, "just like when you beat me at nearly every race."

Then, to his surprise, she laughed. He hadn't realized until that very moment how much he'd missed that sound. Every muscle in Hudson's back and neck loosened as he laughed along with her.

"Well, folks, that was exciting, wasn't it?" Brice called over the rink's loudspeakers. "And believe it or not, we don't have a winner."

"What?" Dakota pivoted, and Hudson released her hands.

"It was a tie," Brice explained.

Kayleigh and Gigi skated over to them, and while Gigi held up a trophy, Kayleigh carried an envelope. They placed both in Dakota's hands.

"We have gift certificates for the snack bar, two bring-a-friend-to-skate coupons, and a trophy," Kayleigh said. "But you're going to have to decide between yourselves who gets what."

"Thanks to everyone for participating. Now — back to the general skate." Brice waved toward the DJ booth.

When hometown music group Kirwan's "Dance All Night" began to play, a collective cheer sounded from the audience. Before long, the rink filled up with skaters moving to the beat.

Hudson held his hand out for the trophy. "I'll take that, thanks."

"Whoa, Garrity," Dakota said. "Who said

you get the trophy?"

"Fine. You can have the trophy, and I'll take the gift certificates."

"But what if I want the trophy *and* the gift certificates? I think we need to share custody of the trophy."

"Share custody?" He couldn't stop his smile.

Kayleigh nodded toward the oncoming crowd of skaters. "I think you two need to take this to the snack bar before you get run over."

They all moved to the side of the rink.

Dakota made a big deal out of her sigh. "Fine, you can have the trophy."

He held his hands up. "No, you keep it."

She shrugged, setting the trophy down on a bench. Then she opened the envelope, sifted through the gift certificates, chose one, and handed the rest to him. "I just wanted a drink."

"Fair enough." Hudson took the envelope and started toward the concession stand.

"Wait up," she called, grabbing the trophy and skating up beside him. "Thanks for racing me."

Hudson cocked an eyebrow. "Uh . . . you're welcome, I guess?"

"Oh, come on, Hud." Dakota gave him a playful nudge. Was she actually flirting with him? Had she lost her mind? "You have to admit it was fun, and you were a worthy opponent."

He shook his head.

"I remember you actually beating me a few times back in the day. And there was that one time when you tried to trip me so you could win."

Hudson stopped and faced her. "Oh no. I didn't try to trip you. You got too close to me and ran into my skate."

"You *tripped* me, Hudson." She shook the trophy at him. "You cheated."

"I never had to cheat, Dakota. I won fair and square. You're rewriting history."

"No, I'm not." She grinned. "I clearly remember —"

"Dakota?"

Parker interrupted her words. He stumbled toward her on the skates, half skating, half walking. "You were fantastic out there. You're like a professional."

Hudson resisted the urge to roll his eyes, then moved along to the snack bar. He used his gift certificate for a large plate of nachos and three drinks before skating to the table where Gavin and Anissa sat.

"Congratulations," Gavin said. "You were impressive out there."

"You're the best, Mr. Hud," Anissa announced.

"Thanks for cheering for me, Anissa. Wanna share some nachos?" Hudson placed two drinks in front of Gavin and Anissa and the nachos in the center of the table, then sat down across from them in the booth.

Anissa bit into a nacho and beamed at him. "These are yummy, Mr. Hud."

"Thanks for the snack," Gavin said.

"You're welcome." Hudson turned toward where Dakota was talking to Parker and Kayleigh. He tried to decode her body language as she waved her arms and seemed to be sharing a story. Her dark eyes sparkled, and Parker hung on her every word, clearly infatuated. Not that Hudson blamed him. He had once been that guy, completely and utterly in love with her.

A coil of envy wrapped around his insides and tightened. He was being ridiculous. Why would he be jealous of his ex-fiancée's boyfriend after the way she'd hurt him?

Hudson lifted his cup before taking a drink.

Gavin studied him. "You and Dakota looked like you were having a good time together. Seemed pretty cozy to me."

Hud shook his head. "Not even close."

"I know it's none of my business, but you two were together for a long time." Gavin lifted his dark eyebrows. "What happened?"

Hudson ate a few nachos and then wiped his hands on a napkin, trying to keep his expression devoid of emotion. "We were engaged, but she broke it off right before I left for New York." His lips formed a sarcastic smile. "And that was that."

Gavin nodded slowly. "That was a long time ago. People change. Circumstances change."

"Not this circumstance. She decided she didn't want to marry me." He said the words simply, as if they weren't still a punch to his gut nearly a decade later.

"Well, as an outsider looking in, it sure seems like there's some serious chemistry between you two."

"There isn't," Hud said tersely. He nodded toward Parker sitting beside Dakota in a booth across the way. "And even if there was, she's obviously seeing someone now."

She already destroyed me once, and I'm not likely to take that chance with her again.

"When I met Jeannie, I'd recently gone through a bad breakup. I was certain I'd never get married. Now I have Jeannie *and* Anissa, and I've never been happier. Who knows? You and Dakota might get a second chance."

Hudson picked up another nacho and

considered his friend's words. He couldn't imagine ever trusting Dakota again.

At the same time, he couldn't deny that he'd felt his heart starting to come back to life tonight.

"Want to skate with me, Mr. Hud?" Anissa said.

Hudson turned his focus to the sweet little girl. "Of course I do."

He wiped his hands, took one more sip of his drink, and followed her back out to the rink.

"Tonight was so fun," Kayleigh said while she and Dakota stood by the party rooms in the rink. "You were amazing in that relay race, Dakota. No one skates backward better than you."

The rink had closed and patrons were filing through the exit doors toward the parking lot. Brice and Parker were only a few feet away, talking while Brice balanced a sleeping Gigi in his arms.

Dakota pulled on her jacket. "You would have beat everyone if you'd raced, Kay. You don't give yourself enough credit."

Kayleigh leaned in close and lowered her voice. "Parker seems to like you a lot."

"Yeah, he does." Dakota was careful to keep her voice soft.

"And . . . ?" Kayleigh prodded.

"And now isn't the time to discuss it." Dakota pointed her chin toward Brice and Parker.

"Well, I'm glad to see you finally dating again."

"We're not *officially* dating."

"You should be." Kayleigh gently bumped her shoulder against Dakota's. "He's a super-nice guy."

"You know how insane my life is right now." Dakota lifted her purse and tote bag, which held her skates, onto her shoulder.

Parker had been funny and attentive all evening, and judging by how he and Brice continued to talk, he was a good fit with her friends. But despite his magnetic personality and his good looks, Dakota wasn't attracted to him. Her heart just wasn't feeling it at all.

And if she were to be completely honest with herself, she hadn't been able to stop thinking about Hudson since they'd held hands after the relay race. She could almost feel his warm skin still against hers, and the way her heart had thundered when they'd laughed together. The race had taken her back to happier times when they were in love — before he'd chosen his career over their future together.

She'd spent most of the evening doing her best to focus on Parker, but her eyes and her heart kept defying her. She marveled at how good Hudson had looked out on the rink floor. He was still graceful and athletic, and she was struck by how he interacted with Anissa. He seemed so attentive when he talked to her and skated with her. It made her wonder about what could have been between them if they'd gotten married, had a family . . .

"Can I help you and Brice clean up before I go?" Dakota asked.

Kayleigh shook her head. "No, but thanks." She pointed toward the rental booth. "Ryan is handling the skate returns, and the cleaning crew comes in on Mondays."

Dakota scanned the last of the patrons leaving. When she saw Hudson talking with Gavin near the rink entrance, her heart hitched.

Brice carried Gigi over to Kayleigh and Dakota. "Me and Parker were just talking about getting together. We should plan a double date for the four of us," he said as he turned toward Parker. "We'll have more time to talk when I'm not at work."

Parker sidled up to Dakota, and she could feel his gaze on her.

Kayleigh widened her eyes at Dakota. "That would be so fun, right?"

Dakota hesitated. She glanced at Hudson again and felt the familiar, frustrating attraction. She tried to dismiss it, then smiled at Parker. "Let's get together at my place next week. Maybe Thursday night?"

"Perfect," Kayleigh said, and Brice and Parker agreed. Then she hugged Dakota. "I'll talk to you soon."

Dakota and Parker said good night to Kayleigh and Brice before making their way out into the chilly night air of mid-March. She shivered and zipped up her coat before pushing her hands into her pockets. The dark sky above them was clear and sprinkled with stars, and the warm yellow glow of the streetlights cast shadows on the pavement.

Parker reached for her tote bag. "Can I carry this for you?"

She shook her head. "No, I'm good."

He pressed his lips together before his expression brightened. "I had a blast tonight."

"Me too."

They weaved past other cars on their way to her Focus, which sat at the back of the lot.

An awkward silence filled the space between them, and she tried to think of something to say. The moments ticked by while the sounds of cars passing on the street and their shoes on the pavement drifted over them.

Unbidden thoughts of evenings with Hudson came to Dakota's mind. She couldn't remember one time when they'd run out of words. Except maybe when they were too busy kissing. Thrills rushed through her at the memory of his lips caressing hers, and she swallowed a groan. Why couldn't she get that man out of her mind?

When they reached her car, she tossed her purse and tote bag onto the passenger seat.

"I look forward to seeing you Thursday," he said.

She pushed an errant lock of her hair behind her ear. "Me too." She tried to smile, but it felt strained.

"Good night." Parker's expression clouded with a serious look, and when he puckered his lips and ducked his head, panic filled her chest.

Dakota quickly threw her arms around his shoulders and pulled him in for a hug. "Good night," she said, patting his back. Then she climbed into her car, started the engine, and lowered the window. "See you Thursday, Parker."

Disappointment flickered over his features. "Drive safe."

"You too." With a wave, Dakota steered out of the parking lot, confusion twisting her up inside.

Chapter 11

Hudson climbed into his SUV the following Thursday afternoon. His legs, arms, and back were sore from another day working with Gavin on framing the new building.

He'd started early Monday morning at the restaurant jobsite. Being the new guy and rusty when it came to working construction, he needed to be reminded of a lot — namely that the job demanded really hard physical labor. He'd naively thought his gym membership and physical trainer would have more impact on his stamina while pouring concrete. He was wrong. He'd forgotten how sore he'd always get when working for Smith's Construction.

Just as Hudson started the engine, his phone rang. His aunt's name appeared on the screen, and he pushed a button to connect to the Bluetooth. "Hello?"

"Hi there, stranger," his aunt's voice rang over the speakers. "I haven't seen you in a week. Did you head back to the Big Apple without saying goodbye?"

He sighed and backed out of the parking space. "No, Aunt Trudy, I haven't left. I just needed time to regroup after the fight with Layla. Figured we could both use some time to cool down."

"Oh, Hud. You'll work it out. Oh! And she just pulled in the driveway. Anyway, I was thinking of you today, so I made banana bread. Your favorite. It's sitting here waiting for you, but you'd better get here quick. I'm leaving soon to go to Marcie's for supper."

His mouth started to salivate at the mere thought of his aunt's delicious banana bread. "I'll be there in ten minutes."

True to his word, he soon nosed his SUV into his aunt's driveway behind her car and Layla's. He loped up the front steps, but the storm door opened just as he was about to knock.

Aunt Trudy joined him on the porch carrying a grocery bag. "In order to get you to visit me, I need to bribe you with food."

Guilt bit into his back. "You know that's not true. I've been busy, but that's no excuse."

"Doing what?"

"Working. Gavin Wallace owns the construction company that's building a restaurant where the music store used to be. He was looking for extra crew, so he hired me."

His aunt's face lit with a megawatt smile. "Does that mean you're staying in Flowering Grove?"

He shook his head. "I figured I needed something to do while I'm here, and Gavin needs the help. I don't plan on staying after the wedding." *If there is a wedding . . .*

She clucked her tongue. "You say that now, but you'll change your mind. You're gonna remember why you love it here."

Not likely. Nothing could keep him in Flowering Grove, especially if staying here meant watching Dakota plan a life with another man.

Layla appeared on the front porch and gave him a once-over. "You're a mess. What happened to you?"

"Hud got a job working for a construction company."

"What?" Layla snorted. "The big CEO is working construction? How'd that happen?" She jogged down the steps and over to her car.

Hudson frowned. "You seem to have forgotten I worked construction when I was in college."

"Right, but isn't that beneath you now?"

He pressed his lips together.

"I bet you won't last a week at that job."

"You bet me?" he asked.

"Yeah, I bet you." She pointed at him. "You're too good to get your hands dirty."

"What are the stakes?" he asked.

Layla rubbed her chin. "How about . . . a sundae from the Flowering Grove Creamery?"

Aunt Trudy shook her head. "That's enough, you two."

"All right." Hudson walked over to his sister and held out his hand. "I'll take that bet."

They shook on it. He'd show her that he wasn't the out-of-touch snob she thought he was.

"Well, I need to run and meet my fiancé. I'll tell him you said hello," she told Hudson before turning to their aunt. "See you later."

"Drive safely." Aunt Trudy waved to her before handing Hud the grocery bag. "Here's your bread. I need to run along to Marcie's, but I'd better see you soon."

He inhaled the appetizing smell of his favorite snack, then kissed her cheek. "Yes, ma'am. I'll enjoy this for sure."

Ten minutes later Hudson parked his vehicle in the driveway of the colonial. The heavenly scent of his aunt's bread had filled his SUV and caused his empty stomach to gurgle. Lunch had been hours ago, and the bread sounded like the perfect supper.

Out of the corner of his eye he spotted movement at the house next door. He killed the engine just as Dakota traipsed toward her front door, balancing a cell phone on her shoulder along with her purse, a tote bag, and several sacks of groceries. He'd seen her in passing a few times during the past week, and they'd shared nods here and there but hadn't spoken.

He shook his head. Dakota Jamison was the most impatient and stubborn woman he'd ever known, and it was just like her to try to carry everything into her house in one trip. He drummed the steering wheel, fighting the urge to help her as she struggled up the steps.

How she chose to carry her groceries wasn't his business. At the same time . . .

Hudson let out a frustrated growl, grabbed the grocery bag with the bread, and strode across the small strip of grass toward her house. He reached the steps just as Dakota started to teeter. Without thinking, he grabbed an armload of her bags before they slipped out of her hands.

Dakota gasped, her dark eyes widening. "What are you doing?"

"Helping you." He arranged the bags in

his empty hand and then reached for the others.

She shifted away from him. "I got it."

"Dakota?" the voice on the other end of her call asked. "Are you okay? What's going on?"

"Everything's okay," she told the caller. "See you in a little bit. Bye." She disconnected the call and studied him. "I didn't ask for your help, Hud."

"It's okay to let people help you." He distributed the weight of the bags evenly in his two hands, then pulled open the storm door. "Lead the way."

She pursed her lips at first, but then her expression softened. "Fine." After unlocking the door, she stepped inside, where her orange cat sat blinking and meowing at her.

"Hi there, Trouble," Hudson greeted the cat. Then he glanced around, taking in the small foyer, den, and dining room. A counter divided the dining room and kitchen.

"Just a minute, Trubs." Dakota pointed toward the kitchen. "You can put the groceries there."

"No problem." He set the bags on the counter while Dakota slipped past him and deposited her purse, keys, and phone in another spot.

Faded orange wallpaper that looked as if

it had been hung in the 1970s decorated the kitchen, along with cabinets covered in chipped yellow paint. A few of the cabinet doors hung at odd angles, while one cabinet door sat on the kitchen table.

The cat moved in circles under her feet, rubbing her shins and meowing.

"Give me a minute, please," she muttered to the cat. She spooned a large glob of fishy-smelling wet food into his food bowl, and after she set it down, the cat began to inhale it. She rinsed off the spoon and peeked over her shoulder at Hudson. "Thank you."

That was his cue to leave, but for some stupid reason, he wasn't ready just yet. He pointed to the cabinets. "Want me to fix those?"

Her nose scrunched adorably. "What do you mean?"

"Those cabinet doors look like they're planning to fall off and hit you on the head. I see that one already has."

"Oh." She shrugged. "I'll get to that eventually. I keep meaning to ask my brother to come by, but then I get so busy at the store . . ."

"There's a screwdriver in the garage next door. I'll go get it."

She waved the idea off. "Don't worry about it. It's okay."

He peered out to her den, taking in her gray sofa, cherry end tables and coffee table, and flat-screen television. The roller-skating trophy from their race sat perched on one of the end tables, and a collection of family photographs hung on the faded off-white walls. He recognized her brother, Nick, and his wife, Eileen, but their three children had grown quite a bit since the last time Hudson had seen them. Both Skye and Aubrey were lovely young women, and Kevin was now a young man.

Debbie and Mitch, her parents, smiled from a portrait nearby, and Hudson recalled conversations he'd had with her father over the years. Soon after he and Dakota started dating, Mitch had become like a surrogate father to him. He'd go to her parents' house for supper every Sunday, and he and Mitch would talk at length about Hudson's plans for the future. In fact, Mitch was the one who'd encouraged Hudson to follow his dream of owning his own software company.

Hudson turned back to Dakota. "This is a nice place."

"I'm sure your place in Manhattan is *much* more impressive."

He cocked an eyebrow at her. Surely her comment was meant as a barb, but she wasn't getting rid of him that easily.

She peeked into his grocery bag and actually smiled. "Banana bread. Did your aunt make this for you?"

"Sure did. I was on my way home when she called and said she had a treat for me."

"I could never match her recipe. Hers was always the best."

He shook his head. "Yours was just as good."

"You're not a very good liar, Hud," she said. "Remember that time I tried to bake you some as a surprise and nearly set my mom's kitchen on fire because I forgot to set the timer?"

"How could I forget?" He chuckled. "We were watching a movie, and I asked you where the smoke had come from."

"All of the smoke alarms went off, and we had to open the windows. It was so cold out too." She leaned back on the counter. "I can still hear my mom yelling at me. She said, 'Dakota Marie, close those windows. Are you trying to heat the entire neighborhood?'"

They both laughed, and it felt good.

"Don't forget the time you gave me a loaf at school on Valentine's Day, and I dropped it in the middle of the hallway. The aluminum foil burst open and sent crumbs everywhere."

"That was such a mess."

"Ms. Lawrence made me get a broom and clean it up."

"I had finally baked you a decent loaf, and you dropped it."

They both laughed again, and when the sound faded away, they stared at each other. For the first time since he'd returned home, he almost felt as if he and Dakota could be friends.

He gestured to the hallway. "Do you have time to give me a quick tour?"

She hesitated, and his smile flattened. Who was he kidding? He and Dakota could never move beyond the past. There was too much hurt between them. Too much left unresolved.

"Never mind." He collected the banana bread and started for the door.

"Wait. I'll give you a quick tour, but then I really need to get ready for guests." She led him down a short hallway and pointed to an open door. "That's my little office slash sewing room."

Hudson stuck his head in the doorway and took in a desk, a few shelves packed with books, and a sewing table where bolts of material, a sewing basket, and a pile of clothes sat. He recognized the gray Singer sewing machine, which used to sit on a similar table in the spare room at her parents' house. He recalled the hours she'd spent creating dresses, skirts, and outfits for herself, family members, and friends. She had even designed her own prom dresses.

She'd been breathtaking in a red gown she had copied out of a fashion magazine. The dress had fit her like a glove, and in his opinion, she'd been more elegant than the model in the picture she'd copied.

He'd been so proud to have her on his arm that night. And they'd danced and laughed the night away. It had been magical. That evening he'd been certain he could never love her more, but somehow he had fallen more and more in love with her with each passing day.

A strange warm feeling rushed over him, and he tried in vain to shake it off.

"And this is my bedroom."

He spun toward the room across the hall.

"Great," she grumbled. "That silly cat has been at it again." She hurried around the bedroom picking up a box of tissues, a book, a bottle of water, and a jewelry box, then set them on her dresser.

"Looks like he earned his name." Hudson surveyed the room containing a double bed, a nightstand, a couple of dressers, and a vanity. The walls were a faded pink, and a border featuring a country scene with a house and a meadow lined the top of the wall, its edges beginning to peel away.

The hint of her flowery perfume wafted over him, and he turned toward her, taking in how pretty she looked in a gray skirt and pink sweater. Her dark hair fell around her face, and her subtle makeup was just enough to accentuate her high cheekbones, full lips, and those bottomless dark eyes.

"Yes, he did." She made a frustrated noise. "You should have been here the other day when I got home and discovered he'd decided to drag the toilet tissue all around the room while I was at work." She pointed to a door. "That's why I have to make sure I close both the bathroom door in here and the one in the hallway before I leave for work."

He tried to imagine what it would be like to be here with her every day. If they had gotten married, would they have settled down in Flowering Grove and had a family?

Her eyes locked on his, and for a moment he wondered if the same thought had occurred to her.

But if he *had* stayed in Flowering Grove, where would he be now? He certainly wouldn't have achieved the success he had in New York City, which now provided for his aunt and sister.

Dakota started toward the doorway. "That's pretty much it. I have a tiny laundry room that really doesn't qualify as a room at all and a small deck and yard. It's nothing like the place where you're staying. In fact, that impressive house doesn't fit on this street at all. I don't know why someone decided to build it here."

"You have a great house. Very homey." He walked behind her, squelching his yearning to reach out and touch her arm.

"Thanks."

Hudson followed her back to the kitchen and picked up his grocery bag. When her phone dinged with a text, he glanced down on the counter and caught a glimpse of it.

Parker: *Looking forward to seeing you again tonight.*

He did his best to swallow back a bite of jealousy and force his lips to curl up. "Did you want any of this banana bread?"

"No, thanks." Her genuine smile had disappeared, and her guarded, forced demeanor was back. "Thanks for your help, Hud."

She traipsed with him to the door, where he bent to give the cat a quick rub.

"Good night," he told her.

"Night."

His heart sank on his way back to the colonial. It was obvious that she had a boyfriend, and Hudson felt like a jerk for allowing himself to believe that he and Dakota might've had a chance to become friends again.

He entered the house and headed for the kitchen to cut himself a piece of banana bread for supper. He pulled out a plate and knife and let the truth fill his mind: Between the issues with his sister and his ridiculous feelings for Dakota, staying in Flowering Grove was clearly bad for his heart and his health. He had to get out of town as soon as he could.

"The first night we opened the rink, we ran out of pizza in less than an hour." Brice grinned at his wife beside him. "We really underestimated the crowd."

Kayleigh chuckled. "The rink had been closed for more than a year when we bought it, and we just knew we'd have to work to get customers. But it seemed like people really missed it!"

Parker, sitting beside Dakota, looked riveted. "That's fantastic. So you never worried about the rink generating enough business?"

Brice scoffed. "Oh, we worried plenty," he

began before launching into another story about the rink.

They decided to take advantage of the unusually warm March weather and sit at Dakota's patio table later that evening. Dakota struggled to keep her focus on the conversation. Instead, her thoughts swam as she picked at her piece of lasagna.

She'd felt out of sorts ever since the afternoon run-in with Hudson. She'd been shocked when he appeared at her side out of thin air, ready to help her with her groceries. He'd been dressed in worn jeans and a long-sleeved black t-shirt, as if he'd spent the day working outside somewhere — and his few days' worth of scruff made it difficult for her to take her eyes off him.

Having him in her house felt strange at first, but then she'd relaxed. It had been natural to reminisce, but the most unsettling part had been when she'd felt her heart coming back to life around him.

For one eerie moment, she'd considered canceling her double date and instead inviting Hudson to stay for dinner and talk all night. She yearned to not only talk about the good times but also ask him where things had gone wrong. They'd been happy — she was sure of it — before he made a choice and left her behind.

And that was the moment when she realized she had to get Hudson out of her house. Her heart and her brain melted into mush around him. It was best that she avoid him. And besides, she had to get ready for her company.

Yet here she was now with her guests, thinking about Hudson while Parker sat beside her, ready and willing to be the kind, steady, loyal, and dependable man she craved.

She needed to have her head examined.

"Dakota?"

"Huh?" Her head snapped up, and she felt all eyes around the table focused on her.

Kayleigh looked at her with concern. "Are you okay?"

"Yeah. Sorry." She leaned back in her chair. "I just have a lot on my mind." She could almost hear Kayleigh's unspoken questions from across the table, but she took a drink from her glass of water and averted her eyes.

"How are things at your store?" Parker asked.

"Good." She nodded. "I had a bride with a large bridal party come in to order fourteen bridesmaids' gowns, plus a flower girl dress and ring bearer tuxedo. Oh, and another seventeen tuxedos for the groomsmen and the fathers."

Brice laughed. "Whoa. That trumps our little wedding with our two attendants, huh, Kay?"

"Definitely." Kayleigh grinned. "Is this the woman with her butter-yellow obsession?"

"That's the one."

Parker's eyebrows lifted. "Butter-yellow obsession? I need to hear this story."

Dakota explained her conversation with the bride's mother. "The mother seemed skeptical about my stock. But when she and her daughter came in, not only did the bride find dresses she liked, but she also decided to purchase her gown at my store. The bridesmaids are coming to order their gowns next week."

"Bravo." Kayleigh gave her a high five.

They ate in silence for a few moments.

Parker forked another piece. "This lasagna is delicious."

"I'm glad you like it, but honestly, it came out of a box." Dakota picked up a piece of garlic bread. "This too. I wish I had more time for cooking."

Yet another reason this double date had been a bad idea. Here she was spending another Thursday night with Parker when she should have been working late. Since she was committed to lessons at the skating rink on her weekend nights, she ought to be spending her weeknights at the store. Among other things that made her feel behind, she'd hardly made any progress on Layla's gown, despite the looming deadline. She was too busy for this double date.

Parker's smile was warm and genuine. "Regardless, the lasagna and the bread are superb."

"Very good," Brice agreed.

Kayleigh's expression was filled with concern. "Should we go get the dessert, Dakota?" Her words were measured, as if trying to convey a hidden meaning.

But a noise next door yanked Dakota's attention away. Across the yard, Hudson stood on the colonial's enormous back deck and leaned over the railing with his phone to his ear. His voice was a deep murmur, and he looked completely engrossed in the conversation and unaware of his audience. He had changed into black sweatpants and a gray hoodie, and his dark hair was wet as if he'd just stepped out of the shower.

Who was he talking to? A coworker? A girlfriend? Jealousy stung her.

"Dakota . . . ," Kayleigh began. "Did you hear what I said? Should we go get the dessert now?"

Brice turned toward where Hudson stood

on the deck. "How awkward is it that your ex is staying next door?"

Parker's gaze toggled between Brice and Dakota. "Wait. Your ex lives next door to you?"

Uh-oh.

Kayleigh began piling up their empty plates. "He doesn't live there. It's just an Airbnb. He's only there temporarily."

"Oh." Parker's brow puckered, and he looked confused or possibly concerned.

"Come to the kitchen with me, Dakota," Kayleigh ordered as she gathered up the rest of the dinner plates. *"Now."*

Dakota picked up their utensils and followed her best friend into the kitchen.

Kayleigh placed the dishes in the sink. "You've been in another world all evening. What's going on with you?"

"I think I'm losing it." Dakota leaned back against the counter and scrubbed her hand down her face. When she felt something soft rubbing against her shin, she glanced down at Trouble, blinking up at her. She gave his soft head a pat. "Remember when I got home earlier and you asked me over the phone if I was okay?"

Kayleigh nodded.

"Hud was here." She pointed toward the house next door. Then she explained how he had helped her with her groceries and taken a tour of the house. "He was so . . . nice. It was weird. Almost like we'd gone back in time to when things were good between us." She cupped her hand to her forehead. "I have to keep reminding myself he's not my friend. He broke my heart. I can't trust him. I can't even be around him."

Trouble meowed, and she filled his bowl with dry food before he began stuffing his face. The cat had a bottomless pit for a stomach.

She took in Kayleigh's concerned face. "I'm still attracted to him, and it's confusing and unnerving. I wish he'd just go back to New York and stay out of my life." She groaned and shook her head. "You don't have to tell me I'm crazy, Kay, because I know I am."

Kayleigh's expression clouded. "I need you to listen to me. Hud hurt you once, and he'll do it again. He's here for Layla's wedding and then he'll be gone. If you get involved with him, you'll regret it. Trust me."

"I know, I know." Dakota held her arms up. "I guess the right thing is to avoid him, because every time he's around, I feel him unlocking another piece of my heart. I can't give him that power."

"Exactly. Parker is here, and it's obvious he likes you. If you like him, then you should concentrate on him and not Hud."

"Right." Dakota stood up straight.

"Now let's bring out dessert and enjoy the rest of our evening."

"Okay." Dakota pulled Kayleigh's cheesecake out of the refrigerator, and as she toted it out to the deck, she found herself wondering if Hudson had enjoyed his aunt's banana bread.

Chapter 12

Later that evening, Parker and Dakota stood beside his blue Kia SUV in her driveway. "I had a great time tonight," Parker said.

Dakota jammed her hands in the front pocket of her sweatshirt and looked up at the stars twinkling in the dark sky above them.

Kayleigh and Brice had already left to relieve their babysitter, and now that Dakota was alone with Parker, she needed to give him all her attention. From what she could tell, he was a good man — and he deserved a chance.

"So did I," she said. She meant it too. The evening had flown by after dinner. They'd enjoyed Kayleigh's scrumptious chocolate chip cheesecake and cups of coffee before playing a rousing game of Scrabble, which involved a lot of laughter.

Though Dakota had enjoyed herself, she was still distracted. Hudson had disappeared from his deck before she'd returned with dessert. She kept searching for him in the house next door, but despite the lights glowing in the large colonial, she hadn't caught another glimpse of him. And though it was a good thing he wasn't within view, she couldn't stop her ridiculous disappointment either.

But it was time to move on. Parker was here. He'd been more than willing to get to know Dakota, and she needed to do the same for him.

Parker turned his attention to the large house next door. "How long is your ex staying in town?"

"Until June. He's here for his sister's wedding." Dakota did her best to sound casual.

He paused as if contemplating the information. "How long were you together?"

This is about to get awkward. "We started dating in high school. Then we got engaged, but we broke up a long time ago."

"So it's over?"

"It has been for years."

His features relaxed, and he smiled. "I'm glad to hear it." He touched her cheek. "I really like you, Dakota."

"I like you too."

He dipped his chin, and instead of dodging his kiss this time, she allowed his lips to brush hers. Closing her eyes, she held her breath and waited for the butterflies, but they never appeared. Instead, once again, she felt nothing. When she gently pulled away and looked up at Parker, the heat in his eyes left her numb.

"I'll see you soon," he whispered, his voice sounding husky. He opened his driver's side door and climbed in.

"Good night," she told him before he drove away. She turned and padded up the front path, then spotted a light glowing inside the colonial.

As she headed into her house, Dakota grappled with why her heart still craved Hudson when Parker was clearly the man she needed in her life.

She hoped her feelings for Parker would morph into something warm and special. Surely they would. She just needed more time.

Hudson's body tensed as he stood at the window and watched Parker kiss Dakota in her driveway. It had been difficult enough witnessing her talking and laughing with him during their apparent double date with Kayleigh and Brice, but he felt physically ill seeing another man touch her.

He had gone out onto the deck to talk to

Darren, but he hadn't expected to see Dakota with her guests. He'd tried to concentrate on what his business partner was sharing about the job opportunities they had in Los Angeles and Great Britain, but he'd been too distracted by his ex-fiancée moving on so happily with her life.

Hudson had then gone back inside, and the more Darren talked, the better the opportunities sounded. Moving far away from Flowering Grove was what he needed. He just had to decide which position to take after he got his sister back on the right track. Then he could pack up and leave Dakota behind for good.

If only he could convince his heart that he needed to go.

Rain peppered Dakota's windshield the following Thursday evening. She steered her car down the street toward her house and tried to hold back the tears that had threatened her eyes all afternoon.

She'd had a bad day — a *really* bad day. Her favorite butter-yellow-obsessed mother of the bride had called her crying, explaining that her daughter had decided to cancel her wedding and elope to Las Vegas instead. Dakota was stunned. This wedding was supposed to make some of her problems go away. She was finally going to be able to recoup some of the money she'd lost on her ruined stock, but instead, she'd lost the entire sale.

Now she had to figure out what to do next. Selling last year's gowns at a discount wasn't helping her situation, and she still hadn't gotten anywhere with her insurance company or her landlord.

She considered calling her father and asking for help, but she couldn't admit defeat. Instead, she'd take a cut in pay and live on ramen noodles and macaroni and cheese until she came up with a solution.

Dakota had stayed late to work on Layla's gown, but no matter what she touched, she messed it up. The beading was off-center, and the sleeves were giving her fits. She had resewn them several times until she realized it was almost eight thirty, and her stomach's growls had nearly drowned out the music playing in her workroom.

She motored into her driveway, and her headlights swept across the front of her house. The rain beat a steady cadence on the roof of her car, and she massaged her forehead, where a headache throbbed.

Hudson's fancy vehicle sat in the driveway next door, and lights glowed in the downstairs of the impressive colonial. She was grateful she'd managed to avoid him during the past week. Every day her stomach had clenched with anticipation when she left for work and when she arrived home. Although she dreaded a run-in with him, she also missed him and wondered what was going on in his life, and that made absolutely no sense to her at all.

After grabbing her umbrella, she wrenched open the driver's side door. Then she sloshed through the puddles in her black heels to collect her mail from the mailbox and dash to the front door. She yanked the door open, expecting to find Trouble there yammering about how he should have been served his supper hours ago. But the cat was nowhere in sight.

"Trouble," she sang on her way to the kitchen. "Trouble, I'm home."

Dakota dropped the stack of mail, and a letter from her mortgage company caught her eye. She opened it, and her heart sank when she found that due to the increase of taxes, her payment was going to jump more than 20 percent in two months.

"No, no, no," she groaned as a shaky, sick feeling doused her. The increase in her mortgage coupled with her business woes could possibly cause her to lose her store and her home.

Her phone buzzed, and Dakota pulled it from the pocket of her raincoat. She had three unread texts from Parker:

Been thinking about you.
How was your Thursday?
Any chance I can stop by real quick?

Her shoulders drooped as she set down her phone and the letter. After the day she'd had, it was best she didn't talk to Parker. She didn't want to burden him with her problems. Although he was sweet and seemed like a good listener, she wasn't ready to open up to him. She'd wait until tomorrow to text him back. Maybe by then she'd have a solution to her problems.

Looking down, she realized she hadn't felt any soft fur rubbing against her legs. She scanned the kitchen for her feline friend. "Trouble?"

She rested her hand on her hip. He had to be hiding somewhere. Or maybe he was punishing her for working late every night this week.

She filled his bowl with a smelly chicken and tuna dinner. Surely the aroma would jostle the kitty from his bad mood or his hiding spot.

"Trouble! Trubs!" she called. "Dinner is served!"

Dakota waited, but no cat emerged.

"Kitty, where are you?" She searched the den, peeking behind the sofa and tables before padding down the hallway. "This isn't funny, Trouble."

After failing to find the cat in her office, she headed into her bedroom, where she checked the cat's usual hiding spots — under her bed, behind her nightstand, and even beneath her dresser, which always astounded her. How did cats manage to flatten themselves like pancakes? But the feline wasn't lurking in any of those spots.

Had Trouble followed her into her closet this morning when she ran back in for her shoes? She opened the door and flipped on the light. "Trouble? Baby, this isn't funny. If you're here, then come out. I'm not in the mood for this. I've had a really rotten day."

When she came up empty, she racked her brain. *Where else would that silly cat hide?*

She recalled how he used to sleep behind the dryer when she'd first moved into the house. Maybe he'd rediscovered that spot and decided to spend the rainy day there.

She peered around the washer and dryer. "Trouble," she sang. "Come out, come out, wherever you are."

She held her breath, hoping to hear the cat's meow, but the house was silent except for the pattering of rain on the roof.

"Trouble, please come out." Her voice shook. "This isn't funny anymore." She whimpered. "I'm sorry for working late, but I'm home now, and your supper is waiting for you. Please, kitty."

The food! Maybe he'd evaded her and snuck back to the kitchen to chow down while she was looking for him like a fool.

Dakota retuned to the kitchen, hoping to find the cat scarfing up his meal, but the bowl remained untouched.

She spun, surveying the kitchen and den, but there was still no sign of her beloved orange cat. A sinking feeling overcame Dakota. What if he got out? And what if he ran away or — worse — what if he got hit by a car and was suffering by the side of the road somewhere?

No, no, no.

Holding back the sting of tears, she grabbed a flashlight from the utility room and made for the back door. Rain soaked her hair as she pointed the beam around the yard.

"Trouble!" she yelled. "Trouble, are you out here?" Her heart pounded in her ears. "Kitty, where are you?"

She continued to call his name and plod around the muddy yard, searching overgrown bushes for any sign of her precious companion.

"Trouble!" she called. "Please come here, kitty. Please!" she pleaded with the animal.

The whoosh of a sliding glass door sounded behind her, but she kept searching, trying to see over her neighbor's fence at the edge of her yard.

"What's wrong?" a voice called, but she ignored it.

She called the cat again.

"Koti, answer me. What's going on?"

Dakota's entire body went rigid. She hadn't heard that nickname in years — seven, to be exact. Only Hudson Garrity had called her by that name.

She spun toward the other side of her backyard. He stood inside her fence while rain soaked his dark hair, blue t-shirt, and jeans.

"H-have you seen my cat?" she managed to ask him. Her voice sounded thin and reedy.

He shook his head. "He's missing?"

She nodded, unable to speak.

"I'll help you find him."

"Th-thanks," she managed, the word scratching its way out of her dry throat.

Hudson peeked over the neighbor's fence and then climbed into the bushes lining the back of her house. Dakota moved to the side of her yard, all the while calling her cat's name.

"Trouble!" she yelled. "Trouble, come on, baby."

Hudson appeared at her side. "I don't think he's out here." He shoveled his fingers through his thick, wet hair. "And you've looked everywhere inside?"

"Yeah."

He hesitated. "Can I take a look?"

"Sure." She wiped her eyes with the back of her hand despite the rain pouring down on her.

His blue eyes seemed to assess her. "You're soaked. You should come inside too."

"No." She shook her head. "Not until I find my cat."

His expression softened. "I'll give your house a quick look and then come back out."

While Hudson jogged toward her back door, Dakota started around her yard again, shining the flashlight toward each shrub and searching behind her air-conditioning unit.

Several moments ticked by, and her hope began to deflate even more. Trouble was surely gone, and her heart began to break.

"Koti!"

She spun toward the back door, where

Hudson stood holding Trouble. The cat's eyes were half-opened, and he yawned before struggling to get free of Hudson's grasp.

With a gasp, Dakota took off running toward her ex-fiancé and her cat. "Where was he?" she demanded.

Hudson grinned down at the offending feline. "This little scoundrel was asleep in the bottom of your closet. He was tucked away behind a few shoe boxes. He seemed pretty annoyed when I picked him up."

"Oh, Trouble." She took the cat into her arms, and as she held him close, the dam inside her crumbled, letting all of the stress she'd carried around go pouring out of her.

The cat wriggled and she released him. He hopped down to the utility room floor, then scampered toward the kitchen and his stinky supper.

Dakota covered her face with her hands and tried in vain to stop her sobs. Her body shook and embarrassment welled up inside her while she continued to cry.

"Hey, Koti?" Hudson's husky voice was next to her ear, sending goose bumps chasing each other down her back. "It's okay. We found him."

Instinctively, she took a step forward to be engulfed by Hudson's muscular arms. She froze as his hands rested on her lower back. Then her body relaxed, and she wrapped her arms around his neck and basked in his familiar scent. Although his shirt was wet from the rain, his taut chest was warm, and her tensed-up muscles began to ease. She rested her head against him and listened to the rhythmic cadence of his heartbeat. She felt safe and protected in his strong embrace.

He moved his fingers up and down her back. "It's okay now. The cat is fine. He just needed a good nap on this rainy day."

"It's not that," she whispered.

"What do you mean?"

She looked up at Hudson, and the urge to tell him everything grabbed her by the throat. She wanted to unload all of her burdens and ask for his advice.

Then warning bells sounded in her head.

Don't trust him!

His gaze roved over her features, and when they lingered on her lips, a thousand butterflies danced in her stomach. Then his focus returned to her eyes. "Go ahead," Hudson prodded. "Tell me."

"It's just . . ."

"Dakota?" a voice asked behind her.

Hudson's arms dropped to his sides, and his warm expression faded.

She spun toward Parker, who was standing in the doorway. He was holding a bouquet of red roses and looking confused.

Dakota sniffed and wiped her eyes. "Parker. What are you doing here?"

"Sorry for just walking in, but I was knocking, and the door was open . . ." Parker divided a look between Dakota and Hudson, and his brow crinkled. "Uh, well . . . And since you never answered any of my texts today, I was worried about you. But I should go —"

"Don't." Hudson held his hand out to Parker. "Hudson Garrity."

Parker paused before shaking his hand. "Parker Bryant."

"Nice to meet you. I was just helping Kot— uh — *Dakota* find her cat." He gave her a curt nod. "Glad we found Trouble. Good night." He slipped past Parker, and his footfalls sounded until the storm door opened and shut with a click.

Parker studied her, and an awkward silence expanded between them.

Dakota pointed to the flowers. "Are those for me?" She hoped her voice sounded more cheerful than she felt.

"Yeah." He held them out to her, and she took them.

"Thank you so much." She breathed in

their sweet fragrance. "They're lovely. What's the occasion?"

"Skye mentioned you've been working long hours on a special wedding gown, and I thought you could use a pick-me-up."

"Th-that's so thoughtful of you." Shame pummeled her. She'd been caught in her ex's arms and had been planning to open up to him, all while this thoughtful man was worrying about her. "I'd better get these in water." She found a vase in the kitchen and arranged the pretty roses before setting them on the kitchen table. "Want a drink?"

"Sure."

She poured each of them a glass of water, and they sat at her table.

Parker pointed to Trouble, who was taking a bath in the doorway after licking his bowl clean. "What happened to your cat?"

"I couldn't find him," she said. When Parker nodded slowly, she figured she'd better explain herself. "I had a bad day, and when I came home, I couldn't find Trouble. I thought he'd gotten out. Hud heard me calling for him in the backyard, and he came over and looked for him."

"Is there anything I can do to help?"

She squinted at him. "We already found the cat."

"I know." Parker smiled. "You said you

had a bad day. Can I help?"

She felt a wash of warmth for this kind man. "No, but thank you." She told him about the bride who'd canceled on her and how it would affect her bottom line. She left out the bigger issues with her store and her mortgage, not ready to share that level of detail about her life with him just yet.

"I'm sorry you lost that sale. I know that was a big one." Parker reached across the table and took her hands in his. "But I'm sure there's another bride with an even bigger wedding party who will come to your store and buy *all* of your yellow dresses."

She smiled. "I hope so."

"I shouldn't have just shown up here, but when Skye told me you were pulling some long hours, I thought you wouldn't mind some cheering up."

She admired her roses. "The flowers are beautiful, and they're just what I needed."

He gave her hands a gentle squeeze. She wished she felt a sizzle at his touch, but instead, it just felt . . . nice.

"I'm sorry I didn't respond to your texts," she said. "I was just so stuck in my own head. I didn't mean to take you for granted. I hope you can forgive me."

"Of course I can." He glanced at the clock on the microwave. "But it's getting late. I should let you rest."

"I'll walk you out." Dakota set the vase of roses on top of her china cabinet so the cat wouldn't eat them or try to knock them over.

The rain outside had stopped, and the cool evening air smelled clean and fresh.

"Thank you for stopping by to check on me."

Parker closed the distance between them and traced a finger down her cheek. "I think about you a lot, Dakota." His brown eyes were intense in the light shining down from her garage. "I care about you."

He leaned down and brushed his lips over hers, and she closed her eyes, waiting for the fireworks to start. Instead, her thoughts carried her back to when she was in Hudson's arms. When she imagined Hudson's lips massaging hers, heat moved up her neck to her cheeks.

When Parker broke the kiss, he smiled. "I'll text you soon."

"Good night," she whispered.

Dakota cradled her arms to her middle while Parker backed out of her driveway. After his taillights disappeared into the night, she spun to face the colonial next door, where golden lights glowed from the second floor.

It scared her how easily she had fallen into Hudson's arms and under his spell. She needed to let him go once and for all. Parker was a good man who deserved her full attention.

Hudson was her past, and Parker was her future. She just needed to find a way to convince her heart.

Hudson had hoped that a long, cold shower would stop his entire body from thrumming with yearning and confusion — but it hadn't helped a bit. He paced the master bedroom, trying to calm his thoughts.

When he'd heard someone yelling outside, he'd been out the door in a flash. As soon as he realized it was Dakota, he recognized the anguish in her voice. He couldn't stand seeing her so upset, and it just seemed natural to call her by the nickname he'd given her when they were sixteen.

He'd been determined to find her cat. The pain and anguish in her sobs had torn his heart in two, and he couldn't help but console her. He'd held her close, soaking in her warmth, and having her in his arms again felt like a dream. He didn't want to let her go. In fact, he'd longed to hold her all night.

And when she'd lifted her eyes to his, he

couldn't take his focus off her lips. For a moment, he imagined resting his mouth against hers and drinking in her taste. The thought made his lips burn with desire. He'd almost kissed her until he realized she was going to talk to him — *actually* talk to him for the first time since he'd returned to Flowering Grove. He'd hoped she might even tell him why she'd broken up with him seven years ago.

But just as she was about to open up, *that guy* showed up with a dozen red roses. Hudson was disappointed and furious until he realized he had no business even dreaming about having Dakota back in his life. That ship had sailed a long time ago, and she was with another man now — which was why he'd tried his best to smooth over the awkward situation and hotfoot it out of there.

He dropped onto the corner of the bed, which creaked under his weight. He was having a difficult time calming down his heart. As much as he wanted to deny it, he still had feelings for Dakota — deep feelings — but that didn't matter. It was best for him to focus on his future.

He glanced at his phone and saw that once again his texts to Layla had gone unanswered. He touched a spot on his collarbone. He needed to figure out how to repair things with his sister, make sure her life was on the right track, and then get out of town.

Hudson needed to finish his business in Flowering Grove and then move on with his life. Now if only he could figure out a way to forget about Dakota.

Chapter 13

"This looks amazing." Layla stood on the podium and moved from side to side, studying her reflection in the full-length mirror the following Tuesday afternoon. She smiled, but it didn't quite reach her eyes. "It definitely resembles my mom's gown." She met her aunt's gaze in the mirror. "Don't you agree, Aunt Trudy?"

The older woman sniffed. "Yes, you look lovely." She turned toward Dakota. "You do fantastic work."

Dakota tapped her chin. "The beading isn't quite right, and I don't like the ruffles on the train." She shook her head. "We're not there yet, but the fit is better." She circled the dress, pinning here and there and making mental notes about what still needed to be altered.

For the past five days, Dakota had been working late at the shop, trying to get Layla's dress ready for the fitting. She hadn't seen Hudson since he'd helped her find Trouble, and she hated to admit she missed him. He hadn't come to the rink Friday or Saturday, but Parker had. And although she had enjoyed her time with Parker, she found herself scanning the crowd for Hudson.

As Dakota pinned the hem, she considered asking Layla and Trudy how Hudson was doing. But she decided it was best not to bring him up at all. She needed to just get over him.

Easier said than done.

"Okay, that's it for now. You can get changed. I'll work on it some more and have you come back for another fitting." Dakota helped Layla off the podium before Layla and her aunt disappeared into a dressing room.

She busied herself with straightening the dressing area until Layla returned with the gown on a hanger.

Trudy wiped her eyes and touched Dakota's hand. "The gown is turning out perfectly. I was just telling Layla that her mother would've loved it. In fact, she looks just like Daphne with that gown on. It takes me back to her parents' wedding day."

Layla sniffed. "Oh, stop it. You're going to make me cry, Aunt Trudy."

Dakota felt her own emotions welling up. "I'm so happy you like it. I'm sure that with some more work it will look even better." She turned and hung the hanger on a hook.

Layla consulted her watch. "My friends and Shane's sister should be here soon to look at their dresses," she said. "I told them they can wear any style they want as long as each gown is light blue." Dakota noticed that though Layla was discussing the details of her wedding, she hadn't really smiled. She got the feeling that something was bothering the bride-to-be.

"Wonderful." Dakota beckoned her toward the racks of bridesmaids' dresses. "Let's look at the options I have. And if they don't find what they want here, we can always check out the online catalogs, and I can order what they like."

Soon Layla's friends Gina and Sheila arrived, along with Shane's younger sister, Melody. Together they searched the racks for dresses they each liked. Dakota took care of fittings for each of the dresses before Layla convinced her aunt to look for a dress of her own. After Trudy settled on a simple dark-blue gown, Dakota rang her and the bridesmaids up before thanking them.

After Layla's friends and Shane's sister had left the shop, Layla and Trudy lingered behind. Layla perused the jewelry case, and Trudy stood by the counter, her lips turned downward. Something definitely was up, and Dakota couldn't help but worry about them.

"Can I help you find something?" Dakota asked Layla.

"I was thinking about getting Shane a special pair of cufflinks for the wedding."

Dakota unlocked the case and lined up a few different pairs. "These are my most popular."

"I like these." Layla picked up a pair of pearl cufflinks.

Dakota rang them up, and Layla handed her a card.

"Did I tell you we're going to the Outer Banks for our honeymoon?" Layla asked.

Dakota gave her a receipt. "You didn't! I love the beaches there."

"I do too. But I haven't been there since I was a teenager." Layla signed the receipt and took her copy. "We're going out to Nags Head. Have you ever been there?"

"I went with my family a long time ago. We had so much fun."

"Shane found a nice hotel on the beach. I just can't wait until the wedding is here and all of the details are handled." Layla leaned forward on the counter. "Did I tell you we're having the reception at the country club?"

Dakota shook her head.

"I thought it would be way out of our price range, but my brother is paying for it all. He's insisting. He says Mom and Dad would've wanted him to pay for it since they can't. Shane and I want to contribute, but Hud is being really stubborn about it — says it's his job to take care of things. I'm sure you remember how bossy my brother can be." She made a face like she was tasting something sour. "He's really being a jerk."

"Layla, you don't seem like yourself today," Dakota hedged. "Is everything all right?"

When Layla sniffed and shook her head, Dakota came around the counter. "What can I do to help?"

"Can you tell my brother to stop being such a jerk?" Layla wiped her eyes.

Trudy kneaded her niece's shoulder, her expression grave. "I can't stand seeing you two on the outs."

"What happened?" Dakota asked.

"Hud has always bossed me around, but this time he's taken it too far." Her expression darkened while she explained that he had been against the wedding from the start. Then she detailed how he'd grilled her and Shane at dinner in front of Shane's family. "He refuses to admit that he's in the wrong. He thinks he's better than Shane. He looks down on him, and I'm over it. He refuses to acknowledge that I'm happy and I know what I'm doing. All he wants is to talk me out of it." Her lower lip trembled, and Dakota's heart wrenched.

"I'm so sorry to hear this," Dakota said. "I know how much you mean to your brother, so he may not realize how bullheaded he's being."

"That's no excuse. I can't let him come between my fiancé and me."

Trudy shouldered her purse. "You and Hudson need to work this out, Layla. He's your only brother." Then she fixed a smile on her face. "Thank you, Dakota." She addressed her niece again. "Honey, time to get back to work."

"Call me when you're ready for me to come back in for another fitting," Layla said. "The gown is my dream come true. Thank you."

The boutique phone started to ring, and Layla waved goodbye. "I'll let you get that," she called before she and Trudy walked out to the street.

Dakota picked up the phone. "Thank you

for calling Fairytale Bridal. This is Dakota. How may I help you?"

As the caller spoke, Dakota glanced down at the counter and realized that Layla had forgotten to take the cufflinks. After she spoke with the customer and made an appointment for the woman, she pulled out her cell phone and shot off a text to Layla.

Hi! You forgot Shane's cufflinks.

A moment later, text bubbles appeared.

Oh no. I'll have to come back for them later this week. I'll see when I can get off work early one day. Thanks!

Dakota studied the cufflinks and contemplated Layla's story about her disagreement with Hudson. Maybe Dakota could find a way to help them work through their differences. They were siblings, after all, and she knew how much Layla meant to Hudson. He always said he was determined to find a successful career so he could take care of her and Trudy. It had to be killing him that they weren't talking, but she also knew how stubborn he was.

She grew more and more determined to fix this. She just wasn't sure how to do it.

She set the cufflinks under the counter just as Skye danced into the boutique.

"Auntie! Gunner asked me to the prom!" She swept across the room and hugged

Dakota.

"Sweetie, that's fantastic." Dakota steered her niece over to the bridesmaids' gowns. "Why don't you pick out a dress?"

Skye grinned. "You know I want pink."

"I bet I have the perfect one."

"I need to head out a little early this afternoon," Hudson told Gavin as they stood in what would become the large dining area of the restaurant. The framing had been completed over a week ago, and now the plumbers and electricians were busy at the site. He enjoyed the work. It felt good to use his hands. As a bonus, he was proving to his sister that he wasn't too good for a blue-collar job. On the other hand, he couldn't help but think about how he could improve the company's software and make their processes easier. He was going to keep pondering that in his spare time. "I need to take care of some business."

Gavin tapped his pen on his clipboard. "Sounds good to me. I'll see you tomorrow."

Hudson nodded to the crew members on his way to his SUV. He'd been planning this for days. He'd called Robertsons' Landscaping to find out where Shane was working, and he was going there to talk to Shane alone, man to man.

He merged his SUV onto Main Street and checked the clock on the dashboard. It was almost five o'clock. Shane should get off work soon.

Hudson drove over to Glenn Avenue and then turned onto Hillcrest Avenue. His thoughts raced with what he would say to his future brother-in-law. Surely Shane knew how he and Layla were rushing into marriage, and he would agree that it was time to slow down. They could postpone the wedding for a year or possibly three.

When he reached the end of Hillcrest, he turned onto Van Dien and saw Shane's faded gray and red Dodge pickup. Another older maroon Ford pickup truck was parked next to it in front of one of the sprawling colonials on the ritzier side of town.

Hudson nosed his SUV behind the truck and killed the engine. Then he settled back in his seat and waited for Shane to come out to his vehicle. When his phone rang, he found Darren's number on the screen.

"Hey," Hudson said. "What's up?"

"I haven't heard from you in a while. What's going on in Flowering Grove?"

"Would you believe I'm back working in construction?"

"Construction?" Darren asked. "Doing what?"

"My buddy Gavin owns a construction company, and they're building a new restaurant. I helped with the framing, and now we're supervising the plumbers and electricians."

"You're telling me you're doing manual labor when you could be running a company? Why would you do that?"

Hudson turned toward the house, looking for any sign of Shane. "Gavin needs help, so I'm helping."

"There's nothing else going on?"

The image of Dakota filled his mind, along with the memory of holding her in his arms, enjoying the feel of her warm body against his on the night her cat disappeared. He hadn't seen her since then, but he'd dreamed about that encounter nearly every night since it happened.

"No. I'm actually enjoying the work, and having lunch at my old haunts is a blast. Have you ever had Carolina barbecue? If not, you need to come down here and eat at the Barbecue Pit. It's the best. In fact, it's known all over the state. And to be honest, I really don't miss the craziness of the city or the traffic." When Darren was silent, Hudson checked to see if the call had dropped. "You still there?"

"Yeah, I'm here. I guess you haven't thought about Bahrain, LA, or London."

Hudson brushed his hand over the stubble on his jaw. "I got your email, and I've been thinking about the options."

"I'm going to need to let Jerry know pretty soon."

Hudson looked up and saw Shane coming down the driveway, walking beside a stocky guy who appeared to be in his early forties.

"Listen, can I call you back later?"

"Sure, man."

"Talk to you soon." Hudson disconnected the call and climbed out of the SUV.

Shane said something to the other man and then started toward his truck. When his gaze tangled with Hudson's, his brow furrowed and his steps slowed.

"Hey." Hudson waved to him, and Shane continued toward him, his expression stoic. "Got time for coffee?"

Shane ran his tongue over his teeth and shook his head. "No, I don't think so."

"Okay." Hudson leaned against his SUV's fender. "We can talk here then."

"About what?"

Hudson leveled his gaze with the younger man. "Are you prepared to take care of my sister?"

Shane swept his hands down his dusty jeans and then gave him a black look. "Me and Layla are prepared to take care of *each other.*"

"I know you got in a lot of trouble in high school. How do I know that you've grown up since then?"

"That was a long time ago," Shane said. "I learned my lesson and got my life together. I got clean, earned my GED, and learned a trade." He gestured toward the lawn and gardens behind him. "I've received nothing but praise from my boss and my customers, including your aunt."

Hudson nodded. "That's good to know. Have you and my sister ever had to work through an argument?" he asked.

Shane gave him a cool stare.

"Are you two truly ready to be on your own? Neither of you has ever lived away from home. Can you even do laundry or cook?"

Shane's eyes narrowed to slits. "Together we do just fine."

Hudson rubbed the bridge of his nose. He wasn't impressed at all. Shane wasn't prepared for this. He just had to figure out how to derail this mess before it happened.

"You and Layla are too young and immature for marriage."

Shane's expression turned menacing. Though several moments ticked by, they remained silent, at a stalemate. This was not going the way Hudson had planned at all.

"Anything else you want to ask me, or is this interrogation over?" Shane seethed. He pulled his keys out of his pocket, and they jangled in his hand.

"Yes —"

But Shane was already walking away.

Jerk. Hudson climbed into his SUV and slammed the door. Now both Layla and Shane weren't talking to him. How could he make them see reason when they were both so stubborn?

Fine. If they wanted to ruin their lives, he would let them.

Hudson glanced over at his aunt beside him in his SUV the following evening while driving her to her weekly bingo game. "What do you really think about Layla's engagement?"

"Well, if that doesn't sound like a loaded question, then I don't know what does," his aunt quipped.

"I had a talk with Shane last night, and he's not ready for this. I don't think he can make Layla happy."

"Don't you think your sister needs to decide who and what can make her happy?"

Hudson shook his head. His aunt was missing his point.

When he slowed to a stop at a red light, Aunt Trudy leaned over and patted his arm. "Hudson, I know Dakota broke your heart—"

"This isn't about me and Dakota. It's about Layla making a huge mistake. I'm just being practical. Layla and Shane are still kids."

"They're *adults,* Hudson." Trudy tilted her head and studied him. "I know you think you're supposed to be her father, but you're not and that was never your job. She might marry Shane and realize she made a terrible mistake. If so, then she'll work through it."

He motored through the intersection and down Goffle Road. "But divorce is not something to be taken lightly, Aunt Trudy. Some of my friends have been through it, and it's an emotional and financial nightmare."

Aunt Trudy nodded. "I understand that, and if she needs our help, we'll be there for her. But have you considered that she might also be wildly happy and build a wonderful life with Shane?"

Hudson scowled.

"Happiness is possible," his aunt sang. "And it's time you found some for yourself."

A country music song, road noise, and the hum of the engine filled the vehicle as they drove in silence for a few moments.

Hudson gave his aunt a sideways glance. "Are Layla and I the reason you never married? Were we a hindrance to your happiness?"

"No, sweetheart. You and Layla *are* my happiness."

"What about love?" he asked. "Did you ever want to get married?"

A wistful expression tinged his aunt's face. "I missed my chance at love, and sometimes I wonder what could have been."

"What do you mean?" As far as Hudson knew, his aunt had never dated.

"His name was Eddie. He was handsome — tall like you but with blond hair and gray eyes. We met when we were teenagers and dated for years." She sighed and glanced out the windshield as if her past love were standing there. "He proposed to me, but my father didn't approve."

"Why?"

"He didn't care for Eddie's family. There was some old dispute about land or something else my father wouldn't let go. Eddie tried to convince me to run away with him, but I refused to disobey my father." Her expression was serene. "There are days when I wonder what would have happened if we had eloped. Would we have been happy and built a family of our own together?" She shrugged. "That was a long time ago. I heard that he married and moved to Bristol. I hope he has a happy life like I do. I'm grateful for my little family with you and Layla."

She touched Hudson's elbow. "But, sweetheart, don't let love pass you by. If you find your true love, hold on to her with all of your might, because love is a precious thing."

Hudson let her advice settle over him as he reeled from the news that his aunt had once been in love.

After a few minutes, he steered into the parking lot of the bingo hall. "Here we are. I'll pick you up at eight."

"Oh no you don't. You're coming with me."

He groaned. "Please don't make me."

"We haven't spent much time together. I think I deserve time with my favorite nephew."

"I'm your only nephew."

"And that makes you my favorite. Now,

let's go play some bingo. All the ladies will get a kick out of seeing you. It's been a long time, you know."

He parked the car, then opened her door and helped her out of the vehicle. He took her arm and led her into the hall, where a gaggle of gray-haired ladies rushed over.

"Trudy, is this handsome fellow that nephew of yours?"

"I don't remember him being so tall."

"Sonny, are you married yet? If not, then you need to meet my granddaughter, Nicole. She's twenty-nine, and she's a pediatrician."

"As a matter of fact, Agnes, he isn't married." Aunt Trudy had the nerve to grin. "But he needs to get married and give me some great-nieces and great-nephews. Maybe we should introduce them."

"Well then," Agnes began, "let's make a date to get them together."

Hudson sighed. This evening couldn't end soon enough.

After several torturous games of bingo and more matchmaking offers than he could count, Hudson drove Aunt Trudy home. He parked in the driveway behind Layla's sedan and walked his aunt to the door.

"Well, that was fun," his aunt said.

Hudson shook his head.

"Are you coming in?"

He shook his head. "I need to get home." He kissed her cheek. "I'll see you soon."

Then he loped to his SUV and drove toward the empty Airbnb.

Chapter 14

Hudson steered his SUV into the driveway the following evening and did a double take when he found Dakota sitting on his front steps, studying her phone. He shifted into Park, and she stood, brushing her hands down her black pants and gray sweater.

Hudson climbed from the vehicle and started toward her. "Are you locked out of your house? Or do you need another tire changed?"

"I was wondering if we could talk."

Well, this is unexpected.

"Come on in." He slipped past her and entered a code on the door before pushing it open. "After you."

She entered the large foyer and peeked into the enormous den. "Wow. I've always wanted to see the inside of this place."

"Help yourself to a tour."

"That's okay." She shook her head. "I don't want to take too much of your time."

"How about a drink?"

"Sure." She walked through the kitchen doorway and stilled, a soft gasp escaping her lips. "HGTV should feature this place on one of those dream home shows." She pointed around the room. "Pristine white cabinets, a huge island with stools . . ." She snorted. "Side-by-side stainless steel refrigerator and freezer, double ovens . . . An oak table with eight chairs that would take up my entire house."

He retrieved two bottles of water from the refrigerator. "It is nice. I like how they decorated it with the black-and-white tile."

She held her arms out. "Kay and I could teach our roller-skating classes in here and still have room."

"Have a seat." He handed her a bottle of water and indicated the table.

She sank down on a chair across from him and took a drink from the bottle. "Thanks."

"So what's up?"

Dakota pulled the jewelry box from her pocket and pushed it across the table. "Layla bought these for Shane yesterday and accidentally left them at my store."

He opened the box. "Nice cufflinks, but I'm not sure why you brought them here." Closing the box, he slid it back to Dakota. "You should have taken them to my aunt's house and given them to Layla."

"No. You need to give them to her and tell her you're supportive of her decision to get married."

So that's what this was about. Dakota was playing mediator between him and his sister. He wasn't about to take the bait.

She moved her fingers over the jewelry box, her dark eyes locked on his.

Without breaking her stare, he opened his bottle and took a long drink.

"Layla was really upset when she came in for the fitting. Why are you two fighting?" she finally asked.

He set the bottle down on the table. "I have a feeling you already know the answer to that question."

"You need to talk to her." She moved the jewelry box to his side of the table again. "Use the cufflinks as a peace offering and tell her you're sorry."

"But I'm not."

"She's your sister, Hud. You love her, and she loves you."

"I do love her. That's why I'm trying to stop her from making the biggest mistake of her life."

"But she's old enough to make her own decisions, Hud. It's your job to be happy for her and celebrate with her, not order her around."

He took another sip of water. "Did you really come here to give me a lecture about my sister?" He folded his hands and rested them on the table. "And I thought this was going to be a friendly visit."

"It *is* friendly."

He could almost read her thoughts. Surely Dakota had already made up her mind about him and Layla, and sharing his side of things would be a waste of time. "I can tell you're dying to give me your opinion, so go ahead and say it."

"I think it's her decision if she gets married." She pushed back her chair and stood. "Go see Layla and tell her you're sorry. You'll be glad you did."

He huffed out a breath. "If I promise to think about it, will you sit down?"

"Why do you want me to sit down?"

"Because it's my turn to ask you questions now." He pointed toward the chair. "Tell me what's wrong."

"There's nothing wrong." She shrugged. "I don't know what you're talking about."

He scoffed. "We both know that's not true. You were going to tell me something last Thursday, but we were interrupted." He lifted his chin. "Now, tell me what's going on, Koti."

He was almost certain she shivered when he said the nickname.

"Please don't call me that." Her voice seemed to plead with him, which he found curious.

"All right. Dakota, it's obvious something's wrong. You were in tears when I found your cat, and I could tell you were upset about more than just Trouble. You can't hide it from me."

She rubbed her elbow and hesitated for a moment. "The pipes burst in my store back in late January," she finally began. "My shipment of new spring gowns was ruined. Well, most of it was."

Empathy rushed over him. "I'm sorry."

She picked up the bottle cap and fiddled with it. "I thought the damage would be covered, but it turns out I barely understand what's in my lease. None of it is covered by the lease after all." She exhaled. "So then I thought it would be covered by my insurance. But last year I stepped down my insurance since the premiums were getting so high, and what I owed for the deductible emptied out my savings. Then I had to max out my credit cards to take care of the damage to the store."

She pointed around the room as if they were sitting in her boutique. "The ceiling, the drywall, the flooring . . . I salvaged what I could of the damaged gowns by steaming them myself, but I haven't been able to get reimbursed for what I lost. I fought the insurance company and the property management company but got nowhere. I thought about hiring a lawyer, but who can afford that?" She sniffed. "Now sales are down since most of the brides are looking for this year's gowns, and I'm losing money by selling last year's at a discount."

She took a shuddering breath. "To make matters worse, I received a notice last week that the mortgage on my house is going up too. That means I might lose my store *and* my home if I don't figure out a solution fast." She absently spun the bottle cap. "I'm cutting back my salary just to pay my niece. Now I'm at my wits' end. I'm working on refinancing my mortgage so I can at least keep my house."

Her posture wilted, but her expression seemed to relax.

Hudson nodded and pulled at the label on the water bottle as a plan filled his mind. He'd rescued companies before, but would stubborn Dakota ever accept his help?

"Now it's my turn to tell you that I know *you* have an opinion." She waved her hand toward him as if waving a white flag. "Go ahead and say what you're thinking, Hud."

He brushed his hand over his chin. "You know, I'm a successful businessman."

"Are you bragging or complaining?" she quipped.

"Would a personal loan help you?"

"Are you offering?"

He shrugged. "Maybe."

She studied him, and those gorgeous dark-chocolate-colored eyes narrowed. "You're not going to just throw money at me to make yourself feel better about the past?"

He almost sputtered at her ridiculous question. "Make *me* feel better about the past?" He pointed to himself. "I'm not the one who broke our engagement."

She pushed her chair back and stood. "I don't have time for this. I need to get home." When she fixed him with a glare, he worked to keep his expression neutral despite the fury boiling in his chest. "Look, I don't want to see you and Layla on the outs. Leave your pride at home, take the cufflinks to her, tell her you're sorry, and be the big brother she needs right now." She gave him a sugary sweet smile. "Have a good night."

She marched out of the kitchen, but Hudson rushed after her. He couldn't let her leave like this.

"Dakota, wait."

When she reached the front door, she pivoted to face him.

He sighed. "Dakota, I never meant to insult you. I just want to help you. I know a thing or two about business."

She looked down at her black heels, and then her eyes met his once again. "Hudson, owning my own business has been my dream for years."

"I knew you wanted to be a seamstress, but you never told me you wanted your own store."

"I've worked hard to get where I am. Losing it would destroy me."

"I definitely understand working hard for something. I've done the same." He tapped the doorframe. "If you want a personal loan, we can talk about it. Or I can take a look at your financials and offer some advice."

She folded her arms, and her brow pinched.

Her anger confused him. "Why are you looking at me like that?"

"Because I don't know what you want, Hud."

"I honestly don't know what you mean."

"What do you want *from me*?" she asked, pointing to her chest.

He couldn't admit the truth when he

seemed to be the only one who wanted to reconcile with her. She'd already burned him once.

He cleared his throat. "I don't want anything from you."

"Then why do you care about my business?" she asked, but he remained silent. "Go talk to your sister. And when you do, tell her I'll see her soon for another fitting."

Then she left him standing there, her pumps clacking on the pavement outside as she retreated to her house.

He sauntered back to the kitchen and pondered the news about her business — as well as her advice about his sister.

Go see Layla and tell her you're sorry. You'll be glad you did.

"Fine," he muttered, pushing the jewelry box into his pocket.

Ten minutes later he knocked on his aunt's front door. Footfalls sounded inside, and when the door flew open, he came face-to-face with his sister. The delicious aroma of his aunt's meat loaf wafted out of the house, causing his stomach to gurgle.

Layla's brows drew together. "What do you want?"

"You left something at the bridal boutique." He held out the jewelry box.

She examined the box and then looked up

at him. "Are those Shane's cufflinks?"

"Yup."

"How'd you get them?" she asked, taking the box from him.

"Dakota delivered them to me tonight." He slipped his hands into his pockets. "Would you consider them a peace offering?"

Layla studied him, her expression impassive. "Is that your sad attempt at an apology?"

He sucked in a breath through his nose. "I'm sorry for embarrassing you at dinner with Shane's family."

"You were a real jerk, Hud."

"You've made that clear, and I'm sorry for hurting you. I still don't agree with this wedding, but I can't stand having you angry with me." He rested his arm against the storm door. "I want you in my life, Layla. You're important to me."

She sniffed.

Oh no. Don't cry.

"Truce?" he asked.

She nodded. "Yeah, truce." Then she grinned. "And how's that construction job going for you?"

"Just fine."

She lifted her eyebrows. "You haven't quit yet?"

"No, and I don't plan to. I'm gonna win this bet, and you're going to owe me a chocolate sundae."

She laughed. "We'll see about that."

"Hud? Is that you?" Aunt Trudy called from somewhere in the house.

Layla turned toward the kitchen. "Yeah, he brought me the cufflinks."

"Join us for meat loaf," his aunt instructed.

"Gladly." He looped his arm around his sister's shoulders while they walked to the kitchen.

"So I took the cufflinks over to the Airbnb yesterday and told Hud to work things out with his sister," Dakota told Kayleigh, raising her voice to be heard over the pounding bass of a spirited pop song. "I told him to use them as a peace offering. I couldn't stand the thought of them not speaking. I mean, they only have each other and their aunt. Sure, Nick used to boss me around and drive me nuts when I was younger, but he's still my brother — my only sibling."

It was Friday night, and she and Kayleigh were finished with their skating classes. Now that the general skate was in full swing, the rink was packed with patrons of all ages, gliding around to the music as the disco ball reflected lights onto the ceiling and walls. Brice was working in the office, and Gigi had insisted on staying with her dad.

Dakota had waited until after their lessons to fill Kayleigh in on her two run-ins with Hudson — the night she lost Trouble and the conversation they'd had about her business woes.

"I just can't believe he had the nerve to call me Koti," Dakota exclaimed, tapping the table for emphasis. "He acts like no time has passed between us. As if he didn't completely annihilate me when he chose New York City over me."

She stopped talking when she realized her best friend was staring at her, seemingly befuddled.

When Kayleigh remained silent, Dakota blew out a frustrated puff of air. "What?"

"Do you still love him?"

Dakota laughed off the question. "No, no, no. That's ridiculous, Kay. Why would you even ask me that?"

Kayleigh looked unconvinced, and she leaned forward. "Then why did you hug him after he found Trouble?"

Dakota was stumped. "Uh . . . I-I-I don't know. He opened his arms, and I just . . ." She had no explanation for why she fell into Hudson's embrace so naturally. "It's no big deal. It was a mistake." She shrugged. "I'm seeing Parker."

"And you like Parker?"

"Yeah, yeah, of course. He's handsome and sweet. And did I tell you he brought me roses?"

"You know, Dakota, you should really —"

"Dakota! Kayleigh!" Layla slid onto the bench seat beside Dakota. "Shane and I wanted to get out tonight, and I suggested we come skating. But he's over at the snack bar." She angled her body toward Dakota. "I wanted to thank you for asking Hud to bring me the cufflinks. He said he was sorry for hurting my feelings, and we're talking again."

"I'm glad I could help." In her peripheral vision, Dakota could see Kayleigh watching her.

Layla glanced back and forth between the two friends. "What's new?"

Kayleigh smiled. "You tell us. You're the one who's getting married in two months."

"I can't believe April is here already, and there's still so much to do." She began counting off the tasks on her fingers. "We have to finalize the menu for the dinner, and then we have to agree on a cake. I think we should go with marble cake, but Shane insists not everyone likes chocolate."

While Layla carried on about her plans, Dakota shared an amused look with Kayleigh. She longed to know what Kayleigh had been preparing to say before Layla had interrupted them. She could feel her best friend's disapproval over her interactions with Hud.

Layla's smile was bright as she continued describing her to-do list. "And then we have the invitations. I'm going to handwrite them in calligraphy. We don't want a super-big wedding, but we want to invite our families and our important friends, including you two, of course." She snapped her fingers and faced Dakota again. "That reminds me. I wanted to ask you. Are you going to bring a date to the wedding?"

Dakota nodded. "Most likely."

Layla's smile faded. "Who?"

"Parker Bryant. We've been seeing each other."

"Oh." Layla's expression cooled. "Okay."

Dakota laughed. "Why do you look so disappointed to hear I'm seeing someone?"

"Don't be silly." Layla laughed in a way that sounded forced. "I'm not disappointed. That's great. Good for you."

Shane skated to the end of the booth, nodded a hello to Dakota and Kayleigh, and slid a drink in front of Layla. "I turned around, and you were gone. I thought you'd left me."

"You know I could never leave you." Layla stood and kissed his cheek. "Join us. We were just talking about the wedding."

Shane sat beside Kayleigh before sipping his own drink.

"I was going to ask their opinion of our cake," Layla said.

Shane smiled. "I'm sure they'll agree with me."

"About the marble cake?" Kayleigh asked, and Shane nodded. "Who doesn't like chocolate?"

Shane tilted his head. "For one, my uncle Larry doesn't like chocolate."

"Then he can have something else for dessert, right?" Layla asked Dakota.

"Sounds good to me."

"Right," Layla exclaimed. "The wedding will be about Shane and me, not his uncle Larry."

Shane held his cup up, and Layla tapped hers to it. "I can't wait," he said.

"I can't either," Layla told him.

When the couple shared a warm look, Dakota found love for each other in their eyes. Then she felt a pang that took her back to her time with Hudson.

"Who wants to skate?" she asked, trying

to table her feelings.

Layla held her hand up. "I do." She scooted out of the booth, and Dakota followed.

Hudson paid the admission fee at the window and then slipped through the door into the rink. The delectable smell of pizza mixed with nachos and popcorn filled the air, along with a blaring pop music song and the buzz of conversations.

He had considered staying home tonight and going through his email, but he was anxious to get out of that big colonial. He moved through the crowd and past the party area, nodding to familiar faces until he reached the rental booth. After renting a pair of skates, he sank down onto a bench to pull them on.

"Hi, Hud," Brice called when he and his daughter emerged from a door leading back to the offices. "You came back." He smiled, and his little girl waved at Hudson.

"Good to see you," Hud said, continuing to lace up his skate.

Gigi pulled on Brice's arm and then pointed toward the rink. "Daddy, I see Mommy skating with Anissa and her mom. Can I go?"

"Yes. Just be careful." Brice touched his

little girl's nose before she gracefully skated off like a mini professional. "It's good to see you too, man." He shook Hudson's hand.

Hud glanced around the rink just as another pop song started, the bass reverberating off the walls. "It sure is hopping here tonight."

Brice looked out toward the crowd. "Yes, it is." Then he chuckled. "My folks and my brothers thought I was nuts when we bought this place, but honestly, I don't have one single regret. It's brought a lot of joy to my family and Flowering Grove."

He pointed toward the rink. "My daughter loves to skate. Kay and I had a blast teaching her how, and she's taken to it like a duck to water. I had worried she would eventually grow tired of coming here, but on rink days, she's ready to leave the house before we are." He folded his arms over his chest. "I also feel like we've helped build a sense of community here. I see many of the same faces every week, and watching everyone interact is rewarding."

"I'm sure it is." Hudson scanned the space. He felt the sense of community Brice spoke of, and it was something he hadn't experienced since he'd left Flowering Grove seven years ago. Sure, he had friends up north. He had his work family and acquaintances. But it wasn't the same as being in his hometown. All in that moment, he realized he missed feeling at home.

He wondered if his aunt had been right when she said he belonged in Flowering Grove. He tried to imagine moving back — buying a house and settling down.

Would he fit in after being gone for so long? Where would he work?

And then there was the issue of Dakota and their awkward encounters. On second thought, maybe coming back home sounded like an emotional nightmare.

"Hey, Brice," a young woman who looked around seventeen called from the snack bar. "The register is acting up again. The screen is frozen."

"Be right there." Brice jammed his thumb in the direction of the snack bar. "Duty calls. Have fun."

"Thanks," Hudson said. He left his shoes under the bench and skated to the rink, where he glided along to a song that sounded vaguely familiar.

Hudson moved swiftly past the slower skaters. He enjoyed the feeling skating provided him — burning off his conflicting feelings about his hometown and his future.

When he came around the curve, he saw Dakota skating with Layla, Shane, Kayleigh,

Gigi, Gavin's wife, and Anissa.

When Anissa saw him, her face lit up. "Mr. Hud! Mommy, Mr. Hud is here."

"Hey there." He smiled as the little girl skated over to him. "Are you having fun?"

"Uh-huh!"

Jeannie beamed as she joined them. "Good to see you, Hudson."

He glanced around the rink while they skated together. "Where's Gavin tonight?"

Jeannie pointed toward the parking lot. "He got called back to work. There was an issue with the plumber."

"Let's skate together, Mr. Hud." Anissa held out her little hand.

"I'd love to."

Hudson, Anissa, and Jeannie fell into line behind another couple, and Hud worked to keep from staring at Dakota. She looked fantastic in a snug pair of jeans and a red sweatshirt, with her thick dark hair in a ponytail.

While he skated he recalled a conversation he'd had with Gavin earlier in the day. When Gavin asked over lunch how things were going with Dakota, he'd relayed their discussion at the Airbnb last night, leaving out the personal details about Dakota's business woes. Hudson also mentioned how their conversations usually seemed to end in a heated debate.

Gavin's response had surprised him. *"If you and Dakota can't talk without getting into an argument,"* he'd said, *"then there's still something between you. Maybe you need to take the first step and address it."*

Hudson shook his head, and when his gaze tangled with Dakota's across the rink, she scowled before looking away.

He tried to imagine having an honest conversation with her, but how could he have a heart-to-heart with someone who refused to listen to him?

Chapter 15

"Layla's friends want to have her bridal shower at my house," Aunt Trudy said. "They're going to decorate and make all of the food. I tried to convince them to have it catered, but they insist it will be fun to get together and cook."

Hudson was driving her home from the grocery store the following Tuesday evening, and he nodded as he drove down Glenn Avenue.

"The shower is going to be so much fun," his aunt continued. "You'll have to stop by."

Hudson gave her a side glance. "Aren't bridal showers for the women?"

"No one said men can't participate."

He'd be sure to miss that.

"I've never seen Layla this happy. I think this marriage is going to be great for her. She'll finally be out on her own, living her life."

He shook his head. "After all the trouble

she gave us when she was younger, you're convinced she can handle this?"

"We won't know until we let her try."

Hudson parked his SUV in the driveway behind Shane's old pickup. He hadn't spoken to Shane since their conversation at his worksite, but Hudson wasn't concerned. He'd shared his thoughts, and that was that.

"You go on inside, and I'll carry the groceries," Hudson told his aunt as he opened the liftgate.

She smiled. "Thank you. I'll take one of the light ones."

"Hud!" Layla raced down the front steps dressed in light-blue scrubs decorated with Disney characters. "I was hoping to see you."

Shane sauntered down the steps behind her with a sour expression — one his aunt would've described as "looking like he'd been sucking on lemons."

Aunt Trudy picked up a grocery bag and started toward the house.

Shane intercepted her and reached for the bag. "Let me carry that for you."

"You're such a sweet young man." She handed off the sack and continued toward the house.

Shane shot Hudson a sneer before following Aunt Trudy inside the house. "Let me get the door for you too."

Hudson shook his head. If Shane wanted to hold a grudge against him, that was his choice.

Layla chose a few bags from the truck. "Thank you again for bringing those cufflinks to me. I'm going to surprise Shane with them at the rehearsal dinner."

"No problem."

Layla grinned and then scooted toward the house with an armload of grocery bags.

Hudson sighed as he stared after her. She seemed to live in an alternate universe — one incompatible with reality. According to her, everything was going to be easy, including her marriage to Shane. With such a rosy, unrealistic outlook on the future, how would Layla ever figure out she was about to make a huge mistake?

Skye stood in the doorway to the workroom at the back of the store Friday night. "Auntie, it's time to close up."

Dakota looked up from the table where she sat trying to fix the beading on Layla's gown. She'd been working on it every night this week, and it still didn't look right to her. Something was off.

"Would you please lock up for me?" she asked her niece, then turned her attention back to the gown.

When she didn't hear the sound of Skye leaving, she looked back over her shoulder and found her niece watching her. "What's up?"

"You've worked late every night this week."

"I know, I know."

Skye sat down beside her at the sewing table. "And you're staying late tonight too?"

"Probably." Dakota sighed.

"Don't you have to teach at the rink?"

"I need to get this gown done before Layla's next fitting, and I'm running out of time. I texted Kayleigh earlier, and Brice is going to handle my class." But the gown wasn't her only problem. She'd been turned down for the refinancing of her mortgage, and she needed to figure out another way to save her house and her store. After she worked on the gown for a while, she was going to hit her books.

"Auntie, I'm worried about you."

The waver in Skye's voice took Dakota by surprise and tugged at her heartstrings. She touched her niece's arm. "Sweetie, I'm fine. I'm just having a fit with this gown, and I don't normally struggle this much."

"Mr. Bryant said he hasn't seen you in two weeks, and he's worried about you too."

Guilt pricked her. She'd been blowing off Parker's messages about setting up another date, using every excuse she could think of. She'd been leading him on, which wasn't fair. It was beyond time to have an honest conversation with him.

But she didn't have the bandwidth for that right now. She hadn't seen her family in weeks either.

"He really likes you," Skye added.

Dakota gave her a solemn nod. "I know. He's a nice man."

"Then —"

She held her hand up. "And that is a conversation I need to have with him. You don't need to share that with him or get involved, okay?" When her niece agreed, Dakota narrowed her eyes. "Promise me, my little cupid."

"I promise." Skye crossed her heart and then stood. "Anyway, I need to go. Gunner is taking me to the rink tonight. I was looking forward to introducing him to you since you haven't come to Nana's in a while."

"I'm sorry, honey. I promise I'll meet him soon."

Her niece crossed to the doorway. "Promise me you won't work too late."

"Okay. Thanks for locking up."

Skye tapped the doorframe. "Good night,

Auntie."

Her niece left, and Dakota turned her focus back to the dress. As she fiddled with the pesky beading, she racked her brain for any solution that would save her house and her store.

Hudson nosed his SUV into the driveway of the colonial later that evening and peered over at Dakota's house. Lights glowed from the inside, and Trouble, the precocious cat, lounged in the front window as if he didn't have a care in the world.

He killed the engine but remained in the vehicle. Hudson had enjoyed his Friday night at the rink. He skated with Anissa until his legs were sore, and he spent time talking with Gavin and Brice. He even ran into some old friends from school and had a blast reconnecting with them.

Yet as much as he enjoyed the evening, he'd noticed as soon as he arrived at the rink that Dakota was missing. He had expected to see her skating with friends, but she was nowhere in sight. He considered asking Brice where she was, but he didn't want to give the impression that he was interested in knowing. Instead he managed to eavesdrop on Kayleigh telling someone that Dakota was working late, trying to finish a gown she was altering.

Hudson climbed from his car and started toward the front door, jamming his hands into the pockets of his jeans. For some reason, he couldn't get Dakota out of his head. He'd mulled over their conversation since last Thursday when he'd offered her a personal loan, and he wondered if she still needed assistance with her finances.

But her money problems weren't his concern. She'd made it clear she didn't want him in her business or her life.

Yet if that were true, why had she wrapped her arms around him and allowed him to hold her close the night she'd thought she'd lost her cat?

He yearned to knock on her front door and ask her if she still needed help.

Hudson growled out a frustrated noise and stalked toward his front door. He had to stop thinking about Dakota and her life. It was best for him not to be tied to her in any way. They weren't meant to be together, and they never would be.

Chapter 16

Sunday evening a week later, Dakota heard a knock on the front door. She yawned and stretched her arms overhead on her way from the sofa to answer it. She had worked late at the store every evening this past week and skipped skating lessons again this weekend, telling Kayleigh she was busy catching up on work. She also had avoided another date with Parker.

She pulled the front door open and jumped back when she found her family spilling all the way from the porch to her front walk — her parents and brother and sister-in-law, along with Skye, Aubrey, Kevin, and a handsome young man she assumed was Skye's boyfriend, Gunner. The late-April evening was warm, and the sun was bright in the cloudless blue sky.

She glanced down at her clothing — worn jeans and a faded concert t-shirt — and scrutinized her den, which hadn't been vacuumed in about three weeks. Then she stared at her parents. "Uh . . . wh-what's going on?"

"Surprise," Mom said, holding up a grocery bag in each hand. Her dark hair was styled in a bob and looked as if she'd recently visited the salon to have her gray covered. "Since you were too busy to come over for a cookout, we brought the cookout to you."

"What?" Dakota demanded.

Mom waved her out of the doorway, and Dakota stepped aside. "We brought burgers, buns, all of the fixings, and dessert."

"We've missed you, sweetheart." Dad, also holding two grocery bags, kissed her cheek on his way to the kitchen. She'd always thought Nick looked just like Dad, since they both were tall and shared the same dark hair and eyes.

"Hi, Auntie!" Aubrey, her fourteen-year-old niece, waved on her way to the den. Aubrey was just as pretty as her mom, Eileen, with her amber eyes and bright smile that always seemed to light up the room.

Eleven-year-old Kevin was the perfect mixture of his parents. He rushed over to Dakota and hugged her waist. "I haven't seen you in forever, Auntie."

"I'm sorry about that." She touched his

nose. "I've missed you."

"I've missed you too." He grinned and faced the den.

"Let me guess," she teased. "You want to turn on your favorite movie since you don't have it at home."

"Is that okay?"

Dakota laughed. "Of course it is." She leaned down to him and whispered, "Just be sure it's rated PG."

"I will." He gave her a high five before making a beeline to the television.

"Auntie!" Skye rushed toward her with the handsome young man at her side. "This is Gunner." She pointed from the young man to Dakota. "Gunner, this is my aunt Dakota."

Gunner nodded. "Great to meet you."

"Likewise," Dakota told him. "I've heard a lot about you."

Skye blushed, and they went inside.

Eileen held up a cake. "I picked up your favorite — carrot cake with cream cheese icing."

"Awesome. You're welcome if you're bringing my favorite," Dakota said with a wink.

Her older brother, Nick, was next. "We need to talk. Come out to the grill with me?"

Dakota and Nick scurried out to the deck while her parents and Eileen moved around the kitchen. With the TV on, the younger ones all got comfortable in the den.

"Skye's worried about you," Nick told her. "She mentioned to Eileen and me about how you're working crazy hours, and Mom's concerned you're missing our Sunday dinners."

Dakota hated the guilt that took hold of her, but she hadn't wanted to share her financial woes with her family. This was her problem, and she could handle it just fine by herself.

"Skye insisted we bring Sunday supper to you, and Mom suggested a cookout. So here we are. We all miss you."

She gazed at the colonial next door, and when she found Hudson sitting on the deck staring at his phone, the muscles in her shoulders pinched. "Please keep it down," she hissed. "My neighbor is outside."

"What's going on, sis?" Nick asked, ignoring her request. "Why are you acting like a hermit?"

She avoided his concerned look by turning the knobs on the grill. "I'm not a hermit. I'm just busy." She pushed the button to light the grill, but nothing happened. "Ugh." She tried again. Still nothing.

"You must be out of propane." He examined the tank. "Yup, it's empty."

"Great," she muttered. "If I had known you all were going to invite yourselves over here for supper, I would have prepared a few things."

Nick shrugged. "No big deal. I'll run out to the store."

"Let me get my purse —"

"There's a propane tank here you can use."

She turned to where Hudson leaned over the fence, and heat prickled her neck. She tried not to think about how long he'd been standing there and how much he'd heard.

"Hi, Hud." Nick waved to him.

"Long time, no see, Nick." Hudson jammed his thumb toward the deck. "I'll bring the tank over for you."

Nick looked at his sister, stunned. "How long has your ex been living next door?" he asked softly.

"Seriously?" Dakota shot her brother a look. "*Now* you whisper?" She blew out a frustrated sigh. "He's just staying at the Airbnb next door, not living there."

Hudson came through her gate carrying the tank. His gray t-shirt pulled nicely over his chest and biceps, and his black basketball shorts showed off his muscular, tanned legs. She couldn't take her eyes off him while he and Nick switched out the propane tanks.

Nick hit the button, and the grill began to heat up. "Thanks, Hud."

"No problem. I'll probably never use the grill anyway. Enjoy your supper." Hudson started back toward the gate.

"Wait," Nick said, stopping Hudson in his tracks. "My mom always overbuys, so we'll have plenty. Join us."

Hudson scratched his cheek. "Are you sure?"

"You provided the propane, and we at least owe you a burger," Nick said.

"Okay, if you insist." Hudson raked his hand through his wet hair, and it stood up at odd, adorable angles.

Stop staring at him! Dakota silently chastised herself.

The back door opened, and Dad walked out holding a metal pan with a stack of burgers and a large spatula. He grinned at Hudson. "Why, Hudson. What a surprise."

"Hi, Mr. Jamison."

"You're an adult too. Call me Mitch." Dad set the pan and spatula on the table by the grill and shook Hudson's hand. "Are you back for good?"

Hudson shook his head. "No, sir. Just for

a couple of months."

"Where have you been living?"

"Manhattan. I started a company, and my business partner and I recently sold it. I'm in between gigs right now."

"Is that right?" Dad seemed impressed. "Is it that software company you always talked about?"

Hudson nodded, and Dakota's heart squeezed. She recalled how close Hudson and her father were when they were dating. Hudson once told her he felt he could tell her father anything, and he always sought his approval as well as his advice.

And as Hudson and her father fell into an easy conversation about Hudson's life, her body suddenly felt heavy with grief and regret for what could have been between them. They could have built a life together — a family, a future . . .

"Dakota?"

Her head swiveled to the back door, where Mom stood looking annoyed. "Yeah?"

"Should we eat inside or on the deck?" Mom's question was laced with a hidden meaning Dakota couldn't quite decipher.

"Well, we can —"

Mom's eyes narrowed. "Get in here, please."

Dakota stepped inside, and Mom took her

arm and pulled her down the hallway toward the kitchen. Skye, Gunner, and the other kids sat in the den while an animated movie played on the TV. Trouble purred on Aubrey's lap, and she scratched his ears.

"You're pinching my arm, Mom," Dakota said in the kitchen. "What's the problem?"

"Why is Hudson Garrity in your backyard talking to your father?" Mom demanded.

Eileen stopped tossing a salad in a large bowl and sidled up to Dakota. "Hudson's *here*?" She looked back and forth between Dakota and Mom. "I'd heard he was back in town. Are you dating him?"

Dakota held up her hands. "Calm down. Hud and I are *not* dating. We're accidental neighbors." She explained that he was in town temporarily and staying at the Airbnb next door. "My grill was out of propane, and Hudson brought over his spare tank. Blame Nick for inviting him to stay for supper. We've spoken a few times, but we're *not* dating. That's it. End of story."

"He broke your heart, Dakota," Eileen said. "You can't forget that."

Mom poured a bag of chips into a large bowl. "Eileen's right. Don't let him worm his way back into your life again."

"I already told you all Auntie is dating my teacher, Mr. Bryant," said Skye, who had materialized with her boyfriend in the kitchen. She leaned on the counter and swiped a chip from the bowl.

Dakota shook her head. "It's nothing serious. In fact, I haven't seen him in a few weeks. I've been too busy with work."

"And he misses you." Skye swirled a chip through the air. "You should call him."

Eileen wagged a finger at Skye. "You shouldn't meddle in your aunt's business."

"But I'm good at playing cupid." Skye took Gunner's hand and led him toward the hallway. "Let's go check on the burgers."

Dakota pointed toward her kitchen table. "How about the adults eat inside, and the kids on the deck?"

"Fine," Mom said, still scowling. "I'll grab the dishes and utensils. But don't expect me to be overly friendly to Hudson. I still remember how he broke your heart."

Eileen's expression also darkened. "And I'll never forget how you cried for weeks after he left." She pointed to the stove. "I'll warm up the beans and prep the condiments."

"And I'll get the tablecloths." While Dakota set to work, she tried to mentally prepare herself for the most awkward Sunday supper yet — all thanks to her annoying brother and ex-fiancé.

■ ■ ■ ■

The appetizing smells of hamburgers and baked beans filled the kitchen as Hudson took a seat beside Dakota. She gave him a shy smile, and his heart kicked. She looked effortlessly pretty in jeans and a faded concert t-shirt. Tendrils of her dark hair fell from her messy bun to frame her beautiful face, and he had to squelch the urge to push a lock of hair behind her ear.

Earlier in the evening he had walked out onto the deck to get a whiff of fresh air after taking a shower. In fact, he couldn't get enough fresh air since coming home to Flowering Grove. Aside from Central Park, the green spaces in New York City were few and far between — so he was soaking up the mild spring weather. When he noticed Dakota and her brother outside, he had almost retreated into the house. But then he reminded himself that he was entitled to sit out on the deck of the house he was paying for.

He had no plans to interact with them until they mentioned the empty propane tank. And he also had no intention of joining them for supper, but when Nick offered, he felt he couldn't say no — especially when

Dakota hadn't appeared horrified at the idea. Shocked, yes, but horrified, no.

And when Mitch started talking to him, Hudson felt an old familiarity. It was as if no time had passed at all, and he started to realize that he'd missed Dakota's family. His heart clutched at thoughts of what could have been. They had almost become *his* family too.

"Would you like some?" Dakota held the container of green salad toward him.

"Yes, please." He took the bowl and scooped salad onto his plate next to his cheeseburger, chips, potato salad, and baked beans.

"Dakota, your cabinet doors look like they're about to fall down." Nick pointed to the cabinet door leaning against the wall. "And I see that one already has. Where's your toolbox? I'll fix them after supper."

"I offered to fix them too, but she turned me down," Hud added.

"Sounds about right," Nick said. "She's definitely independent."

"Tell me about it," Hud muttered.

She waved them both off. "I took my toolbox to work after the flood, and I can't find the screwdriver I used to keep in the kitchen. I'll get to it eventually."

Nick chuckled and shook his head.

"So, Hud," Mitch began from the other side of the table, "I heard your sister is getting married. Is that what brought you back to town?"

"Yes, it is. Layla is getting married in June."

"Layla's getting married?" Nick looked stunned.

Eileen rolled her eyes. "I told you I'd heard that." She pinned him with a stern expression. "You never listen to me."

Dakota cupped her hand to her mouth, stifling her laughter.

"I remember when Layla was tiny," Nick added. "Is she old enough to get married?"

"Well, that's debatable," Hudson quipped, and Dakota shot him a disapproving look. "She's twenty-three, but I think she's rushing it."

"Why do you say that?" Dakota asked.

"They've known each other for only a few months now. That's hardly enough time to make a life commitment."

"They seem to get along well, and it's clear they love each other," she said. "Isn't that enough?"

"Are you serious?" Hudson couldn't stop his bark of laughter. "You're asking me what makes a good marriage?"

Dakota's eyes narrowed, challenging him

like she always did when they argued as a couple.

An awkward hush filled the kitchen. When Hudson turned, he found Dakota's brother and father studying them curiously. But the dark expressions on her mother's and sister-in-law's faces made it clear he wasn't as welcome at the table as he thought he was.

"Are you going back to New York after the wedding?" Nick asked.

Hudson almost smiled, grateful for the change in subject. "Only to collect my things," he said. "My business partner and I sold our company, so I'm looking at options."

"Options?" Nick asked. "For other jobs?"

Hudson nodded. "I'm considering one in Bahrain."

"As in the Middle East?" Dakota's expression seemed to convey both shock and possibly disappointment, which surprised him.

"That's right. My business partner is considering it too. We'd love to buy another company and then sell it."

"Wow." Mitch seemed impressed. "You're big-time, Hudson. Sounds like you've been successful."

"I'm grateful I've been able to provide for my aunt and sister." He shifted in his chair, eager for the focus to be taken off him.

"Skye, Aubrey, and Kevin have really grown up. How are they doing?"

Nick smiled. "Oh, they're great kids."

As Nick talked on about his children and other Flowering Grove news, Hudson felt himself begin to unwind. After their plates were clean, Eileen brought out a carrot cake, and Dakota served coffee. Then they moved outside to sit on the deck, which he noticed could use some TLC.

Hudson talked with Nick, Mitch, and Gunner about working for Gavin on the new restaurant. He also asked Nick about his work as a marketing executive and how Mitch was enjoying retirement.

While he visited with the men, he peeked over to the other side of the deck, where Dakota talked with her mother, sister-in-law, and Skye. Hudson found himself wondering if he would have enjoyed more of these Sunday night suppers with her family if he and Dakota had built a life together in Flowering Grove.

"Well, I guess we should be going," Nick announced a while later, resting his hand on his wife's lower back. "We have to get up early tomorrow for work and school."

Eileen cupped her hand over her mouth to cover a yawn. "That's true. My fifth graders always turn rowdy in April. When the weather warms up, they start getting the itch for summer break. Thanks for having us, Dakota."

"Like I had a choice." Dakota hugged her sister-in-law. "The cake was amazing."

Her mom stood. "We'll have to do this again."

"Or I could just come to your house so you all don't catch me by surprise when I haven't even vacuumed."

"Is that why there's cat hair everywhere?" Nick teased, brushing his hands down his jeans. Everyone laughed and Dakota gave him a playful punch.

Hudson followed Dakota's family into the house, where he said goodbye to everyone before Dakota walked them out to their cars.

Hudson leaned on the back of the sofa while the credits for a movie rolled on the television. He felt something warm and soft brush against his leg and found the cat blinking up at him.

"Hey there, Trouble. Have you given your mom any more scares?" When he scratched the cat's ears, Trouble started to purr. "I hope not. You really upset her."

The cat meowed and scampered off to the kitchen.

Hudson followed the feline. He wasn't

ready to leave yet. In fact, he hoped he could stay and talk to Dakota for a while.

But first he was going to look for a screwdriver and take care of those cabinet doors.

Chapter 17

"You need to join us on Sundays," Mom ordered, standing in the driveway with Dakota and the rest of the family.

"We've been so worried about you."

"I know, and I'm sorry. I promise I'll be in touch."

"You'd better." Mom pulled her in for a hug and whispered in her ear, "Do yourself a favor and steer clear of Hud. If you get tangled up with him again, it will only lead to heartache." Then she gave her shoulder a pat and climbed into the passenger seat of the car.

Dad embraced her next. "I know you say you've been busy, but it's not like you to pull away." His dark eyes studied hers. "Do you need anything?"

She felt the urge to tell him the truth — the *entire* truth — but she couldn't stand the idea of letting him down. He had warned her that she'd taken on too much when she opened the boutique and bought the house, and she was determined to fix this mess herself. Asking for help was like admitting defeat, and she was a Jamison. It wasn't in her makeup to fail.

"No, I'm fine, Dad," she insisted. "But thank you."

"Call me if you need me," he told her before folding his tall frame into the car and starting the engine.

Dakota turned toward Skye and Gunner, who were laughing by a red sports car. "Gunner," she said, and he looked over at her. "Are you going to stop by the store to get your tux for the prom?"

"He sure is," Skye said, resting her hand on Gunner's bicep.

Gunner held up his hand. "Yes, ma'am. I'll be by after school this week."

"Good. See you then." She waved to her brother and his family and then ambled toward the house.

Her heart gave a little kick when she realized she was going to be alone with Hudson again. She stopped in the kitchen doorway and took in the view of him fixing her cabinet doors. "What do you think you're doing?"

He looked over his shoulder and grinned, which sent shivers dancing down her spine.

"What does it look like?"

"I told you I can fix them myself." She walked over to him, and a whiff of his woodsy cologne sent her senses spinning.

He tightened a screw and then opened and closed the door, testing it. "You fed me, so it's only right that I do something to repay you. And I found this screwdriver in a drawer." He looked sheepish. "I didn't mean to go through your things, but my aunt would tan my hide if she knew I stayed for supper and didn't bring something to share." He pointed the screwdriver toward the counter. "I was going to start the dishwasher, but I thought fixing your cabinet doors would be more helpful."

"Thanks." Despite herself, appreciation shimmied through her. "That's really thoughtful."

"Happy to help. Dinner was delicious, and the company was great too." When he turned to face her, he was only a breath away. He stared down at her, and her throat dried. "I guess I should get going."

But she wasn't ready for him to leave — not yet.

"Would you like to sit on the deck?"

"Sure," he said without hesitation.

She poured two glasses of sweet iced tea before handing him one.

He smiled again, and her heart did a jig.

They sat out on the deck just as the sun started to set, sending vibrant colors across the sky. A cool breeze kicked up the smell of moist earth mixed with honeysuckle. Dakota skimmed her hands over her arms and mulled over the evening. How easily Hudson had fit in with her family once again. Then she turned toward him and recalled their last conversation.

"Did you deliver the cufflinks to Layla?" she asked.

"Yes, and you'll be happy to know we've agreed to call a truce. Again."

She smiled. "That's fantastic." She took a long draw from her glass of iced tea.

"I heard your mom say she was worried about you," he said, and Dakota gulped.

Had he been eavesdropping when her mother told her to avoid him? She tried to hide her embarrassment. "What exactly did you hear?"

"Nick said something about how you'd missed a bunch of their Sunday night dinners. Is that why she's worried?"

Dakota nearly blew out a relieved sigh. "Yeah. I've been working late at the store trying to get Layla's gown right, among other things. It's turned into a more difficult project than I imagined." She realized what she said and added, "Not that I can't handle it. It's just taking more time than expected, and I don't want her to be disappointed with the final product. I know how much it means to her."

"I have full confidence the gown will look exactly like my mom's. You always were the best seamstress in Flowering Grove."

Dakota smiled. "Thanks."

"It's the truth." He shrugged. "I remember how busy you stayed tailoring all of your friends' gowns during prom season. Your sewing room was full of dresses."

She sipped her tea while the compliment warmed her from the inside out.

"Do you remember those matching shirts you made us for spirit day in high school?"

"I do. In fact, Layla mentioned them recently."

He looked embarrassed. "Would you believe mine is still hanging in a closet at my aunt's house?"

She guffawed. "You're lying."

"Nope." He shook his head, and she laughed. "Any news on your financials?"

Her happy mood evaporated, and she gave him a tight smile. "Everything's about the same." She turned toward him. "Hey, do you remember the old Franklin farm?"

"Of course. We used to go for hayrides

there every fall."

"Right. I took my nieces and nephew there until they said they were too old for the hayrides, which makes no sense. No one is too old for a hayride." She folded her leg underneath herself. "Anyway, it's for sale."

His lips twitched. "Are you in the market for a farm?"

"Yes and no."

"Dakota, I'm sorry, but you've lost me."

"I know, but just listen. Lately people have been turning their old barns or warehouses into wedding venues. The Franklin farm had this big old barn, and if I had the money, I'd buy the farm, restore it, and open my own wedding venue. I'd hire someone to run the venue part and then I'd open a store on-site. It could be a one-stop shop for gowns, tuxes, bridesmaids' dresses, and all of the accessories, plus the wedding venue." She shrugged. "I know it sounds crazy, but it might bring more weddings to Flowering Grove. Which would be good for our little town."

She folded her hands in her lap, shocked that she'd shared that idea out loud with him. She hadn't told anyone, but when she was with Hudson, she couldn't seem to stop herself from admitting her deepest thoughts and desires.

He studied her and then took another drink of iced tea. "Have you thought about my offer for a loan?"

"Thanks, but no." She picked at a piece of lint on her jeans. Maybe she should have kept her idea to herself.

"Now isn't the time to be so stubborn."

She decided to let that dig go. "Tell me about the company you sold."

"All right." He leaned back in the chair and rested his right ankle on his left knee. "It's called D&H Software Solutions. My partner and I designed a business management system that combines human resources and financial management. Many companies use different applications, which can be tedious, especially when the systems don't talk to each other. This streamlines their processes, and since we were a little bit ahead of our time, the software took off."

"That's amazing. You were always so determined to own your own company, and you did it. You should be proud."

He gave her a half shrug.

"You've always been so modest."

"What?" He laughed.

"You have. I remember when you got all of those scholarships to college, you acted like it was no big deal and you didn't deserve them. But you *did* deserve them."

She couldn't help but be proud of him even though he wasn't hers anymore.

He shook his head.

"No, really, Hud. You've always been humble."

"Well . . ." He grimaced. "Layla would disagree with you."

They were silent for a moment as they took in the sunset. Then she turned toward him again. "Who's *D*?" she asked.

His forehead crinkled. "What?"

"From D&H. *H* is obviously you."

"Oh." He chuckled. "Darren, my business partner."

"How'd you meet?"

Hud set his glass on the small table next to his chair. "We were hired at another software company around the same time and worked our way up together. We just clicked and became good friends. Next thing I knew, I had convinced him to start a company with me. Then we managed to sell it for a nice profit."

"Wow." She nodded slowly. "You got what you always wanted — financial stability and success in a big city."

Hudson took a long drink from his glass and kept those sky-blue eyes focused somewhere across the yard.

Silence stretched between them, and she

considered how much their lives had changed since they'd broken up. She longed to ask him if he was in a relationship, but what did it matter now?

"I overheard you talking to Nick, and I was surprised when you said you're working for Gavin."

He angled his body toward her. "Why would that surprise you?"

"You always seemed to want to be the boss." She set her glass down. "I'm just surprised you're working for someone else."

His smirk made her laugh.

"Do you like working for Gavin?"

"Believe it or not, I do." He drummed his fingers on his calf. "It's nice to not have to shoulder all the responsibility for once. Plus, I'm learning a lot more about construction than I learned back in the day." A strange expression overtook his face. "And I'm determined to prove to my sister that I'm still cut out for the work."

"What does that mean?"

"She thinks I'm too full of myself to do manual labor."

Dakota pivoted to face him. "Too full of yourself?"

"Yeah." He pressed his lips together. "She bet me that I wouldn't stick to the job, so now I have no choice but to do it. You know, pride and all that." He sighed. "I'm trying to show her I'm not the snob she thinks I am."

"Huh." She thought for a moment about all he'd just said. Then she asked the question that had been haunting her all evening. "Why Bahrain?"

He paused before answering. "It's a great opportunity."

"But you'll be so far away."

When he raised an eyebrow, she realized what she'd said.

"From your family," she added quickly, but heat was already creeping into her cheeks. "You'll be so far away from them. Won't you miss your aunt and your sister?"

"Of course I will."

"Didn't you miss them when you were in New York?"

He nodded and sipped more iced tea.

She studied his face and longed to know what he was thinking. *Do you still care for me? Is there any chance we could try again?*

She mentally pulled herself back.

"You look like you really want to say something, Kot— *Dakota.*" He set the glass down again. "So just say it."

"Why isn't Flowering Grove good enough for you?" Her quiet voice wavered.

His eyes narrowed and then recovered. "Is

that what you think of me? That I believe I'm too good for my hometown?"

"Hud, I don't know what to think."

He moved his fingers over the arms of the chair. "I had to move away to make enough money to take care of my aunt and my sister. I couldn't have done that if I had stayed here."

"Yeah, I know that." Her voice was so tiny she could barely hear herself.

He scanned her small backyard. "I didn't realize how much I missed this."

Her stomach dipped. "Missed what?" she asked.

"The stars." He pointed up toward the sky and then around the yard. "The quiet. The sunsets. Don't get me wrong. New York has its perks. I love my apartment and my building, but this — this is nice." He faced her, and his expression was warm, sending a jolt through her. "Do you remember that time we decided to drive out to Coral Cove for the day?"

A bark of laughter burst from her lips. "That was a disaster."

"Well, not the entire day. We had fun walking on the beach and wandering through those junk stores you love."

"They're not junk stores, Hud. They're eclectic."

A smile played on his lips. "Right. *Eclectic.*" He made quotation marks with his fingers.

She gently elbowed him in the side, and he chuckled. "Don't make fun of me," she said with a laugh. "Back then I had a collection of those funny little magnets that I cherished."

"Your brother used to say your folks' fridge was going to fall over because of your magnet collection."

She laughed harder and wiped her eyes.

"After you covered the fridge, you started putting them in a drawer in your nightstand. You had magnets from different states, some with sayings on them, others with cats and dogs. The drawer was so stuffed it would barely close." He cocked his head to the side. "I always think of you when I see a display of magnets. I wonder if you have them all stuffed in your drawer somewhere."

Her heart stuttered at the earnestness in his face.

He grinned. "What on earth did you do with them when you moved out?"

"Well . . ." She tapped her chin. "I think they're in a box in the attic."

He laughed, and she enjoyed the deep, rich sound. She hadn't realized how much she missed it.

"You insisted we stop in every single store to look at their magnets, and we quickly figured out that they had the same magnets at each one. But you still had to check them all out." His eyes sparkled in the low light glowing above the deck. "And when we ran out of stores, we decided to head home."

"And that's when your truck broke down and we had to call my dad for help."

He cringed. "Your folks were not happy about driving three hours to rescue us. Still, your dad was generous as always and offered to pay for the tow truck." He lifted his face toward the sky again and smiled. "Sitting in the bed of the truck and stargazing while we waited was fun."

Yes, it had been. She could almost feel his warm hand holding hers while they pointed out the stars and made up names for the constellations. And then there were those kisses that made her lose track of reality. Her lips tingled at the memory. The night had been magical. Actually, almost every moment spent with Hudson had been magical back then.

She examined his profile — those high cheekbones, that strong jaw, and those lips that she'd once known by heart. A chill that had nothing to do with the weather rushed through her, and she hugged her arms to her middle.

"I loved that old truck, but I had too much faith in it." He tapped his fingers on his knee.

"I loved that truck too."

"We had some good times together." The softness in his voice reminded her of velvet.

She nodded, unable to speak for a moment.

He stared out toward the backyard again, and the quiet hum of traffic sounded in the distance. His expression became pensive, and she could almost hear his mind churning with thoughts.

Concern filled her, and she started to reach for his shoulder. But she held herself back, afraid to be too forward with him. "You okay?"

"Yeah." He focused on her again. "I had to run an errand for Gavin today, and it took me out to Ridge Road. I drove by that old house where I used to live before . . ." He paused. "Before my folks died."

"Oh." She sat up straighter. Hudson rarely spoke about his parents.

"Did I ever show you that house?"

"Once, when we were eighteen or so, we drove by there."

"We moved around a lot when I was little, but that was the house I remember the best." He rubbed his ear. "It looks different now. Better. The porch has been replaced. And the house was painted. It used to be this dull beige color, but now it's blue with white shutters." He stretched his long legs out in front of him. "Seeing that house brought it all back."

"Brought back what?"

"My childhood." He looked up at the sky as if his memories were projected there. "I vaguely recall heated discussions between my parents about my dad's frequent unemployment. My mom would say things like, 'And why does the boss not like you this time, Chan?' Or 'How am I supposed to feed these kids if you're not bringing home any money?'" He shook his head. "I remember feeling the stress and hearing my mom cry. I asked my aunt about it all when I got older, and she said my dad was a good and loving man who just couldn't keep a job."

"That had to be difficult," she whispered.

He was silent for several beats, and his expression became grave. "I remember every detail of that night." He looked down at the deck. "The night when they died."

"You don't have to talk about it," she said softly.

"I know, but I want to."

Her heart squeezed. Hudson had never shared the details except to say his parents were in a car accident.

"Layla and I had been staying with Aunt Trudy while Mom and Dad traveled to Greensboro to find a place to live. Dad was planning to start another new job there." He exhaled through his nose. "It was supposed to be a new beginning for us in a new town. At least, that's what my mom told me when she explained I'd have to start at a new school."

He stared out toward her fence. "I woke up to blue lights reflecting on the ceiling of my aunt's spare bedroom — which eventually became my room. I ran down the stairs and found two police officers standing in the doorway." His blue eyes glittered. "And Aunt Trudy was sobbing." His voice sounded gravelly, as if he was trying to hold back his swelling emotions.

Dakota's eyes stung, and she sniffed before clasping his strong hand. He gave her hand a gentle squeeze in return and then held on.

"After the police left, I asked her what was wrong, and she said, 'Hudson, I'm really sorry, but your parents are gone.' And then she started crying again. I really didn't understand it, but as the days wore on, I realized she meant they weren't coming back."

"Hud," she breathed. "I'm so sorry."

He wiped his eyes with his free hand. "After that, we had to move into Aunt Trudy's house. I remember flashes of the funeral, and the hushed conversations my aunt shared with members of our church." He cleared his throat, and her chest constricted.

She gave his hand another gentle squeeze, and he responded with a sad smile.

"I'm so grateful my aunt stepped up and became the parent we needed."

"Of course she did, Hud. She's your family."

"Right, but it was a sacrifice taking in two kids. She did the best she could, raising us on her limited income. Since my parents died in a single-car accident, there was no lawsuit, no damages awarded to help us financially. And my parents never had life insurance, savings, or any investments. She had to shoulder it all herself."

Dakota released his hand and angled her body toward him. "I understand, but she loves you and Layla like her own. I don't think she sees raising you and your sister as a sacrifice at all." She gestured widely. "I'd do the same for my nieces and nephew without a second thought."

"Still, I'm grateful. That's why I made a promise to myself — that someday I would take care of my aunt and sister. I didn't want Layla to have to move around a lot like I did. I wanted her to have a stable childhood. It was also my life's goal to pay back my aunt for her generosity and prove to her just how much I appreciated all she'd done for Layla and me. Without her, we probably would have gotten separated and then lost in the foster care system."

"Hud, Trudy knows you appreciate her, and you have proven to her how much she means to you." She rested her hand on his broad shoulder. "You've done all you've set out to do. You should be proud of yourself."

He sniffed and wiped his eyes again. "You know, I've never shared any of that with anyone. I just don't talk about my folks." He massaged the back of her hand with his fingers, and his touch set her skin aflame. "It felt good to get that off my chest."

"I'm glad you felt comfortable enough to share it with me."

They studied each other. The air around them seemed electrified, and intensity crackled between them. Dakota's heartbeat zoomed, and she was certain to the depth of her core that she still cared for Hudson

— deeply. She was drawn to his compassion and determination. His loving devotion to his aunt and his sister was his most attractive quality. And despite their complicated past, he had offered Dakota help with her store.

In that moment, she longed for him to tell her he cared for her too.

He suddenly glanced at his watch. "I didn't realize how late it is. I need to get to the construction site early tomorrow." He stood and picked up his empty glass. "Thank you for listening. I had a nice time tonight."

"Me too." She held her hand out toward the glass. "I can take that."

He shook his head and then opened the back door for her.

She slipped into the house and found Trouble blinking up at her.

"Has he hidden on you again?"

"No, he's met me at the door every night since you helped me find him."

"Good." Hudson bent down and rubbed the cat's ear, and Trouble closed his eyes while his purrs rumbled loudly. "I told him not to scare you again. I'm glad he listened."

Dakota chuckled and set the glasses in the sink before they walked out to the porch together.

"Thanks again for supper."

"You're welcome."

A strange expression traveled over his face, and he pushed a lock of her hair behind her ear. His finger traced her cheek, leaving a trail of heat in its wake. The intensity in his blue eyes sent a quiver through her belly. He leaned down, and her breath caught as she waited for his lips to caress hers after so many years. But instead his arm came around hers in a half hug.

"Guess I'll see you around," he said.

"Yeah." She did her best to mask her disappointment. "Guess so."

"Night." He strode down the porch steps toward the driveway.

Dakota leaned on the railing, and her shoulders sagged. Doubt and confusion threatened to drag her under and drown her. Once again she had to remind herself that what they'd once shared had ended years ago. Why did she keep forgetting that when she was around him?

She headed back into her house while her mother's wise words echoed through her mind:

Do yourself a favor and steer clear of Hud. If you get tangled up with him again, it will only lead to heartache.

Dakota pulled her phone out and posed

her thumbs over the screen, ready to text Parker. Then she stopped and let out a long, shaky breath.

Slipping the phone into her back pocket, she continued to her bedroom and contemplated her strange evening with her ex. She had to stop allowing her feelings to run amok. Hudson Garrity had hurt her once and would do it again. After all, he'd made it clear he wasn't going to stay in Flowering Grove.

The smartest thing she could do would be to forget about Hudson. But how could she forget a man who was already imprinted on her soul?

Chapter 18

Kayleigh took Dakota's arm on Friday night and pulled her past the crowd of rowdy patrons ready to hit the floor. General skate was about to begin as Kayleigh steered her best friend into the office at the back of the rink.

Once they were tucked inside the office, Kayleigh closed the door and rested her hands on her hips. "All right, Dakota. We're alone now, so spill it."

"What do you mean?"

"Please." Kayleigh harrumphed. "I've known you since we were kids, which means I can read you. You've texted one-word answers to my messages all week, and you didn't smile once during our lessons tonight. You're usually bubbly and energetic, but you look as if you haven't slept in a month." Her expression filled with compassion. "Tell me what's wrong."

Dakota dropped onto the chair across

from the desk and slumped backward. "It's been a rough week. Things are spiraling out of control for me financially. The store situation has gotten worse." She shared about her mortgage payment rising, how she hadn't recovered from the lost stock, and how sales at the store hadn't improved.

Kayleigh sat on the edge of the desk. "Is there anything I can do to help?"

"I don't think so, but thanks. I've been racking my brain trying to figure out what to do. I almost called my dad and asked for help this week, but I don't want to hear 'I told you so.' " Dakota rubbed her forehead.

Kayleigh leaned forward and rested her hand on Dakota's shoulder. "Sometimes we need to swallow our pride and ask for help. That's not a sign of weakness."

"I know." Dakota sighed. "I'm getting there." She rested her hands on her lap. "But that's not all that's going on." She sniffed and examined her faded blue jeans. "And I think I'm losing my mind because . . ."

Kayleigh gave her a palms-up. "Because what?"

"I can't stop thinking about Hud." Dakota grimaced and waited for the explosion of her best friend's disapproval.

Kayleigh blinked. "You what?" Her nose

scrunched. "Why Hud?"

"I saw him Sunday." She explained how her family had surprised her with a cookout and how Hud wound up staying for supper. "After my family left, he fixed my cabinet doors and then we talked on the deck for a while, and it was . . . wonderful." She bit her lower lip, and Kayleigh frowned. "Now I can't get him out of my mind. I almost stopped by his house the other night, but I talked myself out of it. Seems he's moving to the Middle East. I know he's just going to disappear from my life again, and I'll be left nursing another broken heart."

Kayleigh held her hand up like a traffic cop. "Whoa. Stop right there. What about Parker?"

"I haven't spoken to him in a while. We've texted here and there, but he's been busy at school with exams and grading senior projects. There was also a big field trip he was preparing for last week."

"It's obvious that he really likes you, Dakota." Kayleigh tapped the corner of the desk. "Don't you think you need to be honest with him instead of leading him on?"

The guilt that had followed her around all week pressed down on her, making her posture wilt even more. "Yes, I know I need to." She rubbed the back of her head. "I've been staring at the ceiling at night trying to figure out how I'm going to fix my store and my heart. I'm losing my mind, Kay, and I don't know what to do."

"I thought Hud was your past and Parker was your future."

"I thought so, too, but apparently I don't know how to let go of the past."

A knock sounded on the office door. Kayleigh skated over to open it, and her husband filled the doorframe. "Hey, Brice."

He peeked past Kayleigh and eyed Dakota. "Parker's been looking for you."

"Oh. Thanks." Dakota's stomach pitched. She pushed herself up from the chair and squared her shoulders. It was time to face the truth. She'd been using Parker as a distraction when her heart was truly craving Hudson, and Parker deserved better.

Kayleigh touched her husband's arm. "We'll be out there in a sec, okay?"

"Sure." Brice gave her a curious look, then backed away from the door.

Kayleigh closed the door again and wagged a finger at Dakota. "You need to be honest with him."

"I know, I know, but this isn't the place to do it. I'll ask him to give me a ride home since I rode here with Skye tonight."

"Good idea." Kayleigh's expression

warmed. "My nana always says honesty is the best policy."

Dakota nodded, but the best policy certainly wouldn't be the easiest.

Bile rose in Hudson's throat while he stood by the snack bar and watched Dakota and Parker talking near the rink. A pop song thundered through the speakers, and when Parker touched Dakota's arm and leaned close to talk to her, Hudson's nostrils flared. All week long he'd tried in vain to shove thoughts of Dakota from his mind, but she remained there, lingering at the edge.

He couldn't stop reliving Sunday night, recalling how easily they'd joked and laughed together. How she'd teased him, elbowing him in the side while her eyes gleamed. He'd felt that old connection come alive again. She seemed disappointed when he talked about moving to the Middle East, which surprised him, and when they reminisced, she seemed to enjoy reliving those times as much as he did. But most shocking of all was how willing he'd been to talk about his parents and share his grief. He meant it when he said he'd never opened up to anyone like that before. He hadn't even discussed those feelings with his sister or his aunt. But Dakota always seemed to unlock something deep in his heart and soul.

He'd longed to stay on her deck and talk all night, but he didn't want to risk ruining the progress they'd made. Dakota had gone from shutting down and almost asking him to leave the last time he'd been in her house to inviting him to stay and talk. Too much of a good thing could have ended badly.

When they'd said good night, he couldn't stop himself from touching her hair and running his finger down her soft cheek. He'd somehow squelched the urge to kiss her, even though he had the overwhelming feeling that she'd wanted him to.

At the same time, he knew she was seeing someone. He'd hoped she'd tell him the relationship with Parker was over, but now as he stood in the rink, he could see it wasn't. He could tell from their body language they were still together, and he realized he'd been kidding himself when he started to believe she might actually still care about him. If he confessed to her that *he* still cared, what would stop her from rejecting him just as she had seven years ago? His heart couldn't survive that again. He must have imagined their connection, and it was best that he just leave Dakota and the rest of this town in his rearview mirror when he took off for good.

But for some reason, that idea hurt him almost as much as the thought of leaving his family behind.

"What would you like, mister?"

Hudson swiveled back to face the snack bar, where a redheaded teenager with spiky hair, braces, and freckles stared at him.

"Two Cokes and two pretzels with cheese."

"Sure thing."

He paid the kid and toted the food over to where Gavin sat in what seemed to have become their usual booth every Friday night. Hudson would miss these weekend visits to the rink too.

"You look like you're ready to punch someone," Gavin said before breaking off a piece of his pretzel.

Hudson shrugged at that idea and sipped his Coke.

"What's up?"

He turned toward where Dakota and Parker had been standing, but they were gone. Most likely they had joined the rest of the skaters on the rink. "Dakota is still seeing that guy." He tore off a piece of a pretzel and dipped it in the cheese.

"And this is news to you because . . ."

"We sort of had a moment Sunday night."

He explained how he had supper with her family and then stayed and talked. "I thought maybe —" He stopped speaking because he sounded like a ridiculously lovesick guy, and he didn't have time for this. Besides, he wasn't staying in Flowering Grove, so none of it mattered anyway. "Never mind."

Gavin remained silent for a beat and ate a few more bites of pretzel. "If you care about her, you should tell her."

"There's no point."

"Why not?"

Hudson turned toward the rink just as Dakota and Parker skated past. "She's with him, and I'm leaving town soon."

"She might not be with him if she knew you cared."

Hudson shook his head.

"The attraction between you two is pretty potent. I wouldn't be surprised if Parker has noticed it too."

Hudson sipped his Coke and cut his gaze toward the rink. Gavin was wrong. But doubt still lingered in the back of his mind.

"Come skate with me, Daddy." Anissa appeared at the table and took Hudson's hand. "You too, Mr. Hud."

Hudson couldn't resist her. "Yes, ma'am."

He pushed himself up from the table and allowed her to steer him toward the rink.

Later that evening Parker steered his Kia SUV into Dakota's driveway. She gripped the passenger side door handle and tried to remember the speech she'd mentally prepared during the short ride home.

The evening had passed at a snail's pace. She had tried to stay busy, encouraging Parker to skate so they could avoid getting into a deep conversation at the rink. But now they were parked in her driveway, and it was time for her to be honest with him. The truth would most likely break his heart.

She bit back a grimace and fixed a smile on her face before unfastening her seat belt. "Thanks for the ride."

He moved his fingers over the steering wheel. "You've been quiet tonight. Wanna tell me what's wrong?"

Her gaze involuntarily moved to the house next door, where light glowed in the second-story windows and Hudson's fancy SUV sat quietly waiting for him. She had seen him talking with Gavin and also skating with Anissa, which made her smile. She'd even managed to skate near him a few times during the night, but they hadn't shared more than an awkward hello. She'd longed to have another conversation with him, but his curt greetings spoke volumes. Hudson didn't want to be more than acquaintances, and it was better that way.

So then why did her heart insist on craving him?

"Dakota?" Her eyes met Parker's, and they seemed to plead with her to tell him the truth. "Please talk to me. Have I done something to upset you?"

She shook her head as her stomach lurched. "No, not at all."

"Then what is it?"

"Parker, I'm really sorry I've been so standoffish. The truth is . . ." She gripped the door handle. "The truth is, I'm just not ready for a relationship. You're a sweet guy, and I'm grateful my niece set us up. But I'm just not in a good place emotionally, and I'd really prefer we just be friends."

Her speech, which sounded so awesome in her head, was incredibly pathetic when she said it out loud. She angled her body toward Parker, and to her surprise, Parker's lips formed a sardonic smile.

"Friends, huh?" he asked. "That's what you want?"

Oh boy.

"Y-yes," she stammered. "Just friends."

He nodded slowly as if working through

something in his mind. "Does your reluctance to date me have anything to do with your ex?" He pointed toward the colonial.

Dakota's eyes widened. Had she been that transparent?

"You're really going to act surprised?" Parker gave her a look of disbelief. "I suspected you had feelings for him the day I stopped by and caught you hugging him, but I hoped you were being honest with me." Hurt spread across his face. "That's all I've wanted, Dakota — honesty. I don't think that's too much to ask."

"No, Parker, it's not. And you deserve so much better than me."

He rested his arm on the steering wheel. "I just wish I'd realized sooner that you were stringing me along while you waited for your ex to notice you."

"It's not like that —"

"Please don't say anything else, Dakota."

She pushed the door open and climbed out of the vehicle before turning back toward him. "I never meant to hurt you, Parker."

"Too late," he said before slipping his SUV into Reverse.

She stood in the driveway as he backed out and his taillights disappeared into the dark. Hugging her arms to her middle, she longed for the shame and remorse that crashed inside her to subside. But she knew she deserved to feel as bad as she did. She had led Parker on, and he did deserve better — so much better. She hoped he would find someone who appreciated him for the kind, patient, thoughtful, and sweet man he was.

Dakota swiveled toward the colonial next door, and for a moment, she considered knocking. She longed to sit on the deck with Hudson and talk until the sun came up, but tonight he'd seemingly kept her at a distance, which was probably for the best.

With a heavy heart, she trudged toward her front door. She would stare at her ceiling again tonight and hope that somehow she could get herself through this mess.

Chapter 19

The murmur of conversations faded behind Dakota as she made her way to Trudy's bathroom, which was located beyond the modest family room in her Cape Cod–style house. Ever since she'd arrived for Layla's bridal shower, she'd felt like she couldn't breathe.

She'd planned to send a gift and avoid the shower, but when Layla texted her at the shop earlier in the day to make sure she'd gotten an invitation, Dakota felt obligated to come. She'd done her best to make conversation with Layla's friends and Shane's family members, but she felt as if the memories surrounding her might strangle her.

Every time she looked at the family photos on the walls, she was taken back to when she and Hudson had been a couple. She'd spent hours in this little house with Hud and his family. It seemed like only yesterday that this house felt like her second home, but now she was nothing but a memory, almost a stranger.

She washed her hands before exiting the bathroom, and when she moved past the kitchen, she caught a glimpse of the backyard. She took in the lovely landscaping of flowers along a rock path accentuated by benches.

Dakota crossed the kitchen and pushed open the back door leading to a small deck. She inhaled the fresh air as the warm, late-April afternoon sun kissed her cheeks. It was Saturday, and spring had fully arrived in Flowering Grove. The colorful plants in Trudy's lush backyard danced in the warm afternoon breeze as bees buzzed around them. Three rabbits hopped by before disappearing into a bush, and two squirrels helped themselves to an afternoon snack from a nearby birdfeeder.

But despite the happy scenery, sadness built in Dakota's chest as she leaned on the deck railing. She was still reeling from hurting Parker last night, and now the memories conjured up by Trudy's house were about to send her into a bottomless, hopeless abyss.

She should have told Layla that she needed to keep working on her gown, which was the truth. She was still struggling to perfect the dress, and she only had a little over a month to finish it before the last fitting. The beading on the skirt still didn't look right, and despite hours of work, she wasn't yet happy with the sleeves or the train. Had she lost her touch?

The backyard gate opened with a squeak, and Dakota looked up. Hudson was walking through clad in pressed khaki shorts and a green golf shirt from an exclusive brand that flaunted his sinewy arms. A rush of nerves swarmed her stomach. His face was clean-shaven, and when his blue eyes met hers, he appeared as surprised as she felt.

She pushed her hands down her green sundress and patted her hair, hoping her French braid was still straight. Then she stopped herself from groaning. Why was she always fussing about her appearance around him?

He reached the bottom of the deck stairs. "I didn't expect to see you here."

"I wasn't planning on coming." She grimaced. "That came out wrong. What I meant was, I was going to send a gift so I could stay at the boutique and work, but Layla texted me and asked me to come."

"Interesting. She texted me too." He nodded toward the double glider behind her.

"Want to sit?"

"Sure."

They sat down, and Dakota looked out over the yard. "The yard looks different than I remember," she said. "It's nice." She closed her eyes and pressed her hand to her temple. "Again, that's not what I meant. Nothing's coming out right today."

"It's okay." Hud chuckled at her honesty. "I was never one to make time for helping my aunt with her yard work." He blew out a puff of air. "But apparently, Shane wanted to show off his landscaping skills."

"He did this?" she asked with a gasp, and he nodded. "He's talented. If I had the money, I'd hire him too."

"Yeah, I guess he's pretty talented." Hud's smile dipped downward.

"That sounded sarcastic. Do you not think he's talented?"

He wasn't about to offer up his feelings about Shane when Dakota had made it clear she was Team Wedding. While keeping his focus on the yard, he gently pushed the glider into motion, and it creaked back and forth.

"It's nice that you came to her shower," she said. "Does that mean you've changed your opinion on the marriage?"

He glanced back toward the house, confirming none of the bridal shower guests were within earshot, and faced her again. "Honestly? No, I still think she's too young and not ready for this."

"Hold on, Hud." She rested her sandals on the deck, stopping the glider. "That's just an excuse. What's the real reason you're against the marriage?"

He shook his head and looked out toward the backyard. She didn't want to hear the truth, or maybe he wasn't ready to share it.

"What aren't you telling me?"

He pressed his lips together. "She was a mess in high school." His voice was low and close to her ear.

"What do you mean?"

"She got mixed up with the wrong crowd and was expelled for fighting."

"Fighting?" Dakota cupped her hand to her mouth before angling herself closer to him. "I can't even imagine that."

He fiddled with a loose sliver of wood on the arm of the glider. "I couldn't understand it. She was failing classes, skipping school, and experimenting with drugs and alcohol. I knew how gossip spread in this town, so Aunt Trudy and I kept it as private as we could. Only her school counselor knew the details of what was going on."

"If I had known, I could have tried to help her."

He gave her a look of disbelief. Why would his ex-fiancée help his sister?

"Hud, I adore Layla. When we were together, she was like the little sister I never had."

He continued to watch her, warmed by her admission. Had she truly loved him and his family? If so, why had she done what she did?

She shifted away from him on the glider.

"Aunt Trudy was going out of her mind, and I was in New York City," he explained. As he spoke, all of the worry and helplessness he remembered crashed over him again. "I was brand-new at the company and had no personal time off to use, not to mention the money to travel home to help. So I did what I could from afar. We talked to the guidance counselor so often, I had her number memorized. We got Layla in with the school psychologist, which helped, and signed her up for summer school to make up the work she missed so she wouldn't be held back."

"That had to be horrible, Hud. I'm so sorry."

He scrubbed his hand over his face. "I'd never been so stressed out before, but we got her through it."

"But she's doing great now. I can tell she's gotten her act together."

Hudson's brow wrinkled.

"What else am I missing, Hud?"

"I can't trust her decisions."

"Because of her past?"

He stared out toward the fence line, and when Dakota touched his bicep, he almost jumped.

"Hey," she said. When he turned and met her gaze, he was struck by the softness in her eyes. "Learn to trust her to make her own decisions, Hud. She's not a little girl anymore."

"She'll always be little to me."

"I know how much you care about her. I really do. But she's a young woman now. What's the real reason you don't want her to get married? You're still making excuses. What's the *truth,* Hud?"

"The truth is that this marriage is a mistake, Dakota." He pointed toward the flowerbeds. "Sure, Shane is talented, but he needs to work harder and start making some real money."

"Is money all you care about?" She clucked her tongue. "If so, you're not the same man I fell in love with in high school. You're different now."

Her words felt like a spike to his heart, and he shielded his hurt with a scoff. "Is that what you think?" *Is that why you dumped me?*

"You've always been so focused on making money to take care of your family, and you've done that. But now money seems to be *all* you care about, and there's more to life than that."

He stared at her. "I don't only care about—"

"There you are, Dakota," Trudy called from behind them, interrupting his words. "Oh, hello, Hudson. I saw your vehicle, but I didn't know where you'd gone." She beckoned them toward the back door. "Come in for cake," she sang before disappearing into the house.

Hudson stood and held his hand out to Dakota. She hesitated, and for a moment he thought she was going to reject him. But she accepted his hand and allowed him to lift her to her feet.

He released her hand, and together they walked into the house. He was still reeling from her comment and longing for more time to explain himself, but the moment was gone.

For the rest of the afternoon, Hudson couldn't take his eyes off Dakota. She was stunning in a green sundress that made the most of her trim figure. Her thick dark hair was fixed in a braid with tendrils falling around her beautiful face. Just enough makeup accentuated her captivating dark eyes.

He also couldn't stop mulling over the conversation they'd shared outside on the glider. He was stunned when she said she would've tried to help Layla if she'd known she was struggling in high school. It seemed so unlikely that she still cared about his family after the way she'd ended their relationship without explanation. Had the roles been reversed, would he have done the same? He wasn't so sure. Yet he found truth in her eyes and in the tone of her voice. It seemed she really cared for his family. He then remembered how she'd given his sister the family discount on her gown to help her with the wedding of her dreams.

If she cared about Layla, did that mean she could still care about him?

He almost laughed out loud. To indulge these thoughts was foolish because Dakota was seeing Parker. She belonged to another man.

But still it felt good to tell her about Layla's past and finally get his concerns off his chest. She had listened to him, which hadn't surprised him. She'd always been a good listener — the best, really.

But what had shocked him most of all was when she accused him of only caring about money.

Is money all you care about?

If so, you're not the same man I fell in love with in high school.

Those words had quickly burrowed deep into his soul. Was that who she truly thought he was?

More importantly, was she right about him?

They joined the party in the den, where they sat on the sofa together, ate cake, and talked to some of the other guests. He'd felt strange being the only man at the shower, which made him wonder why his sister had invited him. But when he saw his sister grinning at him from across the room, it hit him — Layla was still holding on to the crazy idea that he and Dakota could rekindle their romance.

When the party ended, Hudson helped clean up the kitchen while Layla said goodbye to her guests. Dakota had disappointed him by slipping away before he'd had a chance to say goodbye. Had she deliberately left when he wasn't paying attention? Had she been that disgusted with him after telling him he only cared about money?

"There's a box for you in my craft room, Hud," Aunt Trudy said, setting a serving tray in the cabinet. "I found a photo album I want you to have."

"Okay. Thanks." Hudson dropped a handful of utensils into the dishwasher.

"You and Dakota were getting awfully cozy out on the deck earlier."

He shrugged. "We were just talking."

"Oh." She sounded disappointed.

He glanced at her. She looked disappointed too.

They worked in silence for a few moments as she washed another serving tray and he stacked the dishes in the dishwasher.

Then he looked over at her again. "Did Layla invite me because of Dakota?"

Trudy paused long enough that Hud thought she wouldn't answer his question. Finally she said, "Well, she's determined to get you two back together."

"Not gonna happen. I've already made that clear."

"It's obvious you still care for each other. I'm sure even a stranger would pick up on the chemistry between you two." She dried the serving platter and set it next to the sink.

"She's seeing someone, Aunt Trudy." He

leaned back against the counter, and when she gave him a disbelieving look, he added, "Dakota has a boyfriend. I've met him."

His aunt waved him off. "That might be true, sweetie, but the intensity I saw in y'all's eyes for each other out there on the deck is something very special. It reminded me of your younger years."

"That was a long time ago." He picked up a few glasses and added them to the top rack. "Plus, I'm not staying here. I've decided to go to Bahrain."

"Blah, blah, blah." She turned and jammed her hands on her hips. "Hudson Nathaniel Garrity," his aunt began, "don't you think it's time for you to stop running?"

He bristled at her words. "I'm not running."

"Are you sure about that? You need to stop trying to prove that you've done enough to take care of your sister and me. You've done right by your parents, Hudson. It's time you stopped running from your feelings for Dakota and faced them instead."

"Running from my feelings for Dakota?" He scoffed. "She *dumped* me without any explanation, remember?"

Aunt Trudy's expression warmed. "Of course I remember, but did you ever ask her why?"

"She said it was over. What else was there to ask?"

"Maybe you didn't ask her because you were too afraid to fight for her and still lose her in the end."

"Aunt Trudy, she made it clear that she'd made up her mind about me. She just didn't love me." He shrugged as if Dakota's rejection hadn't permanently scarred his heart.

"Hudson, listen to me," she began. "After you left, you never came home for Thanksgivings. At Christmas, you never stayed here more than four days. And you also avoided your ten-year class reunion. You always tell me you're too busy working to spend more time with your family, and I understand that you have an important job — but even CEOs take some time off to recharge their batteries." She took a step toward him. "I believe the true reason you didn't want to come for extended periods of time is because you were trying to avoid Dakota. If that's not running away, sweetie, then I don't know what is."

He stared at her as her words soaked through him, but then he shook them off. She was wrong. He didn't belong in Dakota's life any more than he belonged in Flowering Grove.

"Let's finish these dishes," he muttered before turning his attention back to the sink.

Later that evening, Dakota stood in her brother's backyard and aimed her phone at Skye and Gunner as the couple posed for prom pictures.

Skye's thick long hair fell in curls past her shoulders, and her long pink A-line gown fit her perfectly. The V-neck bodice was adorned with an embroidered lace applique, thin straps, and a laced back that complemented her tall, youthful figure. She looked as if she'd just walked off the pages of a fashion magazine.

Gunner was handsome in a gray suit that made the most of his tall muscular build, short blond hair, and bright-green eyes. He seemed completely relaxed resting his hand on her waist as they posed and smiled with three other couples in front of Eileen's colorful flower garden.

"They make the cutest couple," Mom gushed while snapping photos on her phone.

Dakota beamed at her mother and sister-in-law. "I definitely agree."

She took more photos of the posing couples, and when Gunner slipped a corsage onto Skye's dainty wrist, Dakota couldn't help but ponder her conversation with

Hudson at the bridal shower — how they'd sat close together on the glider and how he'd opened up to her about the issues Layla had encountered after he'd left for New York.

She'd felt close to him again, but she knew it was all a façade. She'd meant what she said when she accused him of only caring about money. She missed the man he'd once been, back when they were in love. Back then they'd dreamed of a future together, in the days when his focus was on his family and his former wife-to-be.

But none of that mattered now. Soon he'd leave, and she'd stay behind in her hometown — trying to reckon how to make heads or tails of her business woes.

She tried to bypass her worries while the young couples prepared to leave for the night. Then she walked with Skye to Gunner's sports car.

"Skye, you're absolutely gorgeous." Dakota pulled her niece in for a hug. "Have fun tonight."

"I will, Auntie." Skye touched her shoulder. "Thank you for the dress. I love it."

"It was made for you, sweetie." Dakota stepped out of the way and took a few more photos of Skye saying goodbye to her grandparents, parents, and younger siblings. Her chest squeezed at the tender scene.

"You okay?" Nick asked, sidling up to her.

Dakota nodded. "Yeah."

He shook his head and grinned. "You never were a very good liar." He pointed to the porch. "Sit with me."

They sank down beside each other on rocking chairs and peered out over the driveway, where Mom, Dad, and Eileen were engrossed in a conversation with a neighbor and Aubrey and Kevin stood nearby looking bored.

"Skye mentioned you're still working ridiculously long hours."

Dakota pushed an errant tendril of hair behind her ear.

"I try not to get caught up in the gossip, but I heard Skye tell Eileen that you broke up with her art teacher."

"That's all true."

"Are you okay?"

"Yeah. It was my call." She brushed her hands down her green sundress.

"Still, you look stressed." Nick gave her a hesitant expression. "Want to talk about it?"

"I'm really fine," she fibbed, peering out to where Aubrey had begun turning cartwheels on the front lawn. "I never could master the cartwheel."

"She definitely doesn't get her talent from

me," Nick quipped. "But you are one heck of a roller skater, so not all Jamisons are unathletic klutzes."

Dakota grinned. "Thanks."

His smile flattened. "Eileen says I owe you an apology."

"For what?"

"For inviting Hud to stay for supper last Sunday. She insists I made supper awkward by having your ex there." Nick held his hands up. "I'm sorry. I know I ordered you around a lot and gave you tons of unsolicited advice when you were younger because I thought I was so much wiser than you. I wasn't trying to be your know-it-all brother again. I honestly thought inviting Hud to join us would be okay, but apparently I was mistaken."

"You did nothing wrong. In fact, that's what has me tied up in knots. I broke up with Parker because I can't stop thinking about Hud, but I know it could never work between us."

"Why?"

"Because he chose his career over me once, and he'd probably do it again." She moved her finger over the white-painted chair arm. "We want different things. I want a life here in Flowering Grove, and he wants to run another company in the Middle East."

Nick scratched the scruff on his neck.

"If he really loved me seven years ago, he would've kept the promise he made when he gave me a diamond ring. He would've chosen a life with me instead of a fancy life in Manhattan."

"Dakota, I know how you get when you're fixated on something, so I need to ask you a question."

"Go ahead."

"Did you ever tell Hud *exactly* what you wanted?"

She swallowed. "No."

"Maybe it's time you had an honest conversation with him."

Dakota stared at him as his words took hold. An honest conversation was what she was trying to have with Hudson at the bridal shower. She had been pushing him to be honest with her and himself about why he was really against Layla's wedding. It was obvious to Dakota that he didn't want to let his little sister go. And she suddenly saw the hypocrisy of how she'd never been honest with Hudson about their breakup.

"Who wants pizza?" Eileen called, and Aubrey and Kevin started cheering.

Nick stood. "That's my cue to order supper."

While her brother disappeared into the house, Dakota began to wonder if things could have ended differently between her and Hudson seven years ago if she'd just told him the truth about her dreams.

Chapter 20

Two weeks later, the sound of the bell at the front of the store startled Dakota. It was a Thursday afternoon, and she was working on Layla's gown in the back room. She rushed to the store floor and stopped where Hudson stood by the counter, flanked by Shane and his three groomsmen. She rubbed her eyes and hoped she looked alive. She'd worked late the night before and felt as if she hadn't quite woken up this morning. In fact, she'd even managed to pour salt instead of sweetener into her coffee.

A warm glow filled her as she took in Hud's worn jeans and short-sleeved collared shirt, which sported the logo for Wallace Construction where the breast pocket would've been. His strong jaw was covered in a few days' worth of scruff that she longed to run her fingers over. She mentally pulled herself off the ledge and smiled at the men.

"You must be here for your final fittings," she said, and they all nodded.

"My dad said he'd come tomorrow," Shane said. "He couldn't get away from the office today."

"That's no problem at all. Give me a moment and I'll just grab your tuxes."

She retrieved the garment bags and handed them out before the men disappeared into the dressing rooms. Then, one by one, they came to stand by the platform, and her stomach pitched. The sleeves on Shane's coat were too long, while his best friend Dalton's sleeves were too short. Steve, the groomsman, had trousers so loose he had to hold them up, and to add to her embarrassment, his coat was too tight. Even Hudson's trousers needed hemming.

Oh no.

She'd really messed up this time. The lack of sleep was taking a toll on her, affecting her job quality *and* her reputation.

Heat infused her cheeks as the men stared at her. "I'm — I'm so sorry. I'll make it right." She pointed to the groom. "Shane, let's get your sleeves fixed first. I'll grab my supplies."

She pinned Shane's sleeves and then checked his trousers. After dealing with the issues with Dalton's and Steve's tuxes,

Hudson climbed up on the podium.

Dakota kept her focus on the hemline while working to calm her fluttering nerves.

"Where's Skye?" Hudson asked as she carefully pinned the hem.

"She had a meeting after school."

He was silent for a moment. "Everything all right?"

"Just fine," she quipped. Inside, though, she was falling apart. Having to work on these tuxes again would set her behind, and she still was dealing with final adjustments to Layla's gown. "I can't believe it's the middle of May already. The wedding is only a few weeks away. I'll get these tuxes fixed quickly though."

When she pushed another pin through the material, she missed her mark and stabbed herself. "Ow!" she hollered before shaking her hand and sticking her throbbing finger in her mouth.

"You okay?" he asked, his expression warming with concern.

She nodded and wiped her finger on a tissue.

"Those dark circles under your eyes tell me you're not sleeping, and it's not like you to mess up tailoring."

She returned her focus to his hem. He was right. She hadn't been sleeping, but she couldn't give him the satisfaction of admitting it out loud.

"Have you thought about that loan I offered for the store?"

Anger sluiced through her, and she glared up at him. "Are you trying to throw money at me like you throw money at everyone else?"

"You're really bringing that up again, huh? That all I care about is money?"

"Obviously! Your solution for every problem is to pay for it." Her voice was louder than she'd planned, and when she turned around, she found Shane and his friends staring at her. Her face was so hot she thought it might combust, and her hands quaked as she checked the cuffs on his jacket and the waist of his trousers.

An instrumental version of Alison Krauss's "When You Say Nothing at All" began to play through the sound system, but she ignored it. "You're all set. I'll just take care of the hem on your trousers."

Hudson's face was twisted with a glower.

"You found a house?" Dakota heard one of the groomsmen ask Shane.

Hud's head snapped toward the groomsmen.

"Shh," Shane hissed. "Yeah, I'm going to show it to Layla and see if she likes it. I'm already approved for the loan, and my folks are helping with the down payment."

Hudson's eyes homed in on his future brother-in-law. "Shane, did I hear you say you found a house?"

Shane shot his friend a sharp look before he turned toward Hudson. His expression sparked. "Yeah."

"Where is it?" Hudson asked.

Shane licked his lips. "It's on Catawba Avenue near Red Rock Court."

"How many bedrooms?"

"Two."

"Bathrooms?"

Shane crossed his arms over his chest. "One and a half."

"Huh." Hudson's expression was stern. "Square footage?"

"A little under eleven hundred."

Hudson shook his head. "That's a bit small, don't you think, Shane?"

Anger flashed in Shane's eyes. Dakota could almost feel the tension mounting between the men, and she couldn't stay silent any longer.

"Stop it, Hud." She rested her hand on his wrist and pulled him toward her. "Don't grill Shane that way."

His brow puckered. "What?"

"You sound like a father chastising his son."

Hudson's blue eyes smoldered. "He's marrying my sister. I need to make sure she's well taken care of. That's my job."

"No, it's not. It's your job to love her and support her decisions. Stop standing in the way and let her and Shane live their lives."

"You need to stay out of this," Hudson told her.

She shook her head. "No, *you* need to stay out of Shane and Layla's business."

One of the groomsmen grasped Shane's shoulder. "Listen, I need to get back to work. We can talk about the bachelor party plans later."

The other two groomsmen agreed.

Shane nodded and cast his eyes toward Dakota. "Thanks, Dakota. I'll see you later."

She waved to the men before they disappeared out the door. Then she spun back to Hudson. "Back off of them, Hud, or you'll lose your sister forever."

"You don't know everything I've had to deal with over the years with Layla," he snapped.

"What does that mean?" she asked.

"She's given exes money before, and I've had to bail her out again and again. This could end the same way for her. If they get tied up in a house and default on the loan, then I might be the one bailing her out again — only this time I'll be paying for a divorce too. Her credit will be wrecked to boot." He studied Dakota before he added, "What do you know about getting married anyway?"

Fury burned through her. "You need to leave, Hud." She pointed toward the door. "Hang your tux in the changing room, and I'll take care of it." Then she marched toward the back of the store, her body vibrating.

"We found a house, and it's so cute," Layla told Dakota and Kayleigh on Friday night as they sat together in a booth at the rink. "It has two bedrooms and the cutest little kitchen and den. It's just what we need." She pulled out her phone and scrolled through photos of the happy little yellow house and its modest backyard.

Kayleigh touched her shoulder. "That's so exciting, Layla."

"I agree," Dakota said, pretending she didn't already know about the house.

"But the best part is that we made an offer, and they accepted it."

"Congratulations," Kayleigh told her. She pointed to a photo of the front of the house.

"It looks like the previous owner planted a garden. Look at those pink roses."

"Shane says they're Queen Anne roses. My favorite." Layla beamed.

Dakota leaned over. "It's perfect, Layla. I'm so happy for you."

"Thanks. We showed it to Shane's parents, and they love it. In fact, they offered to help us with the down payment as part of our wedding gift since Hud is paying for everything else." Her smile faded a bit as she said the words.

"That's very generous," Dakota said, and Kayleigh agreed.

"We haven't showed it to Hud yet. Shane said he wanted to wait, but I'm not sure why."

Dakota knew why. She could still see the resentment in Shane's eyes while Hudson grilled him about the house.

Layla set her phone on the table and rested her chin on her palm. "I can't believe I'll be married in three weeks. It seems like just yesterday Shane and I met at the coffee shop. I had accidentally taken his coffee, and when he asked for it back, we both laughed. Then he asked me out, and we spent the entire evening together. I'd seen him around in high school, but we never really talked. But that night it was as if we'd known each other forever. I had a hunch from that night that he was the one. It was so magical." She sighed. "I can't wait to be his wife."

Dakota and Kayleigh shared a smile before Kayleigh took a sip of her Diet Coke.

"Whenever you have time, I'll need you to come in for one last fitting," Dakota told her. "The gown is almost done."

"Awesome. I'll text you to make an appointment. I can't wait to see the finished product."

"I think you'll be pleased." Dakota moved her fingers over her cup. "I finished the beading last night. It was more challenging than I expected."

"I really appreciate it, Dakota. You're the best."

Dakota tried to force a smile, but a yawn overtook her. She pressed her hand to her mouth, then sipped more of her own Diet Coke. If only the caffeine would give her the jolt of energy she needed.

"Oh, Shane's here. Gotta go!" Layla scooted to the end of the bench, then skated off to meet her fiancé by the snack bar.

"Oh, to be young and in love," Kayleigh sang.

Dakota shook her head.

"What's that look for?" Kayleigh leaned

forward.

Dakota slumped back in the seat. "I have a feeling Hud is going to ruin the house for Layla." She explained the conversation she witnessed at the boutique during the tuxedo fittings. "I told Hud to back off, but he wouldn't listen. We actually argued about it, and I told him to leave my store." She shared more details of the incident. "I can't believe I lost my cool in front of Shane and his friends. So embarrassing."

Dakota covered her face with her hands. "I feel like I'm falling apart. I spilled hot coffee all over my suit this morning. It's a good thing I keep a few extra outfits at the store. At least I didn't pour salt into my coffee again." She recoiled at the memory. "Anyway, I just can't stop thinking about how angry Hud made me. I feel like I don't know him anymore. All he cares about is money."

"Do you really think that's true?" Kayleigh asked.

Dakota took another sip of Diet Coke, and her lips twisted. "He keeps offering me a loan to help me out. He thinks that if he throws money at people, it will make everything better. It's like he's trying to prove something." She moved her hand over the cool tabletop. "Maybe he thinks offering money instead of dealing with his real issues will solve all of his problems."

Kayleigh moved her straw up and down in her cup, and the straw squeaked in response.

She could almost hear her best friend's opinions churning in her head. "Just say it, Kay."

"You still care about him," Kayleigh said.

"No, I don't. I thought I did before, but the way he wants to use money to control everything, including his sister, makes me nuts."

Kayleigh shook her finger at Dakota. "Dakota, he's done more than that." She started counting off on her fingers. "He took care of you after you crashed while skating. He found Trouble when he went missing. He fixed your kitchen cabinets. He loaned you a propane tank when your family showed up for a cookout you never expected. And we can't forget that he also changed your tire when you were running late to an appointment."

"Yeah, he did." Dakota blew out a dreamy sigh and rested her chin on her palm.

"You still love him."

"He broke my heart once. Why would I risk it again?"

Kayleigh lifted one shoulder in a half

shrug. "Unfortunately, we can't help who we love."

"I don't love him," Dakota insisted.

"Then you need to stay out of his business." Kayleigh leaned forward and tapped the table. "You're getting way too involved with Hud and his family."

"You're absolutely right."

Kayleigh pushed herself up from the bench. "I need to go find my daughter. Last I saw, she was skating with Anissa."

"I'll come with you." Dakota followed and contemplated her best friend's advice. For many reasons, she really should stay out of Hudson's family issues. She spotted Gavin sitting in a booth with his wife, but there was no sign of her ex. And that was a good thing.

"So — we close in a couple of weeks." Layla held Shane's hand, and together they stood in the middle of the house's small den the following afternoon. "Isn't it perfect?"

Hudson scanned the tiny room, which melted into a small dining area off a kitchen too small for even a table with two chairs. He swept his fingers over his chin and peered out the side window. The house next door was so close that the owners would most likely hear him if he yelled hello to them without opening the window. In fact, he might hear their response too.

He'd been surprised when Layla insisted he come with her and Shane to visit the house with Aunt Trudy. And from the dirty looks Shane had been shooting his way, it was obvious his future brother-in-law was still irritable after their heated discussion at the bridal shop. He recalled how Dakota had thrown him out of the store, and shame stabbed him. He shouldn't have made that impudent remark about Dakota not knowing anything about getting married, but he couldn't stop it from slipping past his lips.

Aunt Trudy engulfed Layla in a hug. "I think it's the perfect starter home for you two."

"I'm so glad you agree." Closing her eyes, Layla held on to their aunt.

Shane smiled at Aunt Trudy. "Thank you, Ms. Garrity."

"I told you to call me Aunt Trudy, sweetheart." She touched his cheek.

Layla pointed out the front window. "Did you see those Queen Anne roses? I'm going to add more flowers and maybe even a birdbath. I also saw these super-cute garden gnomes that would look adorable there too." Then she laughed. "What am I saying? You're the landscaper, Shane. I'm sure you could do a much better job than me with the yard."

"Whatever makes you happy, Layla," he told her. "I may have to draw the line at garden gnomes though."

Layla and Aunt Trudy laughed, but Shane shot Hudson another sharp look.

Ignoring him, Hudson stuck his hands in the pockets of his shorts and peered down the hallway that led to two small bedrooms and a half bath. He snuck down the hallway and peeked into each room. He couldn't imagine more than a single bed and a dresser fitting into the spare room, and a double bed with two dressers would certainly clog the second room.

He frowned. As he suspected, this place was much too small.

"What do you think, Hud?"

He pivoted to where Layla leaned on the doorway, looking expectant. Her fiancé stood behind her with an expression that said, "I dare you to break her heart."

Hudson rocked back on his heels. "It's . . . cozy."

"Thanks." Layla's laugh seemed nervous.

"But it's a little small."

"Don't start." Shane's tone was bitter.

"Why don't you let me buy you a house?" Hudson offered.

Aunt Trudy shook her head from the other side of the room.

"I knew you couldn't keep your arrogant opinions to yourself." Shane spat out the words as if they tasted rancid.

Layla placed her hand on Shane's chest, then turned and gave Hudson a tight smile. "That's not necessary, Hud."

"Just hear me out." Hudson held up his hand. "I checked out real estate listings last night, and there's a nice four-bedroom house for sale on the other side of town. I can pay cash. You'd only have to worry about the maintenance, insurance, and taxes, and if you need help —"

"No." Shane took a step toward him. "We are capable of buying our own house. But thanks *oh* so much." His lips tipped up in a sardonic smile.

"Are you really capable of it though?" Hudson held his arms out. "This place is barely big enough for the two of you. What happens when you have a family?"

Shane shook a finger in Hudson's face. "I am so sick of you and your smug comments. You think you're better than everyone else because you have money. Well, money doesn't buy you class."

Hudson glared at him and tried to act like the comment didn't sting.

"All you want is to control your sister, but she's ready to live her own life. If this is the house she wants, accept it." His voice held a harsh edge.

"It's not about control," Hudson retorted. "I'm trying to make sure she can support herself."

"I've already told you we're going to support each other." Shane moved closer. He stood a couple inches shorter than Hudson, scowling up at him.

"What if one of you were to get hurt or sick?" Hudson made a sweeping gesture toward his sister. "I've seen her make some pretty reckless, impulsive decisions over the years. One mistake can ruin you both financially. That's why living paycheck to paycheck isn't good enough."

Shane was nearly nose to nose with him. "Is *anything* ever good enough for you? Does *anyone* meet your highfalutin standards?" He jammed a finger at Hudson's chest. "You know what, Hudson? You throw your money around like it will solve your problems, but you're the one who's alone."

Hudson balled his hands into fists. Oh, he'd had enough of this guy.

Layla took Shane's arm and tugged him back a couple of steps. "Thanks for your generous offer, Hud, but this is the house we've chosen, and we'd like to buy it ourselves."

"Whatever you say," Hudson muttered.

Aunt Trudy clasped her hands together, looking desperate. "How about we all go to lunch?"

Layla took Shane's hand and steered him toward the front door. "Great idea."

Later that afternoon, Hudson sat behind the wheel and glanced over to where Layla kissed Shane goodbye. They'd had an awkward drive in Hudson's SUV to the restaurant and then a much-too-long lunch during which Aunt Trudy and Layla talked on and on about wedding plans. Shane spent most of his time staring down at his plate when he wasn't shooting daggers at Hudson with his eyes.

The ride from the restaurant to Aunt Trudy's house had been just as uncomfortable if not worse. Since Layla and their aunt seemed to have run out of things to discuss, Hudson had turned on the radio — but every time he looked into his rearview mirror, he found Shane silently glaring at his reflection.

As soon as Hudson had parked his SUV in the driveway, Shane had leapt from the car as if his life depended on it. Layla followed close behind him, and now it seemed she was trying to calm him as he sat in his truck.

"You need to back off," Aunt Trudy warned Hud.

He'd been expecting his aunt to share her thoughts. "I'm just trying to help."

"But your idea of helping is actually causing more harm than good." Aunt Trudy's expression seemed sad instead of angry. "Hudson, you show your love by buying things for Layla and me, but honestly, we love you for *you,* not for the things you can give us with your money."

He grasped the steering wheel.

"Do you want to start off Layla's marriage estranged from your brother-in-law?"

Hudson remained silent.

"If Layla has to choose between her husband and her brother, she'll choose her husband every time."

Hudson pushed the door open. "That won't be necessary."

"Wait." Aunt Trudy touched his arm. "Why were you looking at Flowering Grove real estate in the first place?"

Hudson shrugged.

"Were you looking for a place for yourself or just trying to prove to Shane that you can provide a better life for your sister than he can?"

"I'm not trying to prove anything to Shane." He paused for a moment. "You told me he had gotten expelled from high school. He was deep into drugs and alcohol, and it took him a while to get his life on track — to get his GED and find a trade." He licked his lips. "What if he relapses and takes Layla with him? What if she gets hooked on drugs and alcohol again?" His voice sounded raspy.

Aunt Trudy shook her head. "You've got to trust your sister to make the best decisions for herself. She was in a bad place in high school, but that's not who she is anymore. She's grown up, and you need to accept that. Stop punishing her for her past, Hud. If you keep interfering, you *will* lose her, and that will devastate both you and her, not to mention me."

Hudson climbed out of the car and shut the door.

Layla stood up on her tiptoes and kissed Shane while he sat in the driver's seat of his truck. Then he closed the door, started the engine, and backed down the driveway toward the road. Layla waved goodbye to him and then spun to face her brother.

"Layla," Hud said.

"I'm not a little girl anymore." She

marched over to him. "If I want to buy a house with my fiancé, then I will, and you can't stop me."

"I can get you a bigger house that will give you and Shane room to grow."

"But I want *my* house, the one Shane and I chose *together.* Why can't you understand that?"

"But if I can help you —"

"Stop trying to help me!" Her cheeks reddened. "This is *my* life, Hud."

Hudson stuck his hands in his pockets as aggravation surged in his chest. "I only want what's best for you, Layla. That's all. I don't understand what's wrong with that."

"Why are you so insistent on rejecting every single thing Shane and I do?"

"I'm not."

She touched her forehead. "You're always trying to force us to do things your way."

"That's not true."

She sighed. "Forget it."

As she turned and started toward their aunt's house, Hudson thought back to his conversations with Dakota and realized she'd said the same things to him.

Irritation flooded him. He just couldn't deal with it now. They were both wrong. He wasn't trying to control his sister; he was only taking care of her. Surely she'd come around to that truth eventually.

Chapter 21

Dakota sat at her office desk in the store Tuesday midmorning. She stared down at the stack of bills she couldn't pay, then scrutinized her meager bank account on her laptop screen. When she thought she heard a strange noise, her eyes scanned her office.

Pushing the thought aside, she turned her attention back to her financials. She had considered calling her father and asking for help. Then a memory of Hudson offering her a loan filled her mind, and she growled out her exasperation. She couldn't even think about him right now. She had to *stop* thinking about him.

She heard the odd noise again. *Was that a drip?*

Her stomach dropped. *Oh no.*

Dakota jumped up and scanned her office. Sure enough, drops of water were falling from the ceiling.

"Not again!" She ran to the supply closet,

found two buckets, and hightailed it back to her office. She placed the buckets under where the water had started leaking from the ceiling, then yanked her phone from her pocket. She scrolled until she found the name of the plumber who had fixed the pipes last time. Then she stopped. Could she trust him again or not? Perhaps it was time to get her landlord involved and insist she take care of the issues with the building, despite what the lease stated. She pulled up her landlord's number and poised her finger over the phone.

The bell at the front of the store rang, and Dakota rested her hand on her collarbone. She had to help her customer, and then she would deal with this disaster. But how would she pay a plumber? And how would she find someone she could trust? And would her landlord do the right thing this time?

She plastered a smile on her face before marching out front, where she found a scowling Layla. "Hi, Dakota. I'm here for my last fitting."

Worry sliced through her. She couldn't remember a time when she'd ever seen Hudson's younger sister looking so glum. "Layla, are you okay?"

"I'm just over my brother." She started

toward the dressing rooms.

"I'll grab your gown." Dakota retrieved the wardrobe bag and brought it to Layla.

Layla donned the gown and stood on the platform, and Dakota gasped as Layla moved back and forth, studying her reflection in the mirror.

"Oh my goodness, Layla." Her eyes stung. "You are stunning."

Layla met her gaze in the reflection, and her lips turned up in a smile. "I love it, Dakota. Do you have that photo of my parents?"

"One sec." Dakota rushed to the back to fetch the photo and brought it back to Layla in the dressing area. "What do you think?"

Layla nodded. "It's perfect. Thank you."

Dakota moved around the platform, making sure the hem and train were right.

As Dakota finished her inspection of the gown, Layla's joy seemed to diminish. "Hud is really getting on my last nerve," she said. "Shane and I took him and my aunt to see the house on Saturday, and Hud just offered to buy us a bigger house. Shane was furious. I've never seen him that angry. I was afraid they were going to come to blows."

Dakota began pinning the train where it

needed a slight adjustment. "That's terrible."

"Oh, that's not the worst of it. He said he'd pay cash for the house and let us take over the taxes, insurance, and maintenance. He's always bossed me around, but I can't take it anymore. I keep asking him to just let me grow up, but he thinks I'm too immature to make my own decisions."

"I can relate."

Layla's gaze snapped to Dakota's. "How?"

"My brother, Nick, is twelve years older than me, and he used to boss me around too." Dakota slipped another pin in the train, and Layla shifted her weight on the podium. "Don't move, okay? I might accidentally stick you."

Layla grimaced. "Sorry. But what were you saying about Nick?"

"When I was a kid, he'd come home from college and bark orders at me. He used to check my homework, grill me about my friends, tell me I filled the dishwasher wrong — things like that."

"How'd you get him to stop?" Layla seemed fascinated.

"My folks finally said it wasn't his job to be my third parent." Dakota put the last pin in the train and began adjusting the bustle.

Layla rested her hand on her hip. "I appreciate all Hud has done for me. He's bought me cars, paid for my college, sent me money for clothes and books, and even started a savings account for me."

"Wow." Dakota stopped working and peered up at her again. "I had no idea he did all of that for you."

"I know, I know. I sound like a brat," Layla said. "I do appreciate it all. Really, I do, Dakota, but I'm old enough to decide what's right for me and my future, and if I want to buy a small house with my future husband, then I should be able to do that without him telling me I need something better or different."

"That's very true."

"With Hud, everything comes down to money. But that's not what it's all about. It's about living. I want a family of my own. I want to raise kids. I want to have everything I never had." She sniffed and wiped her eyes.

Dakota stood and patted Layla's shoulder. "I know you do, sweetie, and you're entitled to that."

"I love my aunt. She's the mom I never had. But I want to raise my own family with two parents."

Dakota took Layla's hand in hers and gave it a gentle squeeze. This was exactly what she'd feared — that Hudson would overstep and cause major problems for Layla and possibly risk ruining his relationship with her.

Layla's eyes glimmered. "He's just so stubborn." Her words came out in a croak. "It's like he's not listening, and he doesn't respect me. He thinks I'm still a lost teenager even though I've grown up."

"I'm sorry he has you so upset." She handed Layla a tissue from a nearby box, then stood back and admired the gown. "Layla, you look like a princess. I can't wait to see you walking down that aisle toward your sweetheart."

Layla dabbed her nose with the tissue, then swished the dress back and forth. "Thank you so much, Dakota."

"You're welcome."

Layla stepped down from the platform. "You know, Hud doesn't have a date for the wedding . . ." She shook her head. "Never mind."

"I'm sure he'll find one," Dakota said, ignoring the pang in her heart as she spoke the words.

"I don't care if he does or doesn't." Layla harrumphed, then lifted the front of her gown and disappeared into a dressing room.

As Layla changed, Dakota's attention

turned back toward the pressing problem she had in the back. Once Layla was out of the store, she'd try to figure out what to do about her plumbing issue — again!

"Hey, Auntie," Skye called when she came into the office later that afternoon. "I had the craziest day. I can't believe we have finals coming up next week." She paused in the doorway. "Wait. Did the pipes burst again?"

Dakota pointed toward the line of buckets in her office, along with the furniture that she'd covered with plastic. Her shoulders withered. "I checked with my landlord, and she insists the leak and damage are all my responsibility, which is what it says in the lease. So I've called three plumbers so far, but no one can come before next week. I'm at my wits' end."

"Have you reached out to Grandpa and asked him for help?"

Dakota swiped her fingers under her eyes, hoping she didn't smudge her makeup. "Not yet."

"Call him now. He'll know what to do." Skye yanked her phone from her back pocket. "I'll dial him, and we can both talk to him on speaker."

"No, Skye."

"Why not?"

"Because I can handle this myself. This is my business."

Skye folded her arms over her middle. "Why won't you listen to me?"

"I am listening to you. I'm just telling you I need to handle this my way."

"But your way isn't working. Don't you see that?" Skye gestured around the room. "The ceiling is falling in on us. It's time you got someone to help."

Dakota glowered. "I just told you that I've been calling plumbers."

"But you need to call Grandpa."

Dakota sighed. "Honey, there's no way that —"

"He can help, Auntie. I know he can."

Dakota shook her head. "I can handle this myself."

"No, you can't." Skye's dark eyes narrowed. When her eyes brimmed with tears, she brushed them away. "Your whole problem is that you just won't listen to anyone else. No matter how hard I try to help you, you tell me I'm wrong."

"That's not true."

"It is. You ignore what I say because you think I'm a dumb sixteen-year-old."

"Sweetie, I would never —"

"Don't call me *sweetie*!" Skye's voice

sounded thready. "I can't talk to you because you won't listen, so why should I even try?" She wrenched her backpack up from the floor. "I give up. It's not worth it."

Dakota faltered and her mouth dropped open. "What?"

"You heard me." Tears streamed down her pink cheeks. "I quit."

Dakota's chest clutched. "What?"

"I said I quit!" With that, Skye turned and stomped out of the store.

Dakota stared after her as her world began to crumble.

"Isn't that your sister?" Gavin asked Hudson. The men stood in the middle of the nearly completed restaurant site the following afternoon, the scent of paint hovering in the air. The rest of the construction crew worked at giving the newly built restaurant a fresh coat of bright-white paint.

Hudson turned toward the doorway, where Layla stood. Dressed in purple scrubs, she hugged her arms to her chest. Her eyes were red and puffy, and her expression was grave. A cold sensation washed over him as he took off toward her. "Layla, what's wrong?"

"I'll tell you what's wrong." Her eyes smoldered with fire. "You ruined my life!"

she yelled, and he flinched at her sharp tone.

A hush settled over the worksite, and everyone turned to stare.

"What are you talking about?"

She sniffed and wiped her eyes. "Because of you my wedding is canceled." Her lips trembled. "I guess you got what you wanted. That was your plan all along, wasn't it? You wanted to blow up my life. Well, congratulations, Hud. You did it." More tears poured down her face.

"The wedding is canceled?" He should be ecstatic at the news. Instead he was cemented in place, witnessing his sister's pain.

"Yes! Because of you!" When he tried to reach for her, she pushed him away. "Shane came to see me at work today. He said he couldn't take it anymore. He said he's tired of your issues with money. He told me you went to see him at work last month and grilled him about making enough money to support me. He said he's done arguing with you about how money is the most important thing in life. Is that true?"

"Yes, but I was just trying —"

"You betrayed me, Hud. How could you go behind my back and tell my fiancé he wasn't capable of caring for me?" She pointed to herself. "Now he doesn't want to be with me because he thinks my family will always judge him."

A ball of lead formed in his stomach. *What have I done?* "No, that's not it. It's more than that. I'm worried he'll be a bad influence on you."

She squinted at him. "What does that even mean?"

"You both made some big mistakes in high school. What if he falls back into that pattern and takes you with him? I couldn't bear seeing you like that again."

She gasped. "How could you even think that about me after all I've accomplished in my life since then? You're overbearing, intrusive, and controlling, and you're done controlling me."

Hudson opened and closed his mouth. "Layla, I'm sorry, but —"

"Sorry isn't good enough." She sniffed and swiped away more tears. "I thought you were my hero. I believed you would always look out for me and take care of me."

"I am. You're my baby sister. I would do anything for you."

"Except support my choices." She shook her head. "I'm done with you, Hud." She turned and marched out of the restaurant.

Hudson spun toward Gavin, who watched him with his eyes wide. "I need to go."

"Go on." Gavin waved him off.

Hudson took off running down the street to the parking lot where Layla was climbing into her car. "Layla! Wait!"

His sister turned to face him, her visage pale and ominous.

"Please wait." He held his hands up to her. "Let's talk about this."

She slammed her car door closed and leaned against it. "Talk."

"Everything I've ever done was to take care of you. I wanted you to have a stable life." He blew out a shaky breath. "My earliest memories of Mom and Dad were pure chaos. I wanted to give you security — something I never had."

"You know, I'm glad you brought that up, Hud." She crossed her arms over her chest. "Tell me something. Why haven't we ever talked about Mom and Dad?"

Where'd that come from? "What do you mean?"

"You've never wanted to discuss them. Every time I bring them up, you change the subject."

"No, I don't."

"Yes, you do." She shook a finger at him. "I remember when I was five, and I asked you what Mom looked like. You showed me their wedding picture."

"Okay . . ." He tried to read her hidden meaning. "Why was that the wrong answer?"

She narrowed her eyes. "Then I asked you what Mom sounded like. What did Mom like to sing? What was her favorite color? And you told me you had to do your math homework. Whenever I asked you about Mom and Dad, you had a reason not to answer." She counted his offenses off on her fingers. "You were too busy. You couldn't remember. You had homework to do. You were too tired. Or, my personal favorite, you just weren't in the mood to discuss them."

Guilt punched him in the gut. "I'm sorry, but I don't remember any of this. I never realized I was doing this to you."

"You know, you're so worried I'm going to fall back into my bad habits. Well, did you ever wonder *why* I used alcohol and drugs and cut classes?"

"Of course I did. I spent hours on the phone with your guidance counselor trying to figure out what was going on with you."

"You took off to start a new life, and I felt so alone." Her voice cracked, and she cleared her throat. "You and I were orphans. Yes, Aunt Trudy did the best she could, but she's not our biological parent. You're the only other person who can relate to what it was like growing up without Mom and Dad, but you would never discuss it with me. And that's why I resorted to other methods — trying to find some relief from the constant hollowness and pain."

He was flummoxed. "I drove you to that?"

"You sure did. Then to make it worse, you forced me to discuss my feelings with a stranger. Do you know how hard that was for me?"

"But that's what the guidance counselor told us to do to help you. She said you needed a counselor."

"But I didn't need a stranger, Hud. I needed *you,*" she said, pointing at him, "but you were never available." Her voice rose. "Why is that, Hud? Why couldn't you ever open yourself up to me?"

He stared at her. "I-I-I don't know."

"Well, I sure do." She pulled her keys from her pocket and stood up straight. "You hide behind your money so you don't have to open up to anyone. You pretend that all you care about is 'taking care of me and Aunt Trudy,' " she said, making air quotes with her fingers. "But the truth is, all you care about is taking care of yourself, Hud."

"No, no, no." His throat caught. He moved toward her, but she put more distance between them. "What can I do to make this right? Tell me, and I'll do it," he pleaded. This was his worst nightmare. He couldn't lose her. "Do you want to talk about Mom and Dad now? What do you want to know?"

She took a deep, shaky breath. "It's too late. I thought I found my soul mate, the one person I could open up to completely. But you managed to ruin that for me. Now I'm alone again — all because of *you*." She opened her car door and climbed into the driver's seat.

"Layla, wait. Give me a chance, and I'll fix this. Don't go."

She faced him, her expression darkening. "You've intruded in my life for the last time. I don't need you anymore. And another thing. I give up on trying to get you and Dakota back together. I thought maybe if you realized what you'd left behind here in Flowering Grove, you would actually want to be a part of our family. But it's obvious you never will."

Layla started her car and drove away, leaving him standing in the parking lot.

Hudson felt as if the ground had opened up beneath him and was going to swallow him whole. He'd lost his sister, which meant he'd lost *everything*. He stared after her, his body slack, his mind buzzing with confusion and grief.

Without his sister and without a hope of working things out with Dakota, nothing was left for him in Flowering Grove. It was time to leave.

He dragged himself back into the restaurant and found Gavin, who looked concerned.

"Is everything all right?"

"No," Hudson said. "I need to resign."

"You sure?"

"Yeah. Thanks for the opportunity." He shook Gavin's hand.

Gavin patted his shoulder. "I'm going to miss you. You've done good work here."

Hudson nodded goodbye to his coworkers, then headed out of the restaurant and down the sidewalk toward his SUV. He sat in the driver's seat and typed out a text to Darren:

Hey. I'm ready for Bahrain. Send details.

Then he made his way toward the Airbnb for the last time. He was going to pack up and leave as soon as he could — getting as far away from Flowering Grove and his heartache as possible.

Chapter 22

"Dakota!" Layla burst through the front door of the store with tears streaming down her cheeks.

With a gasp, Dakota rushed toward her and gathered her into her arms. "Layla, sweetie, what happened?"

"My wedding is off. Canceled!" She sobbed into Dakota's shoulder.

"Oh no! That can't be true." Dakota rubbed her back as sadness rocked her. "Did you and Shane have an argument?"

Layla worked to get ahold of her emotions and sniffed. "No, it's worse than that."

"Come with me." Dakota led her to the sofa by the dressing rooms and they sat. "Take your time and tell me everything." Dakota handed Layla a box of tissues, and Layla wiped her eyes and nose.

Layla sniffed. "It's Hud. He ruined everything." She explained how she and Shane had an argument over Hudson's meddling, and how Shane canceled the wedding.

Dakota shook her head as she listened. Everything she had feared would come true had happened. "Layla, I'm so very sorry."

"So now I'm not getting married, and I don't need the dress." She blotted more tears with a fresh tissue. "Hud's impossible. I can't talk to him. No matter what I say, he won't listen to me. It's always a losing battle with him." She moved her fingers over the arm of the sofa. "I'm so heartbroken. I thought I'd be taking vows in two weeks and changing my name to Layla Simpson, but I've lost the love of my life. I don't know how to go on without him."

Dakota shifted closer to Layla and took her hand. "I'm sure you can work this out. Just give Shane time to calm down — then you can talk to him."

"No." Layla shook her head. "He said it's over." She rested her cheek on Dakota's shoulder as her sobs broke free.

Dakota rubbed her back again. "Shane's going to realize he needs you as much as you need him. You can't let Hud's criticisms break you up. And hopefully Hud will realize what a blockhead he's been."

"No, he won't." Layla ripped another tissue from the box. "He's completely into himself. I've been trying to get you and him together ever since he returned, but he can't see beyond himself. He's too self-centered to realize he could be happy with you in Flowering Grove. He'll never change."

Dakota tried to ignore the shiver that Layla's words sent through her. She wanted to believe that Hudson needed her and Flowering Grove, but she also knew he was determined to leave as fast as he could.

She gave Layla's shoulder a tender squeeze. "Honey, you can't give up that easily on Shane. You two are meant to be together."

"You think so?" Layla's expression reminded Dakota of a confused little girl looking for encouragement.

"Yes, I know it for a fact. I've seen you and Shane together, and I can see your love for each other radiating in your eyes and your smiles. You can't let him slip through your fingers. Forget what your brother says and just concentrate on each other and your future together."

"It's too late. The damage is done. And now I have to cancel my wedding. How will I even do that?" Her voice wobbled. "I'll have to ask Aunt Trudy to help me call everyone, but what do I say? Something like, 'This is Layla Garrity. My fiancé broke up with me because my brother's a jerk, and now the wedding is canceled'?" She sniffed and started to cry again, leaning against Dakota.

"Oh, sweetie." Dakota sighed. "It's going to be okay."

"No, it's not. Nothing will be okay ever again."

Dakota held her close, and her heart fractured as her friend cried. She knew what she had to do. She had to tell Hudson to fix this — and as soon as she could, she'd go and do just that.

Hudson dropped a book in a bag and brushed his hand over his face. Everything was in shambles. His sister didn't want him in her life, and he had no reason to stay in Flowering Grove. He just needed to keep moving forward, which was what he planned to do.

After he'd texted Darren, they'd talked on the phone and worked out the details. It was time to put Flowering Grove behind him for good. He was going to drive to New York tomorrow to tie up loose ends and meet with Darren before they headed to the Middle East.

If only he could convince himself he was making the right decision. The strange niggle of doubt lingered at the back of his mind. He set two more books in the duffel, and when a knock sounded on the front door, he headed to the foyer.

Pulling the door open, he found Dakota standing on the front porch with a scowl pinching her face. "Dakota. What a surprise."

"We need to talk."

He gestured for her to come in, and she followed him through the large foyer and into the enormous den. "Have a seat."

"No, thanks." She remained standing and crossed her arms. "Layla came to see me this afternoon."

He leaned against a pony wall separating the hallway from the den and studied her, waiting for her admonishment.

"She was really upset," she said.

He swallowed. "And I'm sure she told you that her wedding is off because I interfered with her relationship."

"Exactly." She eyed him. "Why are you here instead of working things out with her?"

He held his hands up. "She made it clear that she doesn't want me in her life."

"And you're okay with that?" she asked. "She's your sister, Hud."

His eyes narrowed, and his anger sparked. "I'm aware of that, Dakota."

"You should be doing everything in your power to work things out with her before you lose her forever. She's positively heartbroken."

His posture wilted and his throat thickened. "I know. I messed up, so the best thing I can do is leave and get out of her way. If I stay, I'll just make it worse."

"That's what you think?" She pointed a finger at him, her voice rising. "Your solution is to just run away from your problems like you always do."

"What does *that* mean?"

"You heard me," she insisted. "You're running toward more money because that's all you care about, Hud."

He stood to his full height and shook his head, glaring at her. "I'm so tired of hearing that all I care about is money. That's *not* true."

"Isn't it though?" Her voice cracked. "You told me you couldn't possibly make it here in this tiny, dead-end town, so you had to leave. But you never even asked me what I wanted." She sniffed. "You never asked me where I wanted to live. You assumed we wanted the same things, but we didn't."

He studied her for a long moment, his thoughts whirling as silence swelled between them. The words hit him so fast and hard that he couldn't quite comprehend them. The past filled his mind, and he felt his heart break all over again when he remembered how she'd thrown the ring in his face and said, *"It's over. I'm done. Go to New York without me."*

Finally, he took a step toward her. "So that's what you think happened between us?"

"Yes, it is." Her words wobbled, and she wiped her eyes with the back of her hand. "You never considered me or what I wanted. It was always about you."

He kept his expression solemn, hoping to hide how deeply her words cut him. "No, it wasn't always about me, but you made it clear when you broke off our engagement that you never really loved me."

She clucked her tongue and shook her head. "You're so wrong, Hud," she whispered, her eyes filling with fresh tears.

He swallowed as the lump in his throat expanded.

"I've *always* loved you, Hud, but you chose your career and money over me."

Shock rocked him to his core. "That's *not* true, Dakota." His words vibrated with his heartache.

"It *is,* Hud. You've been obsessed with making money ever since you got your first job. You've made it the focus of your entire life. But when will you have enough?" Tears spilled down her face, and she brushed them away. "Make things right with your sister. She's devastated, and running away won't fix this."

She pointed to the suitcase. "Layla is convinced she's lost you *and* Shane, and you can't abandon her this way." She wiped away more tears. "She's your only sister. Do the right thing. If not for her, then do it in memory of your parents, Hudson. They wouldn't want you and Layla to be estranged. Your sister and your aunt are all the family you have left in this world."

She started toward the front door, and he took off after her. He couldn't leave things like this. He cared about her too deeply.

"Dakota," he called after her. "Please wait."

When she reached the door, she spun to face him.

"I need to know something," he said, holding up his hand.

She blinked. "What?"

His hands fell to his sides. "I never understood why you broke it off with me. You said we wanted different things, but tell me what I did wrong. How did I drive you away?"

"That's the past, which doesn't matter

anymore," she said, her words barely audible. "What matters is your sister and her happiness, which you're destroying."

"Dakota." He moved closer to her. "Tell me why you broke up with me. Please. I need to know the truth."

"I thought it was obvious, but my brother recently told me it was time I had an honest conversation with you. And you know what? I think he's right."

He tilted his head. "I hope you'll always be honest with me."

"I broke up with you because you insisted on moving away," she said. "I didn't want to go to New York. I wanted to stay here and live my dream of owning a business in Flowering Grove, and that's what I did. But now that dream is falling apart too."

He shook his head. "Why didn't you tell me that?"

"Because I thought you knew," she explained. "I was certain you were choosing your career over me."

He felt his heart begin to crumble all over again. Why hadn't he asked her what he'd done wrong back then? Why hadn't he pushed her for answers? "That's not true." He rubbed his eyes. "I wanted you with me in New York City. It all meant nothing without you. You should've known that."

She stared at him, and something unreadable flashed over her face.

"Listen to me," he began, "you *never* came before my career. You were everything to me." His voice was hoarse, and he felt the truth bubbling to the surface. "You're the love of my life, Dakota, and I never got over you."

"If that's true," she whispered, "then why did you leave me?"

"You left me no choice. You told me it was over and gave the ring back."

"Why didn't you fight for me, Hud? Why did you just leave?"

"What choice did I have?" He held his arms up. "You made it clear that we were through." He paused for a beat. "You know what, Dakota, if you're honest with yourself, you need to realize that you chose *your* career over *me*. You never considered coming with me and opening up a business in New York City."

They stared at each other, clearly at a stalemate.

And then his aunt's words from the day of the bridal shower echoed in his mind:

You were too afraid to fight for her and still lose her in the end.

Was his aunt right? Had he been running from his fear of losing her only to lose her anyway? And what if she *had* gone to New York City with him? Would he still have built a company with Darren while she opened a successful business of her own? Would they have gotten married and started a family?

None of that mattered. The past was behind them, and they needed to face the futures they had created for themselves.

"Look, Hud. Go talk to your sister. Do whatever's in your power to fix this." Dakota pushed open the storm door, her hands visibly shaking. "Good night."

He stared after her, unable to speak. The door clicked shut behind her, and her quavering voice filled his mind:

I've always *loved you, Hud, but you chose your career and money over me.*

Her declaration had rocked him. He'd spent the past seven years convinced she'd never truly loved him, but now he'd learned the truth.

Why hadn't he pursued her and demanded to know why she'd broken the engagement? Why had he let her go so easily?

He wiped his eyes with a napkin as the complete truth came into clear focus in his mind: His pursuit of money and success caused him to lose not only the love of his life but also his sister.

And now he had to figure out what to do. Was it possible to clean up the messes he'd made, or should he just pack up and head to Manhattan?

He let that question settle over his soul for a few moments, and then he stood up straight. Leaving seemed like the only logical step.

Turning toward the den, he continued to pack.

Chapter 23

Dakota sat in her car in her parents' driveway and tried to stop her body from vibrating. After leaving Hudson's, she'd stalked toward her house and rushed inside. Trouble had met her at the door, singing his usual chorus of meows.

While she fed him, her hands still shaking, she pondered everything Hudson had said to her.

I wanted you with me in New York City. It all meant nothing without you.

You were everything to me.

You're the love of my life, Dakota, and I never got over you.

Dakota had dropped onto a kitchen chair and held her head in her hands. She'd always thought that Hudson had left her, but the truth was, she'd pushed him away. It was all her fault that they'd missed their chance at happiness.

And then the hypocrisy of it all smacked

her in the face — her stubbornness had driven away not only the love of her life but also her niece and her business.

And now it was time to fix it. But first she had to swallow her pride and ask for help.

She'd picked herself up and driven to her parents' house. And now, as she stared at her parents' front door, she sucked in a breath. It was time for her to tell them everything.

She knocked on the door, rocking back on her heels as she tried to mentally rehearse her speech.

Mom opened the door and hugged her. "Dakota. What a nice surprise." Then her expression flickered with worry. "What's wrong?"

"I need to talk to you and Dad."

Her mother held the door open wider. "Of course, sweetheart. Come on in."

"Why didn't you tell us this sooner?" Dad asked after Dakota had shared everything with her parents — the money she'd lost on her stock, her loss of sales, her higher mortgage payment, the new leaks in the pipes, and her argument with Skye. The only thing she left out was her argument with Hud.

She rubbed her forehead. Sitting at the

kitchen table with her parents made her feel like a little kid again — vulnerable, immature, lost, and confused. But at the same time, a tremendous weight had been lifted off her chest and shoulders. She wasn't alone in this debacle anymore.

Mom touched her hand. "Dakota, you should already know we're always here for you. You, your brother, Eileen, and our grandchildren are the most important people in our lives, and we'd do anything to help when you need us."

"I know." Shame squeezed Dakota's throat, making her words come out in a squeak. "I guess I was afraid of hearing 'I told you so.' "

Dad's brow puckered. "Why?"

"Because you said I bit off more than I could chew when I bought the house right after I opened the store. And in the end, you were right. I did take on too much, and now I'm dealing with the repercussions."

Dad's expression turned contrite. "Sweetheart, I'm sorry I made you feel that way. You shouldn't ever be afraid to tell us if you need help."

"Yeah, I'm learning that." Dakota drew invisible circles on the table. "The truth is that I'm in over my head. My dream was to work as a seamstress, but I don't have the business sense to run a store. The twenty-three-page lease makes no sense to me, and I had no idea I'd made a terrible mistake when I lowered my insurance coverage. My true love is creating and altering clothes, not worrying about financials, but I was too stubborn and too proud to admit that I had taken on too much." She sank back in the chair. "The worst part is that I feel like I let you both down."

Mom shook her head. "Honey, you could never let us down."

"She's right," Dad agreed. "Now tell me, Dakota, how can we help?"

She clasped her hands together and sighed. "I think it's too late to save my store and my house. I'm going to have to break the lease on the store and then try to find a job." Her lips puckered. She couldn't imagine going back to working for someone else, but what option did she have?

"Nope, that's not what you're going to do."

Dakota's head popped up. "Huh?"

"You're giving up too easily," Dad said, and Mom nodded.

"What do you mean?"

"First off, are you sure the lease says you're responsible for the damage in the store? The landlord is truly off the hook for everything?"

She nodded. "Yes, I'm sure."

"Okay. That means we're going to get the plumbers to fix their mistake. You need to call them and demand they make it right. Also, you need to insist that the plumbers give you a refund for the work they've done to this point."

"You think they'll do that?"

"*Make* them do it, Dakota," Dad told her.

"Okay." She sat up straighter as renewed confidence filled her.

"To save your store, how much money would you need?" Dad asked.

Dakota sat forward in the chair. "I'd have to think about it."

"Let's figure that out now." Dad crossed to the counter, picked up a notepad and pen, and then returned to the table.

They discussed her expenses in broad strokes, and when they came up with a figure, her head began to ache. It was more money than she could ever imagine earning.

"You're sure that's what you need?" Dad asked.

She sagged in the seat again. "Yup."

"Sounds good to me. We can go to the bank tomorrow, and I'll cosign on a loan for you."

She shook her head. "I hate asking you for so much help."

Her parents shared a look.

"Am I missing something?" she asked, her gaze bouncing between them.

"When we were expecting Nick, we were going through similar circumstances," Mom began. "Your dad had started his own business, and it wasn't going as well as expected."

Dakota's eyes widened. "What? You never told me this. What business?"

"It was a printshop," Dad explained. "I'd purchased the machines, and I was going to run the place myself." He pursed his lips. "I refinanced the house and cleaned out our savings."

"And then it was a total flop," Mom said matter-of-factly.

Dad blew out a dramatic sigh. "She's right. There was another printshop in town, and it was much more efficient and affordable. So I had to ask my folks for help."

"Really?" Dakota tried to wrap her mind around this new information. "I had no idea."

"That's because we never talked about it," Mom said. "It was a real test of our marriage. Right, Mitch?"

Dad kissed her cheek. "But it made us

stronger in the end, didn't it, Debbie?" He leaned over and gave Dakota a hug. "We're happy to help you, and you shouldn't feel bad about it."

Dakota held on to him and sniffed. "I love you guys."

"We love you too," Dad said.

"That goes without saying, sweetheart," Mom agreed. "We love you dearly."

Dad patted Dakota's shoulder. "Now. Let's meet at the bank tomorrow morning and see about that loan."

"Right." Dakota rubbed her eyes and stood. "Thank you both. I'm so grateful for you." With her parents' help, she was going to get her store back on track.

The following morning, Hudson hit the code on the garage door, and it hummed as it closed. He glanced over at Dakota's driveway and sighed when he found it empty. It was probably best that she wasn't home. They'd said everything they needed to say last night.

But that didn't stop his heart from fracturing at the thought of not seeing her again.

Last night he had called his aunt to say goodbye, and he could still hear her sobs echoing in his mind. The sound had been a stab to his heart, but he had to go. It was the only solution that made sense. Shame mixed with his guilt. He was a coward for not telling her in person that he was leaving, but he just couldn't bear to do otherwise.

After talking to his aunt, he'd stared at the ceiling all night long, replaying his arguments with his sister and with Dakota while the minutes ticked by at a snail's pace.

Climbing into the driver's seat, he slipped on his sunglasses and started the engine. When he peeked over at Dakota's house one last time, he spotted her cat lounging in the window.

"Bye, Trouble," he said, a little lump expanding in his throat. "Take good care of your mom."

Hudson motored out of the driveway and down Oak Street with country music playing through his speakers. He turned the music up, hoping to drown out his warring thoughts. Then he pushed the button to lower the window, and warm late-May air filled the SUV, bringing with it the scent of moist earth.

When he merged onto Glenn Avenue, a sliver of doubt took root in the back of his mind. Was he running away again like Aunt Trudy and Dakota had said? He tried to lose himself in the words of the country song, but the doubt remained, morphing and taking hold of his thoughts.

He clenched his teeth.

Pow!

A sound like a gunshot startled him. He continued on and then heard a *flup, flup, flup* as the car tugged to the left along the residential two-lane road. When it was safe to do so, he pulled onto the shoulder. He jumped out of the car and confirmed his suspicion.

A flat tire. *Great. Just great.*

Hudson peered into the trunk of his SUV, which was packed full of his luggage. He released a long, exhausted breath. This was not how he imagined his road trip would start. Of course the tire iron and jack were in the compartment under all of his belongings.

Hudson grabbed his duffel bag and set it on the curb. Then he picked up a small cardboard box marked "Hudson," and it came apart in his hand. A photo album fell out, hitting the pavement and bouncing open. He bent down, finding photos of himself as a little boy posing with his parents. He examined the album closer and gasped.

He turned the page to find more photos of himself as a toddler — playing on a swing set, paddling in a small plastic pool, blowing out birthday candles.

He hadn't seen those photos in years. Only then did he realize he was holding the photo album that Aunt Trudy had given him at the bridal shower. He had shoved the box in a corner and forgotten about it. Then he'd tossed it into the SUV this morning before leaving.

Hudson turned another page and grinned at a photo of himself sitting on Santa's lap. Leaning against the rear bumper, he perused the album as traffic moved past him on Glenn Avenue. A dog barked in a yard nearby. Birds sang in the surrounding trees. And the warm morning sun beat down on his face.

Memories flashed over Hudson while he flipped through the pages. Photos of him and his parents at the beach, at the park, posing by a Christmas tree at Trudy's, and standing together on a sunny day dressed in red, white, and blue. When he came to a photo of himself holding an infant Layla, emotion swelled inside him, and his eyes filled with tears.

He sniffed. "We were so happy," he whispered as a car passed by. "And now . . ."

His chest constricted, and he wiped his eyes. He'd ruined his sister's life, and now he had to live with that knowledge.

He refocused his attention on the album and discovered a picture of him with his parents and Layla at church the day she was baptized. He grinned at the camera as he stood at the altar with baby Layla, his parents, and the pastor.

He recalled how Layla cried when Pastor Chris sprinkled the water on her head. She was so tiny, but she had a strong set of lungs.

When he turned the page again, he found a collage of photos featuring him and Dakota. His stomach did a somersault at the sight of them together. In one photo they snuggled on Aunt Trudy's sofa, in another they laughed while posed in the bed of his pickup truck, and in a third they held hands on her parents' porch swing.

They looked so happy. Back then things had been so easy between them. They were in sync and so in love.

But that was another time. They'd missed their chance, and his heart would never recover.

He closed the album, set it atop the duffel bag, and returned to the trunk of his vehicle.

He finished emptying it out before retrieving the scissor jack and tire iron. Then he removed the spare from where it was stowed underneath the vehicle.

He removed the flat, set the spare, and then retightened the lug nuts. After lowering the car and setting the flat tire and equipment in the trunk, he loaded his luggage back into the SUV.

Back behind the wheel, he placed the photo album down beside him on the passenger seat and stared at it for a moment. The memories the book held rushed over him, and he found himself once again doubting his decision to leave town.

Then he turned over the SUV's engine and slipped it into Drive.

Chapter 24

Relief permeated Dakota later that afternoon as she drove down Main Street. Not only had she and her father been approved for her loan, but she'd also received good news from the plumbing company. They were going to fix the leak for free *and* reimburse her for the work she'd already paid for.

Things were looking up. She had a plan for getting her business back on track — but first she needed to talk to her niece. Skye had been on her mind since their argument on Tuesday afternoon. A pit expanded in her stomach. Dakota's texts and calls to Skye had gone unanswered, and now she needed to make things right with her precious niece.

After parking in her brother's driveway, Dakota knocked on the front door. She looked out over the front yard and breathed in the scent of freshly cut grass and flowers.

Nearby, the engine of a lawn mower whirred.

The door opened, and Aubrey appeared on the other side. "Auntie." She hugged her and then turned and yelled, "Auntie's here!"

Eileen poked her head out from the kitchen. "Hi, Dakota. What's up?"

"Sorry for just showing up, but I was wondering if Skye was around."

"She's on the deck studying for a final."

"Thanks." Dakota slipped past her younger niece and headed toward the back door.

As she peered out toward the deck, she bit her lower lip. In her store that afternoon, so many emotions had swirled inside as she worked. Remorse over her fight with Skye, worry for Layla now that the wedding was canceled . . . and then there was her conversation with Hudson. She was still trying to figure out a lot of things, including how she ought to feel about him and whether she should let him go.

But right now it was time for her to apologize and beg for her niece's forgiveness. She knocked on the sliding glass door before pulling it open. Skye sat at a table with a pile of books surrounding her. The large deck looked out over the spacious, lush green backyard. When Skye met her gaze, Dakota slid the door open.

Her niece's eyes narrowed. "What do you want?"

"To apologize," Dakota said, her voice stricken. "I've been too controlling, and it ruined my precious relationship with you. I want to make things right."

Skye lifted her chin. "Keep going."

"You were right." Dakota held up her hands. "I'm too stubborn for my own good. I should have asked for help a long time ago, and I finally did."

Skye's eyes rounded. "What do you mean?"

"I talked to my parents, and my dad co-signed on a loan for me." Dakota sat down beside her. "I met Grandpa at the bank today. I also called the plumber, and he came by and started fixing the leak this afternoon. He's going to finish up tomorrow and reimburse me for some of the gowns I lost, in addition to the damage the first leak caused."

"You're kidding."

"Nope, I'm not." Dakota beamed. "Now I can order more gowns and possibly start a marketing campaign. I'll talk to your dad about that since he's the expert." She touched Skye's shoulder. "And I want to talk to you about instituting online sales and special orders — if you'll still work for me. Correction — work *with* me."

"And . . . ?"

"I'd like to put you in charge of my online sales. You can design the webpages and help me figure out the best way to promote them. You can even be the dress model if you want."

Her niece studied her. "And will you finally trust me to help measure the customers for tuxes and gown fittings?"

"Yes, I will. In fact, I can teach you how to tailor the tuxes and eventually move on to the gowns if you're interested." She held her breath, and a moment ticked by.

"Hmm." Skye twisted her lips. "I'm not sure . . ."

"Skye, tell me what else you want."

Her niece fiddled with her pencil.

The anticipation was killing Dakota. "Well, what do you think?"

Skye tapped her chin. "I'll do it, but only for a raise."

Dakota pulled her in for a hug as relief washed over her. "You got it."

"How about a partnership?"

"Now you're pushing it," she said, and they both laughed. "I don't know what I'd do without you."

"You'd be very bored, and your store

wouldn't be nearly as cool."

"That's true."

Skye tilted her head. "I heard my folks talking about the night Hudson had supper with us at your house. My dad made it sound like you and Hudson might get back together. Is that why you broke up with Mr. Bryant?"

Dakota shook her head. "No, I broke up with him because I really only liked him as a friend."

"Oh." Skye seemed to consider that. "Are you dating Hudson now?"

"That's over."

Skye tapped her chin. "Well, I guess I need to find you a new boyfriend."

"Let's worry about getting the store in order first."

Skye folded her hands. "I can't wait."

Hudson sat in the driver's seat of his car and studied his aunt's house. After putting the spare tire on his SUV, he had headed straight to Barton Automotive. While he waited for Carter Donovan to fix his tire, he remained in the showroom and flipped through the family album again, contemplating his conversation with Dakota.

As the happy memories he'd carefully avoided for so long stared up at him from the album, he could no longer pretend his aunt and Dakota hadn't been right. He *had* been running away. He'd been trying to escape his childhood grief for his entire life, and for more than seven years, he'd tried to live without Dakota. And when he'd come back to town for Layla, the one person he couldn't bear to lose, his controlling ways had led to just that. He *had* lost her.

As he took in the happy family photos, he knew deep down he didn't want to go back to his lonely life in Manhattan or build an even lonelier life in Bahrain. Why hadn't he been willing to acknowledge how lonely he'd been? He had earned the money that enabled him to take care of his family, so working nonstop was no longer his purpose. He needed a new reason to live. What if it could be to find his own happiness for himself?

It also dawned on him that his pursuit of money *had* led him to lose his family and Dakota. Even if he didn't love money, his pursuit of it sure looked like love. And that was why he had to make things right. He had to heal the rift between him and his sister before he lost her forever.

He jogged up the front steps of his aunt's house and knocked on the storm door.

Aunt Trudy appeared and gasped. "Hudson. You're back."

"You were right about everything." He held his hands up as if in surrender. "I have been too focused on money and success, and I have been running away from my grief for a long time. But I'm not running anymore."

"I'm glad to hear you say that." His aunt opened the door wider and pulled him in for a tight hug.

"I also need to trust Layla to make her own decisions, and I'm here to do that. I'm going to apologize and tell her that I support her in everything she does. Please let me try to repair things with her." His throat burned. "I can't lose my family. You and Layla mean everything to me."

"I know you'll fix this. I have faith in you."

Hudson knocked on Layla's bedroom door. His heart thumped, and his palms began to sweat.

"Who is it?"

He placed a hand on the cold wooden door. "It's me."

"Go away."

He grimaced. "Please, Layla. Let me talk to you."

"No," she exclaimed. Something that sounded like a pillow hit the door with a soft *thunk.*

"Okay then," he said. "I'll talk here."

"You can talk, but I'm not listening."

"Fine." Hudson took one long, slow cycle of breath to steel himself. "Layla, I remember every detail of the day Mom and Dad brought you home from the hospital. It was late September, but it was as hot as the Fourth of July. Mom and Dad were so overjoyed, and I remember one of the neighbors telling Mom, 'Daphne, you finally have a girl you can dress in pink and buy dolls for.'"

A vision of that day filled his mind's eye, and he heard someone sniff. Turning toward the end of the hallway, he found Aunt Trudy wiping her eyes with a tissue.

"You've asked me about Mom before. Earlier today I was going through a photo album, and I remembered something you'd want to know. She had an amazing voice," he said. "And she loved '80s music. I remember hearing her in your room singing Cyndi Lauper's 'Time After Time' to you every night. Actually, she'd sing it to you whenever you'd cry. If I ever flip to the '80s station and hear that song, it always takes me back." He rubbed his eyes. "She had this infectious laugh. No matter how silly her joke was, you couldn't help but laugh along with her."

A little sob sounded from inside Layla's room, and he imagined her wiping away tears.

"From the day you were born, I've felt responsible for you, Layla, but it wasn't a burden," he continued. "It was a job I wanted. I was determined to be there for you and guide you as best I could. And when Mom and Dad died, I was confused, devastated, and lost, but the one thing I knew for sure was that I wanted to take care of you." He paused for a moment and swiped his fingers over his wet eyes.

"I thought it was my calling to make sure you had everything you needed — a safe and secure home, clothes, a good education, a reliable car — but I never stopped to think about what you needed emotionally. It never entered my mind that I was hurting you by not talking about Mom and Dad and sharing my grief with you until you brought that to my attention yesterday. I've always thought that talking about it would make me seem weak.

"Or maybe I thought that if I let that grief seep out of the depths of my heart, somehow I'd drown in it. And that's why I've been running away from it for so long. I lost Mom and Dad, and then I lost Dakota. For seven years, I've been trying to avoid that grief too. I thought that if I kept moving forward, I would outrun it — but instead, I just let it fester. And I pushed away the people I love most."

A rustling sound came from the other side of the door.

"All I know is that I never meant to hurt you, Layla." He leaned his forearm on the doorframe. "And I've realized that my goal of always taking care of you and Aunt Trudy was to my detriment. I was so focused on being successful and providing for you that I lost sight of those most important to me — you . . . and Dakota too."

Hudson squeezed his eyes shut as the truth came to the surface. "But the worst thing I did was trying to sabotage your wedding because I thought I knew what was best for you." He glanced down at the toes of his shoes. "Only you know what's best for you, and I'm sorry. The truth is, I was afraid of losing you, and that's exactly what happened anyway."

Another sob sounded from the other side of the door, and his heart wrenched.

The door opened with a whoosh, and Layla threw her arms around his neck.

His tight muscles began to unwind as he hugged her.

"You're such a moron," she said into his chest. "A really big, dumb moron."

He chuckled. "Yes, yes, I am, but morons can fix things and change too."

"You can't fix it." She stepped out of his embrace and wiped her puffy red eyes. "Shane has made up his mind about the wedding. Aunt Trudy said she'd start calling the wedding guests to let them know it's canceled."

Hudson shook his head. "Don't give up yet. I'll talk to Shane and convince him that I'm not going to interfere anymore."

"It won't help." She returned to her room and sank down on the edge of her bed.

"Where's he working today?"

"I don't know." She picked up a purple throw pillow and hugged it to her middle. "He started a new job today, but he didn't tell me where."

"Can you call him?"

She held up her phone. "I've tried, but he doesn't answer."

"I'll be back," Hudson said as a plan took shape in his mind.

"Where are you going?" Layla called after him.

"Just trust me." He hugged his aunt, gave her a peck on the cheek, and then hurried to his SUV.

■ ■ ■ ■

Hudson parked beside Shane's pickup truck and switched off the ignition. His plan of calling the main number for the landscaping business and imploring the receptionist to share Shane's location had somehow worked. He was grateful she believed him when he said he needed to discuss a serious family matter with Shane.

His shoes crunched along the rock path that led from the front of the large home to the back, where Shane and another man were planting shrubs in the hot late-May sun. Bees buzzed past him, and a couple of frogs croaked in the large pond at the center of the lush green yard.

The man working with Shane said something to him, and when Shane turned around, he cast a baleful look in Hudson's direction.

I deserve that.

Shane jumped up to his feet and pointed toward the road. "I have nothing to say to you."

"Hold on." Hudson held his hands up. "Please give me five minutes."

"No." Shane turned his back on him and picked up his shovel, his movements jerky and deliberate.

Hudson continued forward, determined to have his apology heard.

Irritation flickered over Shane's face. "Just leave, man. I'm begging you."

"Please, Shane," Hudson began, "listen to me."

Shane continued to work, his back to Hudson.

"Fine. You plant, and I'll talk." Hudson slipped his hands into his pockets. "I'm here to apologize."

Shane continued digging a hole, his jaw set in stone.

"I was completely out of line, and I'm sorry. I never should have butted into your plans with my sister. I had no right to treat you as if you weren't good enough for Layla. Your work is important. There's so much to be said for working hard all day and seeing the fruits of your labor."

"Is that right?" Shane tented his hand over his forehead and glared at Hudson. "You believe that working outside all day has as much merit as sitting in a cushy office ordering your employees around?" His tone was acid-laced.

"Yes, I do."

Shane stood his shovel upright and propped an elbow on its handle. "And how did you come to that conclusion, Mr. Manhattan?"

"I worked for my friend's construction company. He helped me remember that manual labor, building something tangible, is rewarding."

Shane shook his head. "You're some piece of work."

"What do you mean?"

"You only came out here to tell me what you think I want to hear in order to clear the air with your sister." Shane pointed to the road again, and rage flared in his eyes. "Do us both a favor and get out of here."

"I'm not done, please." Hudson hedged to gather his thoughts. "My sister loves you, and she's crushed that you canceled the wedding. I'm here to grovel and beg for your forgiveness — and if you can't forgive me, at least forgive Layla."

Shane glared at him. "Why should I listen to you?" He ground out the words.

"Look, Shane. You and Layla belong together, and I need to stop running her life." Hudson explained how he'd always felt responsible for Layla after their parents died, but he took his responsibility too far. "I was afraid to trust Layla to make her own decisions, and now I see how wrong I was. She's a mature young woman who's ready to live her life, and she wants a life with you." He cleared his throat. "I messed up, and I'm here to ask you to please forgive me."

Shane lifted his ball cap, wiped his hand over his forehead, and set the hat back on his head. "It's not that simple."

"It *is* that simple," Hudson insisted. "I promise I'll stay out of your lives. I won't give you my opinion or advice unless you ask for it. And I promise I'll stop trying to pay for everything. I understand now how thoughtless and arrogant I've been."

Shane kicked a stone with the toe of his shoe. "I don't think she'll take me back after everything I said."

"Shane," Hudson began, "my sister loves you and wants you back. Please just return her calls. Don't let me stand in the way." He turned and started across the grass toward his SUV.

"Hey, Hudson!"

Hudson pivoted to face him.

"Thanks, man," Shane said.

He waved and climbed back into the driver's seat. While he drove back toward the Airbnb, his thoughts turned to Dakota. Though the two of them had likely missed their chance, he wanted to make things right with her anyway.

Maybe there was no path forward.
And yet his soul craved her.
A seed of hope took root in his heart.
But first he had to get his life in order.

Chapter 25

Two weeks later on a Saturday afternoon, Hudson paced outside the parlor at the church. Life had zoomed by as he'd gotten his affairs settled. He touched the pocket inside his tuxedo jacket to make sure his surprise for Dakota was still tucked away in there, and his pulse quickened. He couldn't wait to put the rest of his plan into action, but first he had to walk his baby sister down the aisle.

The parlor door opened and Aunt Trudy appeared, dabbing her eyes with a tissue. "She's the most stunning bride I've ever seen. She looks just like Daphne."

Hudson's heart squeezed at the sound of his mother's name.

"Come see her, Hud." His aunt beckoned him to enter the parlor.

He walked into the room and found his sister standing in front of a full-length mirror surrounded by her best friends, the wedding coordinator, Shane's mother, and Shane's sister, Melody. He took in his sister's reflection, and his eyes stung with tears. She truly was the prettiest bride he'd ever laid eyes on, and seeing her in a gown exactly like his mother's was almost too much for him to bear.

He held his breath, hoping to hold back the tidal wave of emotions that threatened to break loose.

Layla met his gaze in the mirror and rushed over to him. "Hud." She held her arms out, but he took a step back. Her brow pinched. "What is it?"

"You're perfect, Layla Grace, and I don't want to mess this up." He gestured toward her makeup and her gown.

"But I need a hug from my favorite big brother."

Leaning down, he gave her a loose hug. "You're beautiful, Layla."

"Thank you, Hud," she whispered. "Thank you for always taking such good care of me. I love you."

"I love you too."

Aunt Trudy appeared beside them, sniffling. "Oh, you both already have me in tears, and we haven't even heard the vows yet."

Hudson and Layla laughed.

"Your parents would be so proud of the two of you."

"Stop it," Layla said. "Don't make me cry. My makeup is exactly how I want it."

Hudson smiled as his aunt enveloped them in a group hug.

"Layla," said Judy, her wedding coordinator, "we need you to get your bouquet so you're ready for Hud to walk you down the aisle."

Aunt Trudy took Hudson's hand and smiled up at him. "It's time to marry off your sister."

Dakota's eyes filled with tears when the wedding march began to echo around the large sanctuary. She stood and faced the back of the church just as Hudson started down the aisle with lovely Layla on his arm. She was breathtaking in the gown, and just as Layla had hoped, she looked exactly like her mother had all those years ago when she'd also walked down the aisle toward her sweetheart.

"Oh my goodness," Kayleigh whispered. "Her dress is spectacular. You really outdid yourself."

"Thanks," Dakota said.

When Dakota's gaze found Hudson, she couldn't look away. He was drop-dead gorgeous in his traditional black-and-white tuxedo. His dark hair had been trimmed, and his angular jaw was free of any scruff. He beamed as his sister held on to his strong arm.

Kayleigh jabbed Dakota in the ribs. "Hud looks really hot."

"Shh," Dakota hissed. "Your husband is on the other side of you."

But Kayleigh was right. Hudson *was* hot. He moved smoothly down the aisle. When his sky-blue eyes locked with Dakota's, her legs felt like cooked noodles. She gripped the back of the pew to steady herself.

Dakota had been so relieved when Layla appeared in her store two weeks ago and told her the wedding was back on. Layla hadn't shared any details of her reconciliation with her brother, and Dakota hadn't asked for any. However, she'd noticed his SUV at the Airbnb next door, and she'd hoped that he'd come to see her. But since he hadn't, she assumed he was moving on. They'd said what they'd needed to say the night of their argument. He hadn't even bothered to stop by the store for his tux. Instead, Shane had picked it up for him. It broke Dakota's heart to accept that they had wasted their chance to reconcile. She missed him, and she might never get over him.

When Hudson and Layla reached the end of the aisle, Shane wiped his eyes and smiled at his bride. The love in his eyes for sweet Layla took Dakota's breath away.

The music stopped, and the minister stood by Hudson and Layla. "Who presents this woman to be married to this man?"

Hudson turned to Trudy in the front row and said, "Her aunt and I do."

Layla hugged Hudson and whispered something in his ear before the minister took Layla's hand and moved it to Shane's. After Hudson joined his aunt in the front pew, the minister instructed everyone to sit, and the ceremony began.

Dakota had a difficult time keeping her tears at bay during the service. When it was over, the minister presented Mr. and Mrs. Simpson to the congregation. The newlyweds kissed before they proceeded down the aisle in front of their attendants.

After the wedding party had disappeared into the narthex, the guests began spilling out of the pews toward the receiving line.

Dakota spotted Parker at the far end of the church, and she touched Kayleigh's arm. "I'll meet you outside."

"Where are you going?" Kayleigh asked.

"I need to take care of something," she said before slipping through the crowd, excusing herself on her way to Parker.

When he saw her, he tried to turn on his heel.

"Please, Parker, wait."

He stopped and turned back to her, his face clouding with a dark expression.

"Can we talk?" she asked when she reached him.

He hesitated and gave her a curt nod. "Sure."

They found a quiet corner away from the receiving line, and the all-too-familiar pit filled her stomach once again.

"I didn't expect to see you here," she said.

He stuck his hands in the pockets of his suit trousers. "My date happens to be one of Shane's distant cousins."

"Oh, wow. You brought a date." Dakota pushed a lock of her hair behind her ear. "That's so . . . awesome." *Great. I made it weird.*

He pressed his lips together. "What do you want, Dakota?"

"I, uh . . . I want to apologize to you. I was unfair to you when we were seeing each other. You were genuinely kind to me, and I was really . . . distracted." She glanced across the room to where Hudson gave an older woman an awkward hug. Then the woman reached up and pinched his cheek.

Parker nodded. "You were distracted by your ex."

"That's true, but I never meant to use you or mislead you. You deserved better than that, and I'm truly sorry."

He paused for a beat, but then his lips formed a tentative smile. "I appreciate your honesty."

"So you're seeing someone?"

"Yup." He pointed toward a pretty blond lingering near the doorway. "Her name's Bonnie. We're still getting to know each other, but I don't think she's jonesing for her ex."

"Ouch." Dakota blanched. "That stings, but I deserve it."

He chuckled. "Have you and Hudson worked things out yet?"

"I don't think that's going to happen."

"Well, if you want my opinion, I'll give it to you."

"Go ahead." She steeled herself against his truth. "I can take it."

But Parker's smile was warm. "If Hudson's smart, he'll scoop you up and never let you go, because you're pretty special."

"I appreciate that."

Parker opened his arms, and she stepped

into his hug. "Good luck," he told her.

"Thanks. You too."

While Parker started back toward his date, Dakota peered across the room to where Hudson greeted another elderly lady. An ache deep inside gnawed at her. She hoped she'd get a chance to talk to him alone today — and if she did, she hoped he wouldn't tell her goodbye.

Hudson stood by the bar while Layla and Shane danced in the middle of the country club's reception hall to Elvis's "Can't Help Falling in Love."

He was grateful to have made it through the receiving line, which included not only Shane's and Layla's friends and Shane's extended family, but also at least a dozen of his aunt's bingo hall friends, who enjoyed hugging him, pinching his cheek, and promising him dates with their daughters, granddaughters, and nieces.

Once the receiving line was over, he had posed for at least a hundred photos with the wedding party. Hudson had managed to get Shane alone before they drove from the church to the country club, not only to congratulate his new brother-in-law, but also to thank him for giving Hudson a second chance.

Now that he was at the reception and his brother-of-the-bride duties were completed, Hudson was anxious to talk to Dakota. She hadn't gone through the receiving line, and he hoped that didn't mean she planned to avoid him all day. He couldn't take his eyes off her, sitting at a table with Kayleigh, Brice, and a few other folks who looked familiar. She was breathtaking in a red sequined dress that looked as if it had been made for her. Her hair was pulled back from her face with soft curls cascading to her shoulders.

Layla had insisted Dakota didn't have a date for the wedding, but when he saw her hugging Parker earlier, he'd almost lost his mind. Soon after, though, he'd noticed Parker with another woman. He hoped that meant Dakota was single, but if not, then all of his plans were in vain.

"And now, folks," the DJ announced, "the bride and groom would like to open the dance floor up to all of the couples out there. Please help Mr. and Mrs. Simpson celebrate their special day."

The opening bars of Etta James's "At Last" started playing, and Hudson couldn't stop himself. He made a beeline to Dakota's table and stood next to her, nodding hello to Kayleigh, Brice, and the other guests.

When Dakota looked up at him, her deep brown eyes widened.

He held his hand out to her. "Would you please dance with me?"

Dakota froze, continuing to look shocked.

He felt his courage start to wane, and he hoped she wouldn't reject him in front of a table full of people.

"Dakota." Kayleigh gave her a nudge. "Go."

"Right." Dakota took his hand, and he lifted her to her feet before leading her out to the dance floor.

He opened his arms, and she snuggled against him. Hudson rested his hands on her lower back, and when she wound her arms around his neck, every nerve in his body sparked to life.

He felt her relax as they swayed together to the music. With his eyes closed, Hudson tried to imagine what it would be like to have her in his life forever — to date her again, propose to her again, marry her, own a home with her, have a family with her, grow old with her.

Could that be possible? Could she give him another chance to prove how much he'd always loved her?

She moved her fingers over his neck, sending heat shimmying up and down his back.

The feel of her warm fingers against his skin was almost too much for him to take.

All too soon, the song came to an end, and the loud bass of a livelier song rang out over the speakers.

Dakota stepped out of his embrace and stilled as if waiting for him to make the next move.

"Can we go somewhere and talk?" he asked.

She nodded. "I'd like that." She took his hand, and they walked through the crowd toward the balcony overlooking the golf course.

Dakota's pulse fluttered like the wings of a hummingbird as Hudson guided her by the hand to a quiet corner of the balcony. The sky above them was bright blue and cloudless, and the humid June air smelled fresh.

She'd been overcome with a heady rush of emotions when Hudson had asked her to dance. Had Kayleigh not nudged her, she might have sat there staring at him like a wordless idiot for the rest of the reception.

It felt like a dream when he held her close and they swayed to the music together. In fact, it had felt like old times — as if no time had passed and they were still in love. But once the music stopped, she'd come back down to earth. Almost a decade had passed, and they had changed — in fact, *everything* had changed.

Surely this was his goodbye. He was going to tell her he was leaving for the Middle East or some other exotic place, and he wanted to thank her for being such a great friend. She tried to prepare herself, but her heart started to shred.

"You look beautiful."

"Huh?" She looked up at him. Had she heard him right? She blushed as his smile almost melted her. "I'm sorry. What'd you say?"

"You're beautiful."

"Oh." She looked down at her dress, which she'd chosen off her clearance rack at the boutique. "Thanks. You look . . ." *Gorgeous. So hot I could die.* "Really nice too."

"Thanks." He reached into his pocket. "I have something for you. Hold out your hand."

She did as she was told, and he set something cold and metal into her palm. She looked down and found an "I Heart NY" magnet. She laughed and looked up at him. "What's this for?"

"I told you I think of you every time I see a rack of magnets. My business partner had arranged for movers to bring the rest of my stuff here, and I asked him to pick this up and send it too."

"I love it." *And I will cherish this for the rest of my life.* "Thank you."

"You're welcome." He turned toward the doorway leading to the reception hall. "Did you break up with that guy — I mean, Parker?"

"We broke up a while ago. We were never exclusive."

He looked relieved, which surprised her.

"Is this goodbye?"

His brow furrowed. "What do you mean?"

"This." She motioned between them. "Are you going to tell me goodbye and that you're leaving for some faraway place and a fancy new job?" Her breath paused, and she prayed he'd say no.

"I don't plan to."

"Wait." She held her hand up. "Did you say your business partner arranged for movers to bring your stuff down to you?"

"That's right."

"You're staying here?" She pointed downward.

"Yup."

"Why? How?" She shook her head. "I don't understand."

He smiled. "I've spent the past two weeks tying up loose ends. I wanted to make sure

I was settled here before I told you how I feel." He hesitated. "I had a lot to work through. I realized I've been running away from my grief for a long time, including the past seven years. First I lost my parents, and then I lost you. I was so afraid of losing Layla that I tried to control her — almost driving her away in the process.

"After you and I last talked, your words finally took root. I've been running away like a coward. I made things right with my sister and Shane. Then I asked Darren how he'd feel if he went to Bahrain without me. I can consult from here, which works just fine for him. I'm helping him get the company in shape so we can sell it, but I'll do it remotely. I'm also working on some software upgrades for Gavin's construction company, and I have an idea for another business to start here in Flowering Grove, helping mom-and-pop shops with their business operations."

He paused and took a deep breath. "Aside from that, I've spent the last couple of weeks making sure Layla and Shane understand that I support them and want to be part of their lives. Then I sent for my things and made a ridiculous offer on the Airbnb." He chuckled. "I mean, I offered a lot more than it's worth, and the owners happily accepted.

I'm closing on the house in a couple weeks, and then we'll officially be neighbors."

Happiness rolled through her. "You're really staying here in Flowering Grove for good?"

"Yes, I am." He cupped his hand to her cheek, and she leaned into his warm touch. "Dakota, I never got over you. You're the love of my life, and if I could, I would go back in time and tell you that you mean more to me than money and my career ever did. I wish I had run after you and made it clear I wanted you more than a career. I'm sorry I was too focused on the wrong things and too afraid of losing you all over again. But I can't go back in time. I can only look forward."

She sucked in a breath. "It's not only your fault, Hud. I should have told you how I felt. I could have gone with you and opened a business in New York instead of telling you it was over."

"Dakota, it's okay. That's the past, and we can't change it. But the truth is that I still love you, and I would do anything to have you back in my life."

She sniffed. "I love you too, Hud."

His eyes sparkled with unshed tears. "I fixated on work because I didn't want to be like my dad, jumping from job to job and moving around a lot. But now that my family is secure, I need a new purpose — and I've found it. My purpose is to build a life for myself. And I want to plant roots here because Flowering Grove is my home."

Dakota set her magnet on a small table beside them, and Hudson took her hands in his. "Someone told me that if I found my true love, I needed to hold on to her, since love is a precious thing." He moved his fingers over the backs of her hands. "I was selfish when we were younger and blinded by so much. If you'll give me a chance, I want to try again. I promise I won't be stubborn or selfish this time. I'll put you first."

"I'll do the same." Her words were strained. "I've been stubborn and selfish too. I was too stubborn to tell you I wanted you to stay, and lately I've been so stubborn I nearly lost my niece, my business, and my house." She sniffed. "I even went and opened a bridal boutique without admitting to myself that I knew nothing about running a business."

Her voice faltered, her mouth turning to cotton. "But the worst thing I ever did was not tell you what I wanted when you said you were going to New York City. If I had been honest with you, we could have made it work. I'm so sorry, Hud. I was too young and immature to see how wrong I was."

He brushed a tear away from her cheek. "Dakota, I'm sorry I had tunnel vision back then. I love you, and I've *always* loved you."

"Call me Koti. You're the only person who can call me that, and I miss it."

"Okay, Koti." He gave her a mischievous grin. "I love you, Koti."

"And I love you too."

"I'm glad we've finally established that." His fingers traced the line of her neck before he cupped her face in his hands. Then he leaned down, and his mouth covered hers. For a moment, she was convinced she was dreaming, but the kiss was as real as the desire plunging through her body. She lost herself in the feel and taste of his mouth. She wrapped her arms around his neck, and he pulled her in and held her close.

Hudson's lips began a slow exploration, and the world around them faded. All that existed was Dakota and Hudson, and she felt certain she would float away. When he broke the kiss, she drew in air, working to slow the shock waves still rocking her body.

"I feel like I've waited a lifetime to do that again," he said.

She grinned. "Then don't stop. We have nearly a decade to make up for."

"I couldn't agree more," he told her, gathering her up in his arms again.

Epilogue

One year later

ABBA's "Dancing Queen" pulsed through the speakers in the Flowering Grove Rollerama as skaters moved to the beat out on the floor. Dakota glanced around at the crowd and grinned. The walls were decorated with streamers, peace signs, and disco balls, and the patrons had gone all out wearing their minidresses, jumpsuits, sequins, fringe, shiny shirts, and bandannas.

She leaned on Hudson beside her. "I think '70s night was a great success."

"I've never seen so many bell-bottoms in one place in all my life."

She laughed and gave his hard bicep a squeeze. "And you look amazing in that silk shirt and vest."

"That's because you made them for me." His gaze raked over her before he kissed her cheek, sending heat curling through her.

"By the way, I'm loving that minidress on you."

The past year had flown by at lightning speed. After their wedding, Layla and Shane moved into their little house. Layla was still serving as a hygienist for the dentist's office, and Shane still happily worked for the landscaping company. Shane and Hudson had worked out their differences and somehow had become good friends over time.

Dakota and Skye worked together to institute both in-person and online sales in her shop, including custom orders. The business was so busy that Dakota had to hire two more saleswomen to help. Dakota was able to concentrate on what she loved — creating and altering the gowns — while Skye and the other staff handled the store floor.

After purchasing the colonial that had once been an Airbnb, Hudson continued working remotely with Darren. They were already making plans to sell the company in Bahrain. He also kept busy designing software to help local companies in Flowering Grove, and from his profits, he donated laptops to the local school system.

Dakota and Hudson also kept their promise to always be honest with each other and put their relationship first. Dakota couldn't remember a time when she'd been this happy, and she looked forward to a future with him — a real future this time.

Hudson rested his hand on Dakota's waist and kissed the top of her head. "I love being here at the rink with you."

"It's where our story began." She smiled up at him.

A strange look filled his face. "Yes, that's very true."

"You okay?" she asked, touching his cheek and enjoying the feel of his stubble.

Kayleigh and Brice skated over to them, and Dakota couldn't help but think that Kayleigh looked adorable in her pink mini-dress covering her tiny baby bump. It was hard to believe she'd be a mother of two in only a few more months.

"What are you two doing over here?" Kayleigh pointed to the rink. "Let's go skate." When "Stayin' Alive" by the Bee Gees started playing, Kayleigh grabbed Dakota's arm. "For real. Let's go, girl."

"Hang on." Hudson held up his hand. "I need Koti for just a few more minutes."

Dakota's heart melted at the sound of his nickname for her. She would never get tired of it.

Kayleigh's eyes widened as understanding overtook her face. "Oh."

"What's happening?" Dakota looked from her boyfriend to her best friend and back again.

"We'll meet you out there." Brice took his wife's hand and led her out to the floor to skate.

Dakota studied her handsome boyfriend. "Am I missing something?"

"I just wanted to talk to you for a minute." He pointed toward the door leading to the party rooms. "Follow me."

Curiosity threaded through Dakota as they skated hand in hand to the first party room. She followed Hudson inside. "Tell me what's going on, Hud," she insisted.

He rubbed his hand over his neck. "I wanted to tell you something."

"Okay . . ." She waited, then made a frustrated noise when he didn't speak. "Hud, please stop stalling." When he remained quiet, worry gripped her. "Tell me what's wrong."

"Nothing's wrong. In fact, everything is right." He huffed out a breath. "When I first came back to Flowering Grove, my plan was to convince my sister not to get married and then get out of town as fast as I could. But once here, I started to realize how much I missed this place. I missed my friends, I missed the community, but most of all, I missed you. And when we reconnected, I figured out that I didn't only miss this place — I also needed a home, and I needed you."

She smiled. "I need you too."

"Koti, I've already told you you're the love of my life. My sister once said that you and I never married other people after we broke up because we belonged together. I thought she was crazy at first, but she was right." He reached into his pocket and pulled out a bright-blue jewelry box.

Dakota gasped, pressing her hand to her chest.

Hudson knelt on one knee, which he impressively managed on roller skates. Then he held up the box. "Dakota Marie Jamison, I don't want to spend another day without you. In fact, I want you by my side forever." He opened the box, and a large round-cut diamond, resting in a diamond-encrusted platinum setting, twinkled up at her.

She sniffed as her eyes filled with tears.

"Koti, will you marry me?"

"Yes, yes, yes!"

He blew out a breath. "Thank goodness." He took the ring out of the box and slipped it onto her finger, and it was the perfect fit. "Dakota, with this ring, I pledge my heart to you, and I promise I'll love you and cherish you for the rest of my life."

"Oh, Hudson, I love you."

Then he pulled her into his arms, and when his lips began caressing hers, her stomach fell into a wild swirl.

He pulled away and touched her cheek. "I have another question to ask you. I was looking into real estate yesterday, and I saw that Helms Farm is up for sale." He took her hands in his. "We used to go apple picking there in the fall. Mr. and Mrs. Helms are ready to retire, and I heard their family isn't interested in keeping the place. I remember you said you wanted to buy the Franklin farm last year and turn it into a wedding venue. We missed our chance with that one, but I think this one might work too." A sheepish expression flickered across his face. "Did you still want to do that?"

"Oh yes! That would be the perfect project for us. The farm has an amazing barn that would make a terrific space for weddings."

"What if we bid on it? If they accept our offer, Gavin's company could probably restore the barn. And we could turn the farmhouse into your boutique." He gave her hands a gentle squeeze. "Then you could hire people to run the venue and the store while you manage the alterations and —"

She threw herself into his arms and kissed

him, cutting off his words and making the blood sizzle in her veins.

When she finally released him, he grinned. "I guess that's a yes?"

"Yes, I'd love to buy that property with you — but most of all, I want to be your wife."

He touched her cheek. "Now kiss me again, my beautiful fiancée."

Hudson wrapped his arms around her waist and pulled her close, and his lips continued caressing hers. Somehow through the fog of his kiss, Dakota heard a sound behind her.

"Yay!" Layla sang. "I told you so, Hudson. I knew you two would get married someday."

Hudson released Dakota, and they looked toward the doorway where Layla, Shane, Skye, Gunner, Kayleigh, and Brice all stood, clapping and cheering.

"Let's plan a wedding," Kayleigh called.

Skye held up a finger. "I can get you a deal on a wedding gown."

Dakota cupped her hand to Hudson's cheek. "I can't wait to spend the rest of my life with you."

"Then let's start right now," he said.

And when he kissed her again, Dakota closed her eyes. Happiness flittered through her, and her heart felt light. She couldn't wait to see what the future held for her and Hudson.

ACKNOWLEDGMENTS

As always, I'm thankful for my loving family, including my mother, Lola Goebelbecker; my husband, Joe; my sons, Zac and Matt; and our five spoiled indoor cats and our one outdoor cat. I'm blessed to have such an awesome, amazing, supportive, and purring family.

To my critique partner, Kathleen Fuller — I can't even find the words to properly thank you for your help with this book. I've learned so much from you, and I look forward to working together on our future projects. I don't know what I'd do without your encouraging texts and phone calls.

Casey Parker — I can't thank you enough for not only covering my gray and keeping me blond but also lending your amazing insight and ideas for my stories. Thank you for always being willing to brainstorm with me. You were a tremendous help with Dakota's story. Everyone needs a super-awesome stylist like you.

To my dear friend DeeDee Vazquetelles — your friendship is a blessing. I don't know what I'd do without your daily texts and endless emotional support. As we always say, I'm so grateful our kids brought us together. You're my ride or die!

I'm so grateful to my wonderful church family at Morning Star Lutheran in Matthews, North Carolina, for your encouragement, prayers, love, and friendship. You all mean so much to my family and me.

Thank you, Zac Weikal, for your help with my social media plans, my website, my online bookstore, and all of the other amazing things you do to help with marketing. I would be lost without you!

To my agent, Natasha Kern — I can't thank you enough for your guidance, advice, and friendship. You are a tremendous blessing in my life. I hope you enjoy your retirement with your family — especially your precious grandsons.

I would also like to thank my new literary agent, Nalini Akolekar, for her guidance and advice. Nalini, I look forward to working with you on future projects.

Thank you to my wonderful editor, Lizzie Poteet, for your friendship and guidance. I appreciate how you've pushed me and inspired me to dig deeper to improve both my writing and this book. I'm a better author because of you, and I'm excited to keep learning from you.

I'm grateful to editor Jocelyn Bailey, who helped me polish and refine the story. Jocelyn, I'm thrilled that we're able to work together again. You always make my stories shine. And I love our fun conversations about the details. Your friendship is such a blessing to me. Thank you for being amazing.

I'm grateful to every person at HarperCollins Christian Publishing who helped make this book a reality.

To my readers — thank you for choosing my novels. My books are a blessing in my life for many reasons, including the special friendships I've formed with my readers. Thank you for your email messages, Facebook notes, and letters.

Thank you most of all to God — for giving me the inspiration and the words to glorify You. I'm grateful and humbled You've chosen this path for me.

DISCUSSION QUESTIONS

1. At the beginning of the novel, Hudson believes his sister is too immature to marry Shane. He says she isn't capable of making good decisions for herself after her rebellious past, but by the end of the story, he realizes he's just afraid of losing her. What do you think causes Hudson to change his opinion of his sister's wedding throughout the story?

2. Hudson and Layla lost their parents when Hudson was eight and Layla was a year old. They both have struggled with their grief over the years. Have you ever lost someone close to you? If so, how did you cope?

3. By the end of the story, Hudson realizes that he was so focused on being successful to take care of his aunt and sister that it caused him to lose those most precious to

him. What do you think inspires him to accept that he must change to save his most beloved relationships?

4. Dakota is close to her niece Skye, who works with her at the bridal boutique. Do you have a special relative with whom you're close? If so, who is that relative, and how does he or she influence you and your life?

5. Hudson returns to Flowering Grove after selling his company, and he finds himself struggling to decide which adventure to choose next for his career. Have you ever experienced an overwhelming change in your life? If so, how did you adapt to it?

6. At the beginning of the book, Dakota is convinced Hudson picked his career over his relationship with her. Have you had your heart broken by someone close to you? If so, how did you handle that devastation, and what did you learn from it?

7. Dakota has always loved to sew. Do you have a special hobby or interest that you have loved since childhood? If so, what is it, and why is it special to you?

8. Dakota and Kayleigh have been best friends since they were in kindergarten. They're each other's support, especially during rough times. Do you have a special friendship like that? If so, what do you cherish the most about that relationship?

9. Layla always felt alone in her grief for her parents since Hudson would never share his emotions with her. When she was a teenager, she turned to dangerous alternatives instead of asking for help. Have you ever helped a family member or friend who struggled with grief or other overwhelming emotions? If so, how were you able to assist them?

10. Have you ever visited a small town like Flowering Grove? If you could go anywhere for vacation this weekend, where would you choose to go?

ABOUT THE AUTHOR

Amy Clipston is an award-winning bestselling author and has been writing for as long as she can remember. She's sold more than one million books, and her fiction writing "career" began in elementary school when she and a close friend wrote and shared silly stories. She has a degree in communications from Virginia Wesleyan University and is a member of the Authors Guild, American Christian Fiction Writers, and Romance Writers of America. Amy works full-time for the City of Charlotte, NC, and lives in North Carolina with her husband, two sons, mother, and five spoiled rotten cats.

Visit her online at AmyClipston.com
Facebook: @AmyClipstonBooks
X: @AmyClipston
Instagram: @amy_clipston
BookBub: @AmyClipston

The employees of Thorndike Press hope you have enjoyed this Large Print book. All our Thorndike Large Print titles are designed for easy reading, and all our books are made to last. Other Thorndike Press Large Print books are available at your library, through selected bookstores, or directly from us.

For information about titles, please call:
 (800) 223-1244

or visit our website at:
 gale.com/thorndike